The Killing Club

The Killing Club

Angela Dracup

ROBERT HALE · LONDON

First published in Great Britain 2010

ISBN 978-0-7090-9046-5

Robert Hale Limited
Clerkenwell House
Clerkenwell Green
London EC1R 0HT

2 4 6 8 10 9 7 5 3 1

*For Roger Mayo – friend, fellow dog-walker and deer-spotter,
literary critic extraordinaire. I miss you.*

Typeset in 10.5/13.5pt Palatino
Printed in Great Britain by the MPG Books Group, Bodmin and King's Lynn

DAY 1

Christian Hartwell started to climb the hundred and four steps which would bring him to the head of the crag. The steps were crazily uneven, having been roughly hollowed and shaped by the relentless tramp of feet over the centuries, then in more recent times purposefully hacked out of the steep flank of the crag with pickaxes and spades. He began to puff as he made his ascent. He had put on some weight recently and he knew he was out of condition for a man still in his thirties. He resolved to cut down on the beer and the high-fat diet and to take more walks.

He had a special love of the countryside, having spent his early life in a cramped flat near the railway station in Leeds, a setting which had always seemed to him a world away from the grandeur of the windswept lonely hills of the Pennines which he had glimpsed from time to time in the summer holidays. His early childhood had been unsettled and miserable and it was not until he was free of the moods and indifference of his mother that his personal development had begun to flower. A career in journalism had brought him a degree of success. But it was with the forthcoming publication of his first book that things had really begun to hot up. His editor had said more than once that the book would 'touch a nerve in the public imagination'. Already there had been offers of publication from the States, Germany and Japan. His agent had phoned him with the news and taken him out to dinner. The warm camaraderie of the evening still clung to him. A book was something tangible, something to put on your shelves and finger if your confidence ran low, far better than a pile of yellowed newspaper clippings in a cardboard box. Just the thought of it made him smile.

This was the third morning he had done this particular walk and as he approached the summit of the crag he considered choosing an alternative descent to the one he had used before. He decided against it, anticipating the moment when he stepped around a holly bush dangerously perched on the edge of the rock and reached a point where the drop was vertiginous and the view across to the distant hills simply too good to miss.

He paused to take a breath. The earth beneath his feet was dry and so well trodden that it was like the sand on a beach. As he moved forward each step felt springy and joyous. He stopped when he reached the viewpoint. Green farmland below him, dotted with cows. Above, in a vast sky, the rising September sun was huge and veiled, its colour that of the flesh of a watermelon. And across to the west a frail silver moon was in the gentle process of vanishing. He drew in a long breath of sweet early morning air, relishing the silence, drinking in the picture before him.

The intermittent drone of anxiety which had overshadowed the past few days was beginning to ease. He had always been sceptical of some of the tales and warnings people shared with him and, whilst the recent cautionary tales had troubled him more than most, now that he was back on his own territory he was beginning to see them for what they were – the stuff of fantasy.

He was aware of footsteps coming up behind him. He turned, preparing to smile at a fellow walker who had passed him and exchanged greetings on previous mornings. There was a sudden sharp slam on the curve of one shoulder, just enough to send him hurtling down the side of the crag. Then blackness as he hit solid rock.

The fellow early riser looked down and saw the eager rush of blood from the head as the body landed far below, having been buffeted from one ledge to the next. There were some moments of frozen stillness, and then all there was left to do was simply walk away.

The summer breeze tickled the grass on which the body had fallen. In a tree beside the pathway where the dead man had walked a few minutes before, a small brown bird rose up with a high-pitched scream, circling away towards the stream at the base of the valley.

The blood which had seeped from the head of the corpse formed a pear-shaped pool which glinted in the strengthening rays of the sun. The muscles of the body were becoming soft, ready to melt back into the earth if they were left for any length of time.

The world carried on.

Detective Chief Inspector Ed Swift took a glass of champagne from the silver tray offered to him by a young waitress with an unmistakably flirtatious manner and decided that this birthday party was the most ostentatious bash he'd been to for a long time. He wondered if the birthday boy had rolled out the red carpet for the big five O milestone. It was hard to tell; Jeremy Howard could have been anything from forty-five to fifty-five. Swift had only met him briefly a couple of times but he hadn't struck him as the kind of guy he would have expected his colleague and friend Cat Fallon to be knocking around with. Cat's many credentials included being a perceptive, down-to-earth operator who was a shrewd judge of character. She was also warm, funny and attractive in both looks and personality. What did she see in Jeremy? He recognized a sharp tinge of envy and resentment in his feelings and instantly squashed them.

Taking a sip of his champagne, he looked around him, assessing the venue and its ambience – an expensive but somewhat soulless hotel on the outskirts of Leeds, Michelin star food, unlimited Bollinger, fabulous flowers, women in what looked like seriously pricey dresses wearing tiny scraps of feathery nonsense on their expensively cut hair. He had been taking mental notes from the word go, partly from simple curiosity and habit, but also in order to provide his daughter, Naomi, with an answer to the barrage of questions she would undoubtedly subject him to when they next made phone contact.

Seeing Cat coming towards him, he smiled and raised his glass. She reached up and kissed him lightly on the lips. She was wearing a deep-red gown which curved very pleasingly around her figure. Her shoes were dark red too and skyscraper high. Around her neck was a flashing collar of diamonds which looked as though they might have cost as much as the average semi-detached house, and must surely have been given to her by Jeremy. The sort of present, he thought uneasily, which some rich men might give to their girl-friend as a symbol of control and patronage rather than love.

He recalled his initial disquiet on learning about Cat's having suddenly fallen for Jeremy Howard, ten years her senior and, from what he had heard, a multimillionaire. A chain of restaurants had done the trick, apparently. Not her type, he had thought, wincing at his own prejudice. Who was he to make judgements about her 'type'? He supposed the truth was he had once considered that he, himself, might be her type.

He tilted his head and smiled at her. You look beautiful, he thought, wishing he could say it out loud. But she was a colleague, such remarks would be inappropriate. And, of course, now there was Jeremy in the picture. 'You're looking well,' he said.

She smiled back, reached out for his glass, took a sip from it and returned it to him. 'Thanks. And you?'

'I'm fine.'

'How's life in Bradford Central?'

'It's OK.'

He sensed an undertone of brittleness in their conversation. Everything seemed to be so different from a couple of years back when they had almost got together and become an item. Cat had been working as a DI with the drug squad in Durham and had been extremely helpful and supportive when his daughter had become entangled with the drugs squad there whilst she was a student at Durham University. There had been a frisson of feeling between him and Cat during the fraught two days they had worked together to ensure that Naomi didn't fall foul of the law because of something her racy boyfriend had done. And Naomi had made it clear that she would be only too pleased if her lonely widower father and the likeable Cat became more than just good friends, maybe even going as far as marriage.

Around that time, Cat been virtually headhunted for a DCI job in Bradford Central but at the final interview had been passed over in favour of a bright young Oxbridge graduate. He knew that her disappointment had been keen, not just from being denied a promotion but also because she was eager to get away from the difficult, possibly bent, DCI heading up her team in Durham. When the interview panel offered her the chance to transfer to Bradford Central as a DI in their Homicide and Major Enquiry section she had decided to accept it. She had moved to live in a village on the west side of Bradford and soon settled in. She and Swift had had several dinners out together and things had been going rather nicely. And then Jeremy came along.

'Actually,' she said, her voice low and confiding, 'I have been thinking of giving up the job.' She paused. 'Only thinking!' She curved a strand of hair behind one ear and shot him a swift glance to assess his reaction.

Pressure from Jeremy, Swift wondered, instantly reminding himself that Cat had always been perfectly capable of making her own decisions.

'Is your superintendent party to this thought yet?' Swift asked, picturing her superintendent's habitually grim expression on the reception of any news whatsoever, good or bad.

Cat grinned. 'Not yet. But if I did decide to go, he'd probably be glad to get rid of me. Mouthy, stroppy cows aren't his favourite thing.'

Swift spotted the silver-haired Jeremy gliding up, as smooth as silk, and with all the subtle resilience of that luxury fabric. He placed his arm around Cat and pulled her against him. She smiled up into his eyes and Swift could feel the sexual electricity sparking between them. He was reminded of the day he and Kate had married, the sensations of disbelief that he could have persuaded the most exciting woman in the world to marry him. And he hadn't been disappointed.

'I've picked myself a peach,' Jeremy told Swift. 'Isn't she just the most gorgeous creature imaginable?'

Cat shook her head in despair. 'I'm training him up to stop making comments like that. Just give me a few more months.'

A tall blond man with a lazy aristocratic air strolled up and tapped Jeremy on the shoulder. 'Hullo there. Sorry to interrupt.'

'No, no, Julian, no problem at all.' Jeremy held up his hands and laughed. 'We were just having a little shop talk. Let me introduce you to Ed, who is one of Cat's old friends and a Detective Chief Inspector, no less.'

The blond man nodded to Swift and chuckled. 'Better steer clear,' he drawled, grinning from Cat to Swift. 'Jeremy, some new guests have just arrived. Your presence and that of your lovely lady are required.'

Jeremy gave Cat a little pinch on the end of her nose. 'Time to be circulating, darling.' He smiled at Swift. 'I do hope you're enjoying yourself, Ed. There'll be a light supper served later on in the blue room. We'll catch up with you again then, no doubt.'

The two of them and Jeremy's friend moved off into the throng. A string quartet had assembled on a raised platform at the far end of the room. They began to play one of Haydn's quartets. One or two guests moved forward to listen. Others simply carried on drinking and chatting.

Swift decided not to be available to be caught up with later. He moved with leisurely steps towards the door, having long ago mastered the art of slipping away unobtrusively when such behaviour was required.

Later that evening he poured himself a glass of red and thought about the renovation work he was about to start in his kitchen the next day. Physical work was invariably helpful in pulling him out of the sadness which occasionally seized him when some current event reminded him of the past: of the happiness he and Kate had shared, of the terrible loss when she had been killed in a train crash, of the crushing grief that had followed. As far as he could judge, time didn't heal, it merely kept the wound in a state where it could be kept in check.

His phone bleeped.

'Dad?'

He smiled. 'Offspring! How are you?'

'Maybe that's not for me to say.'

'You sound fine to me. Perhaps your young charges could enlighten me further.' His daughter Naomi was in the States, working with Camp America, and having a poke around the terrain.

'I seem to have the knack of keeping them amused. I'm absolutely whacked at the end of the day.'

'Good for you.'

'I could take that two ways.'

'Indeed.'

'What have you been up to?'

'Attending a very posh birthday bash.'

'Hey, cool. Whose?'

'Cat Fallon's new boyfriend.'

'Oh!' There was a pause. 'I had hopes for you there, Dad.'

'How was it I never guessed?'

'So who is this guy who got there before you?'

'One Jeremy Howard. Single. Eminently eligible.'

'So, what makes him any better catch than you?'

'I'm at a loss to guess.'

Another pause.

He could tell she was thrown and disappointed with the news. She really liked Cat.

A few moments and then she rallied. 'Hey, Dad. Gotta go. Kids waking up from after lunch kip. Keep busy, keep happy.'

'You too.'

'Love you,' she murmured, then was gone.

He sat for a while, poured another glass of red.

Bertrand Morrison was a widower, a father, and a grandfather. He was a man who felt happy to wake up and know that there was some shape to the day which stretched out before him. Mondays, Wednesdays and Fridays were grandson-minding days. Saturdays and Sundays were for newspaper reading, gardening and having a frame or two of snooker at the local pub with his friends. Thursdays were for supermarket shopping, which left Tuesday as a flexible day for fitting in whatever else needed to be done.

On this particular Tuesday he had had an appointment with the practice nurse at his GP surgery for a check-up on his blood pressure and cholesterol level in the morning and a session of swimming in the afternoon. By 5.30 he was feeling in good shape and decided he would take his dog for a walk before he started to think about supper. Arriving at the entrance to the woods in which he regularly walked, he had to wait whilst council vehicles bearing nodding branches of lopped oak and sycamore trees made their way through the five-bar wooden gate.

'You're OK, sir,' one of the drivers called out. 'We're all done now.' He revved up the engine, adding, 'Thank goodness, we started at 8.00 sharp this morning.'

Bertrand waved to the driver and he and his golden retriever walked forward on to the broad woodland path beyond the stout five-bar gate. Barney was no longer in his bounding prime and preferred to amble and sniff at his leisure. Sometimes he would freeze into stillness, head cocked, listening for movements in the grass, awaiting the opportunity to track some of the small creatures inhabiting the wood. He never caught anything which was still moving, but he would occasionally bring Bernard the sad dead body of a rabbit or a wood pigeon, held gently in his long jaw.

Bernard went ahead, leaving Barney to snuffle to his heart's content. This evening there was a pale lemon rind moon rising, a nip in the air and the sweet smell of freshly cut and sawn wood pervading the atmosphere. Bernard's heart lifted with the pleasure of it all. He reflected on his day, recalling the kindly smile of the practice nurse, the exhilaration of cutting through the water in the pool. And then he thought ahead to the next day when he would be in charge of his grandson for several hours. Life's not so bad, he thought, even when you're on the wrong side of seventy. He walked on, making steady progress, occasionally glancing back to check that Barney was following.

As he approached the turning to the stone steps leading up to the crag, he turned once more – but Barney was nowhere to be seen. Bernard waited. Elderly dogs could take their time sniffing, and he had the patience to wait. Five minutes went by. Then five more. Bernard felt a twinge of anxiety. He turned and retraced his steps, calling out to Barney as he went. He got back to the gate and there was no sign of the dog. This had not happened before, Barney being the most reliable and biddable of dogs. Had he been stolen? There'd been a spate of pedigree dogs going missing lately. And Barney was an amiable chap; maybe he'd go with someone who knew how to put a dog at ease, someone with a pocketful of cooked steak.

He squared his shoulders. He pulled himself together and walked back again the way he had come until he was almost back again to the base of the steps. His heart was beating hard now. He tried not to picture a life without Barney. That would come in time, but not yet, the old boy had a few years left in him.

As he stood very still, he became deeply aware of the quietness all around. Well, it was getting on for 6.00, a time when workers were coming home, when folks were preparing supper, when families were already eating. It was always quiet at this time of day.

He heard a rustling sound, the noise of twigs snapping. His heart leapt. 'Barney – here boy!' There was only silence again. He moved off the path, walking towards the noise he had heard. The terrain was carpeted in thick grass, interspersed with small hilly folds of land, which provided a perfect home for bilberry bushes. The head of the crag loomed above, but the approach was still mainly flat. And then suddenly there was one single plaintiff howl, followed by an indignant outbreak of barking. And then dead silence. Bertrand followed the sound. Behind one of the bushy outcrops at the start of the steep hill he saw the flash of a blond tail. He hurried forwards. And there he was. His lovely Barney. Thank God! Nose down, tail wagging – as right as rain.

'Ay, what are you doing, lad?' Bertrand was half amused, half angry to have been caused all this unnecessary angst. And the dog was still not taking a blind bit of notice of him, his tail wagging in excited alarm rather than simple pleasure.

As he walked forward, Barney suddenly turned, eyeing his master and letting out one single bark, before returning to the focus of his attention.

What the hell had he found, Bertrand grumbled to himself. He halted in his tracks. The answer lay before his eyes. He felt a sensation of icy cold water trickle down his spine. It flashed through his mind that there was a first time for everything. And he wished he had not been selected to be on the receiving end of this particular one.

DAY 2

Home for Ed Swift was currently a cottage on the edge of the North Yorkshire moors. Following the dramatic events of the year before, when his daughter had been held hostage in his apartment by a mentally disturbed murderer, he had decided to make some changes in his life. He had told his superintendent that he would take three months' unpaid leave, starting as soon as permission was granted by the Chief Constable. Superintendent Finch had been none too pleased, but he had nevertheless done all he could to implement Swift's decision. By the spring of the following year, Swift had cleared his desk, sold his apartment on the north west side of Bradford and settled into his new place.

The cottage had been recommended to him by one of the administrative staff who had a farmer friend looking for a reliable tenant for one of his cottages. He had driven out into the National Park to have a look at it one April evening when the sun and the moon had both been out, regarding each other across a sky of soft baby blue. Sheep, which he later learned were Swaledales, were tearing at the grass at the sides of the narrow roads. They leapt about as the car approached, displaying blind panic rather than any sense of purpose or direction.

The road curved its way down a hill to a ford where a silver tongue of water glinted over the lowest point, then wound back up the hill and gradually disintegrated into a stony track ending at a tall, rusty gate. There was a wooden sign saying *Ferndale Farm* in letters that looked as though they had been carved by a six-year-old. A muddy, shaggy-haired white horse stood behind the gate, regarding Swift with solemn brown eyes. He left the car and made his way through the gate, following the stone footpath that led down to the cottage which stood in a hollow some way behind the farmhouse. Its thick stone walls were brushed with gold from the setting sun, and the dark-green moors beyond looked majestic, peaceful and curiously enticing.

The farmer had arranged to leave the cottage key in what he had referred to as the conservatory, which to Swift looked like little more than half a greenhouse, leaning against the wall at the side of the front door. Security not an issue here, he thought, as he located the large old-fashioned key beneath a clay pot housing a pretty cyclamen which he guessed had been put there earlier in the day.

Inside the cottage was exactly as he had expected an unrenovated cottage in the Dales to be – the bathroom furnished with a cracked porcelain lavatory and an enamel bath weeping rusty stains, the kitchen housing little except a pot sink full of dead flies and an old gas cooker. In the sitting room there were sturdy wood beams running across the ceiling, a bare wooden floor and a small, but rather fine cast-iron fireplace. The main bedroom had two windows, one facing south towards the farmhouse, the other due north to the moors.

He walked around for a while, imagining waking up in the morning to a view of the protective hills. And then he began to consider what restoration work he might do in the place, and a surge of excitement sprang up within. He recalled the early days of his marriage, the small flat he and Kate had rented, the skills he had learned in painting and joinery in order to make the place a pleasure to live in. Skills long out of use, but which he was sure would soon come back.

The farmer, a lean man in his forties, now making the major part of his living from renting out agricultural machinery, had been most apologetic for what he considered the shortcomings of the cottage and had asked for a ridiculously low rent. Swift had protested and had embarked on a curious, inverse bargaining session, attempting to persuade the farmer to up the fees. He had not been very successful, but the farmer had reassured him that any renovations he wished to make would be absolutely fine.

On this particular July morning Swift was painting the skirting boards in the hallway. He had the front door open so he could appreciate the sweet morning air at the same time. Looking up to check out the way the weather was going, he saw a woman making her way across the field towards the farmhouse. She was tall and straight-backed, wearing spiky-heeled shoes totally inappropriate for making progress along a stony path. As she came nearer, he recognized her and smiled to himself. Parking his paint brush in a tin filled with turpentine, he went into the kitchen and filled the kettle with water. As she arrived at the front door, he was there to greet her before she had time to knock. 'Superintendent Stratton.' He offered her his hand. 'Come in.'

For a moment she looked startled, although her grasp was firm and confident. 'Ah, I see news travels fast around here.'

'I still have the occasional drink with members of my team,' he said, as he ushered her through the door. 'They like to keep me informed on items of importance. Like a new boss.'

'Then you'll know I'm only standing in whilst Damian's … recovering,' she said, clearly unhappy about using the word 'stroke' with regard to their colleague's recent medical problems.

Swift nodded and pointed to the sitting room. 'Do go through and sit down. I was making coffee; do you want some?'

'Yes.' But she declined his offer to sit in the front room and followed him through to the kitchen, leaning against the counter and watching him put coffee beans in the grinder. She stared around, noting the pale granite work tops and the dazzling white paint. 'So,' she said, 'besides being a detective you're a DIY man.'

Swift felt the vibrations beneath his fingers as the beans whirred against the grinder blades. The alluring scent of fresh coffee crept into the atmosphere. He smiled and made no comment.

Stratton seemed to have made herself at home. She moved to stand at the window which looked out towards the moors, running her fingers along the inner stone sill which was six inches thick. 'That is the real deep dark countryside out there,' she commented. 'The back of beyond, is the term, I believe. Don't you feel a little isolated?'

'I've taken to it like a duck to water,' he said. He poured coffee into two mugs and glanced at her.

'Black, two spoons of sugar,' she commented.

He placed a mug and a sugar basin in front of her. She dug her spoon into the golden crystals, stirred thoroughly, then took a swallow of the resultant dark, sweet mixture.

'So what can I do for you, Superintendent?' he asked.

'This is an informal visit, so please call me Ravi,' she said.

Informal, he thought. I don't think so.

'I know that you're on leave, Ed. I've looked through your file and I'm aware of the reasons for your wanting to take some time off. I'm also aware that I'm making a big presumption in dropping in on you like this, so I won't waste any of your time beating about the bush. You'll already have guessed that I'm going to try to persuade you to consider cutting short your leave and heading up a case.'

He glanced out of the window, registering the dark comforting bulk of the hills. 'Go on.'

'Have you caught up with the local news this morning?' she asked.

'I did hear a brief item about a body being found at Fellbeck Crag.'

'That's what I'm referring to. We had to release information of the death speedily, and also remove the body. As you know, the crag is a very well-used leisure area. Cordoning the whole of it off for an extended period wasn't really an option.'

Swift agreed. Cordoning off a large area, with numerous entry points, which contained a white investigation tent which in turn contained a body was a sure-fire way of drawing the crowds and possibly creating public panic.

'SOCOs have been working through the night,' Stratton told him, 'but there's not likely to be much in the way of useful evidence.'

'Death in open ground,' Swift said, recalling a case some years back when a young girl's body had been found on Howarth moors. 'My very first CID superintendent used to say it was one of the most difficult crime scenes to squeeze information from.'

Stratton nodded. 'And the weather has been dry for the last few days, so little chance of getting footprints.'

'And, of course, the area is daily trampled over by hundreds of feet, paws, bicycle tyres … you name it!' Swift observed. 'Any witnesses come forward so far?'

'No,' Stratton said. 'Not a good start, I'm afraid. But still, it's only early days.'

'So what are we looking at?' Swift asked. 'Foul play? Murder?' Clearly, a superintendent in the Homicide and Major Enquiry team would not be dabbling in accidental death enquiries.

'We're not sure until the pathologist's examination is complete. However, we are able to say at this stage that the dead man has severe injuries to the back of the head and that his clothes had been set alight, causing significant damage to his trunk and arms.'

So hardly likely to be an accident, he thought. He watched her as she patted the hair at the back of her neck, as though checking that it was all in order. She had no need to worry on that score. Her long black hair was arranged in an immaculately sculpted upended cone shape running down the back of her head. He thought the style was called a French pleat, and that it had been fashionable back in the 60s. He'd ask Naomi next time they spoke. And he guessed that the superintendent's patting of her hair was more to do with her sense of unease in interrupting his period of leave and offering a potentially thorny case than her concern regarding the neatness of her hair.

'Do we have an ID?' Swift asked.

She shook her head. 'No. And his pockets were empty apart from £30 in notes and some loose change. No wallet, no phone, no credit card.'

'So our perpetrator wasn't some youngster after cash,' Swift observed, his interest now fully aroused.

'It wouldn't seem so.'

'And my team?' Swift asked, adding wryly, 'I presume you wouldn't expect me to me to come out of my country hidey-hole and conduct a one-man investigation?'

'Of course not.' Stratton looked deeply concerned and held up her hands in recognition of the absurdity of this proposed job description, giving Swift the impression that she was not a woman who thrived on irony. 'Your team colleague, Laura Ferguson, is on a development course in Bristol and Doug Wilson is in Australia visiting relatives,' Stratton elaborated.

Swift thought of the young, bright Laura, and the stoical middle-aged Doug, always ready to do the footwork which others slued away from. He would miss their support but there would be other cases to work on with them, in the future.

'I've been doing some careful thinking on whom we might draft in to work with you.' Stratton's words were enunciated with slow and almost laboured carefulness. Swift found himself wondering how she fitted in with her high-ranking colleagues who were mainly male and given to sardonic one-liners with a generous peppering of blasphemy.

He nodded acknowledgement and waited for the result of her deliberations.

'I have got in mind Inspector Catherine Fallon,' Stratton said. 'You'll probably know that she has been working in our team in Bradford Central division for some time. She's recently indicated a wish for a transfer in order to support us in the North West division. I spoke to her earlier this morning and asked her to consider a place on our team and to be available as soon as possible to assist you on this case. She agreed – quite readily, in fact.'

Swift sensed an inward jolt. 'I've worked with Inspector Fallon before,' he told Stratton, deciding to leave it at that, not to mention anything of his and Cat's close friendship in the past. He wondered how it would feel to work with her, and soon decided that the phrase 'mixed feelings' best fitted the bill. 'She's a very good detective,' he said, formally. 'I'd be glad to have her on the team.'

'Naturally, I shall give you access to any other support you need,' Stratton said. 'And, of course, I shall be pleased to act as consultant and supervisor as long as I'm in post here.'

Swift glanced out of the window. In the field beyond the strip of back garden a hawk hung in the air, still and menacing.

'Will you at least think about it?' she asked.

He turned back to her. 'Yes.'

Her eyes widened. 'Yes, you'll think?'

'Yes, I'll agree to your proposal,' he said, reaching for the coffee pot and giving them both a refill.

DAY 3

Craig Titmus heard the tap on his door. There were just two taps, and then the sound of feet moving on to the door of the next cell. Again two more taps, the noise of knuckle bones on steel, then more footsteps, more taps – on and on the same signal. 'I'm here. It's me – Blackwell. Look out.'

He jerked bolt upright on his bed, sweat breaking out in his armpits. Blackwell rarely worked on the isolation block now, but when he did it was always the same old routine, letting his fingers and feet tell them who was there. That *he* was there, and that he could see *them*, but they couldn't see him.

Blackwell had been on when a guy on the block had hung himself up by a rope he'd made from shredding his blankets. Craig knew that Blackwell had watched the wretched bloke through the Judas hole, and that he'd not raised the alarm until it was all over. Well, he hadn't seen it with his own eyes, but he *knew*.

Craig would be out the next day and he knew there would be plenty of Blackwells waiting for him. A howling mob would find him, or the papers would let on where he was. They'd hunt him down like a fox and tear him to bits.

He should be glad to be getting out next day. But he'd been shut up so long the whole idea of it freaked him out. No one had been to visit him for years. He sometimes screwed up his eyes to try to see his mum in his head, imagine how she might look now. Blackwell had told him she'd gone crazy because Craig had murdered her bloke. He'd been a security guard, which was almost as hallowed as a policeman. Everyone would be out to get him,

Blackwell said. He made it sound as though he was famous – him, Craig. He supposed that was something, at least, but not exactly a good thing.

He heard footsteps coming back, stopping at his cell. Blackwell had always liked to watch him. He jumped back on to his bed, flung himself down and faced the wall. *Don't react, just wait. He'll go away.* He covered his ears, just to be on the safe side. Blackwell liked to trickle filthy words and thoughts through the hole. *Titmus, Titmus, they'll come and get you, murdering bastard.* And then, in time, he went away, giving a final two raps on the door as he shuffled off to torment someone else. Craig waited until morning, his thoughts milling and stirring into a boiling stew of anxiety.

Blackwell was off duty when it came to leaving. Dave Lofthouse came to escort him to the desk at the outside door where the guards would give him his stuff and get him to sign a paper. He didn't mind Dave – he was new to the job, young and not yet broken in by the older screws.

They walked in silence, past the cells where the inmates called out goodbye as he passed. A lump came into his throat and he could manage no more than a grunt to let them know he wouldn't forget them. They went through corridors and doors which Dave unlocked and then locked again after they'd passed through. When they passed the kitchen he could smell the warm softness of cooking: mince and onions, sponge and floury custard.

And then, as if he was in some kind of dream where things happened in no particular sequence, he'd been given a bag to carry and he'd reached the big grey metal outside door. As they waited for the guards at the outside desk to buzz it open, Dave put a hand on his shoulder. 'Good luck, Craig. Don't let's be seeing you back here, eh?'

And then he was out in the yard and there was blue sky above him and a bright sun. He screwed his eyes against the light, shying away from it. He looked around him; there was no one there, no one waiting to get him. No sign of any Blackwells. Not yet.

The sense of aloneness scared him. He'd had years of being watched, told what to do, never having to make a decision for himself. He made himself move forward, because that was all he could do, just walk away. He didn't know yet what he would be walking to. He remembered one of the guards saying he had to get a bus, get to the probation office. He'd been given some directions to put in his bag, along with enough money to keep him afloat for a week or so. They'd told him the probation officer would help him. But Blackwell said he'd be all on his own a like fox on the run, with a pack of hounds behind him, catching up, catching up.

He tried to picture his life, running on ahead of him like an endless road. What would happen to fill all those minutes and hours and days until he got old? He didn't know. He wanted a family to go to, but there was no one. His mum hadn't ever been married and he had no brothers or sisters, not that he knew of anyway. His gran and grandad had died, the prison officers had told him that. But his mum was still alive. But she wouldn't want him, Craig, back ever. Because he had murdered her bloke and therefore driven a pile of nails into his own coffin.

DAY 4

The drive from Swift's cottage to the station just outside the market town of Ilkley was a match for any recommended scenic route you could pick from a tourist handbook of the Yorkshire Dales. And the weather was typical too; a bleak chill in the air, the sky low and glowering, turning the hills to brooding dark monsters. Streams sparkled beneath humpback stone bridges and dips in the road had become glinting splashy fords following the heavy rain through the night. A photographer's dream.

By 7.45 a.m. he was settled behind the desk in a tiny office, the only space the superintendent could find for him at present. It was on the top floor of the building, which was currently undergoing a re-fit. The walls were bare and ready for painting and the room smelled of dust and stale cigarette smoke. The single window was about the size of a tea tray. But the room had a computer and a phone and a pleasing air of quietness, being removed from the hub of activity of the work being carried out on the floors beneath.

Swift was well aware that the waters had partly closed over him since his decision to take time off work. That happened with everyone who had a long absence from the team: no one, however good at their job and valued as a person, was irreplaceable. He imagined the comments on his file; queries about possible post-traumatic stress disorder, about his ability to deal with it, about his future in the force. Curiously none of this worried him. His main concern was to get to grips with the case in hand and to make good of the opportunity to test himself out once again.

The sergeant at the front desk had told him that Inspector Fallon was finishing off paperwork in her current station and would not be joining him until the beginning of the next week. Swift was not sorry about that: getting his feet back under the work table would be easier on his own.

Not that he intended to sit behind his desk all day. Having reviewed the brief details in the file Stratton had given him, he made an appointment to visit the mortuary and speak to the pathologist, then turned his attention to the issue of doing some research regarding the scene of the crime.

His first port of call was a well-heeled bungalow in a small cul-de-sac about a hundred yards from the base of Fellbeck Crag. The man who opened the door was a tubby, baldheaded man with a grandfatherly appearance. A toddler who looked like a good candidate for fulfilling the role of grandchild was standing behind him, peering curiously around his right leg.

'Good morning, young sir!' said the tubby man. 'And who might you be?'

'Good morning, to you,' Swift said, thinking it was a long time since he had been called a young sir, and showing his ID. 'DCI Swift.'

'Bertrand Morrison,' the man responded, waving Swift through the door, whilst the toddler continued to stare in solemn silence. In the sitting room, a large blond dog raised an untroubled head as the three of them filed in.

'Sit down, sit down!' Morrison said. 'What can we do for you, Chief Inspector? I'll guess you're here about the poor beggar who met his maker on the crag.'

'You're quite right. I'm investigating the circumstances of the man's death.'

'Checking out that there was no foul play, I'll be bound,' Morrison replied.

Swift nodded, making no comment.

'Do you know who he was?' Morrison asked.

'Not yet. I take it you didn't recognize him.'

'Never seen him before in my life.' Morrison shook his head regretfully. 'Poor chap, toppling off the crag and then being set alight. What a terrible business.'

'Yes,' Swift agreed. 'And a troubling experience for you, Mr Morrison.'

'Oh well, it wasn't too jolly, I have to admit. But that's life isn't it? You take the good with the bad.'

Swift wondered if Morrison was more upset than he admitted. 'One of our Liaison Officers could have a talk with you if that would be helpful,' he said.

'Thanks for the offer. I don't think I'll be needing anything like that.' He paused. 'But then if your officer were a pretty young blonde, I might change my mind.' Immediately he looked ashamed of having made this frivolous remark. 'Sorry, we mustn't speak disrespectfully of anything to do with death.'

Swift judged that Mr Morrison had no need of any counselling, being resilient enough to counsel himself. Or was there another reason?

The toddler, having carried out his own check on Swift, now sidled softly up to him and held out his hand, offering Swift the Lego brick he was holding in his hand.

Swift received it with due gravity. 'Thank you.'

'His name's George,' Bertrand Morrison said. 'They're all coming back, the good old traditional names. Say hello to the Chief Inspector, George.'

George stared for a few moments, declined to speak and wandered away to the pile of toys stacked in a box beneath the window.

Swift looked at the benign, slumbering dog. 'I gather that it was your golden retriever who found the body.'

'Indeed he did,' Morrison declared. 'Barney has a nose like a bloodhound.'

'I see,' Swift said. 'Do you walk regularly around the crag?'

'Oh, yes. Every morning, every evening, regular as clockwork.'

'Can you tell me what happened on the evening you, or rather Barney, discovered the body?'

'We set out around teatime. It takes about five minutes to walk from here to the entrance to the woods at the foot of the crag. We'd been walking around fifteen minutes, when Barney did one of his off-piste sloping off away from the path and into the under-growth. I didn't think anything about it as he regularly goes off on a nose-to-the-ground job. I went on at my usual plodding pace, and all of a sudden I heard this bark. And then I realized that it was him – and that he sounded excited and somehow worried. I followed the noise and there he was, standing beside the body, barking his head off.'

He stopped, his amiable, carefree expression stilling into serious-ness. 'Well, I stepped forward to have a look and I was pretty sure the poor chap had had it. But I didn't touch him. Well, to tell the truth I felt squeamish and anyway they always say you shouldn't interfere with funny goings-on, don't they. I put Barney on the lead and calmed him down. And then I got out my mobile phone and contacted the police and the ambulance service. Barney and I sat and waited until someone came. One or two runners came past, but they didn't cotton on what was happening. Well, I suppose me and Barney were blocking the view. Anyway, the police were there in minutes, and one of them had a bit of a feel at the body and said he thought it was dead. After that they cordoned the body off, then took some details from me. And that was it, really.'

'Thank you, that was a very clear and helpful account,' Swift said. He let a small silence fall. 'Mr Morrison, do you have any reason for saying that the dead man toppled from the crag.' Swift had checked the wording of the press release and there was no mention of the possible reason for the man's death, or the way he had met it.

Morrison looked faintly surprised to be asked that question, as though it were quite unnecessary. 'Well, it makes sense – to me anyway. You see, I do a circular walk with Barney. We walk almost to the top of the crag and then we turn along a narrow path which has a point on it which I've long regarded as a death trap. I'd certainly never walk near it without having the little one on reins and even then I'd keep right to the other side of the path.'

His answer was so ready and straightforward that Swift put Morrison on the furthest back burner of being a suspect as regards the killer he was searching for.

'So presumably you have a good idea of the location from which the body might have fallen?'

'Oh, yes. I know exactly the spot,' said Mr Morrison. 'Exactly! Me and Barney pass it every day. And that body was as near-as-damn-it directly underneath that very spot.'

'Would you show it to me?'

'Absolutely would – no problem. Do you mean now?'

'If that's convenient for you.'

He wrinkled his forehead. 'Well, we'll have to take the little 'un along. I can't leave him when he's on my watch. Child-minding duties are my new career, you see, seven and a half hours, three days a week. He fills my days with gold does that little lad. And then Barney'll have to come too.'

Swift smiled. 'No problem.'

Twenty minutes later, having wrestled the child into his shoes and outdoor gear, then got himself and the dog ready for walking, Mr Morrison carefully locked the front door behind him and the little party set out. As Swift had guessed, progress was very slow. By the time they reached the site where the body had been found, Swift was familiar with a good deal of Bertrand Morrison's family history and his views on a number of issues ranging from childcare to the disgraceful state of the British economy. He noted that the site, which was still cordoned off with white tape bearing the blue police logo, was not in full view of the path, as it lay in a channel of hollow ground which formed part of the modulations of the terrain just beneath the slope of the crag. Morrison was understandably reluctant to walk up close to the site in the company of his grandson and his dog. He stood waiting whilst Swift took a few moments to glance at the area and form a general impression.

They then commenced the climb which would take them to the high reaches of the crag. The toddler made a valiant attempt with the first few steps, then fell and began to cry. Morrison swept him into his arms and stomped forwards up the steps, clutching his burden. Swift found that it required quite an effort to keep up and was impressed with the older man's stamina.

Towards the top of the steps Morrison indicated that they were to take a left turn, which took them up an earth path patched with outcrops of rock. There was another climb and then they made a second left turn joining a high path which ran parallel to the path they had started out on. Glimpsing down, Swift was surprised at how much height they had gained. The view across the valley was sweeping and impressive. To the right of them the path was separated from the hilly farmland by tired-looking wire netting. In the distance, Swift spotted two deer, standing on the high point of a ridge, dramatically outlined against the sky.

'Just here,' Morrison said, gesturing to the left with a nod of his head, keeping the child firmly grasped in his arms.

Cautiously approaching the cliffside edge, Swift saw that he was standing on the brink of a jaw-dropping precipice. Below him the land curved inwards slightly, giving almost immediately on to serried ranks of bluish-grey rock which ran all the way down to the plateau below – and the place where the body had been found.

He stepped back a little.

'That poor chap must have fallen from there,' Morrison said. 'It's the only place along here that's truly dangerous – a death trap, if you like.'

Swift agreed. He stepped forward again, knelt down and looked at the point just beneath the jut of the land. If a person were to stumble and be taken off balance they would have every chance of falling on to the small platform of grass-covered earth immediately below. But if they were pushed, they would miss breaking their fall and land on the rock. He imagined the horror of it; bouncing down the rock, clutching at emptiness, hurtling on to further injury, powerless to prevent their inevitable fate.

He got to his feet and brushed the earth off his hands.

'I've written to the council once or twice to suggest they put some warning signs or barricades up, but nothing's happened,' Morrison said. 'I suppose in all fairness it's not a very much-frequented path. Too goatlike for most folks.' He shifted the child's position on his hip. 'Well, that's enough of all that. Let's move on, shall we?'

They resumed their walk, which would eventually lead them on a long gentle slope back to the lower path. After negotiating two streams, the land began to flatten out and Morrison let the child get down. He sped off with glee. 'Run, run, run!' he shouted, chasing after the dog.

'If it were up to me to offer an opinion,' said Morrison, 'I'd say that your body had a helping hand to send him on his way. You've just looked at the lie of the land, Chief Inspector, you'll have seen that a person would need some force behind his fall to hit the rock.'

Swift was impressed. 'Do you know of other fatal incidents that have taken place at that spot?'

'No, strangely enough, I don't, and I've walked all over the crag for years. Still, you'll be able to look it up on your computers, won't you?'

Swift nodded confirmation.

'I'm always around,' Morrison said. 'Minding the little 'un and walking the dog. And while I enjoy every minute of it, I wouldn't say no to a little more excitement from contact with the outside world. So if you need any more wise words from a willing old pensioner, just give me a call.'

'I will,' Swift said.

Morrison suddenly stopped dead and struck his forehead with his hand. 'There's something I haven't told you, Chief Inspector. Blow it, I'm such a befuddled old codger these days. You see, on the day Barney and I found the body this part of the crag had been cordoned off all day for some tree cutting. I saw them leaving when I came along with Barney. So that's maybe why someone didn't spot it sooner. I mean, if the poor chap had been killed the night before you'd have thought he'd have been found much earlier in the day. There are dozens of dogs being walked in this little spot, which means he must have been killed sometime after dark on the Monday or very early Tuesday before the council tree-cutters got here. That is, after all the general public and all other traffic had departed to bed and the workers had started, which was eight o'clock so one of them told me. I'd say a slot between 11 p.m. Monday and, say, around 7 a.m.Tuesday. Dirty deeds can happen in the night, you know. It never gets really dark this time of year, and I should know – I'm an insomniac.'

Swift digested all this and committed it to memory. He hadn't expected to be given an estimated time of death with such cogency so soon. He would ask for a written statement from Morrison later and it would be interesting to compare his evaluation with that of the pathologist. 'Did you ever think of taking a job with the CID, Mr Morrison?' Swift inquired.

Morrison beamed.

'How come the council workers didn't find the body?' Swift mused.

'Number one, it was well hidden from the path. Number two, they were cutting trees quite a few hundred yards from where the body was lying. Number three, they don't take dogs to work.' Morrison beamed again, getting well into his stride now.

'I take your point,' Swift said, thinking it almost laughingly ironic that council workers should have been crawling around the crag and not discovered a body lying yards away from them.

He made a mental note to contact the SOCO team without delay and ask for a further examination on the crag, focusing on the possible point from which the body fell, and the rocks below. He'd advise them they might need climbing gear.

As they walked on, Swift was aware of a little throb of excitement of his own, a sense that this was a case which merited investigation. It was a few months since he had experienced the rush of purpose and curiosity which came at the start of a murder enquiry. And he realized how much he had missed it.

The town mortuary was an unobtrusive single-storey building situated close to the local hospital. Rectangular and built out of red brick, it had one single door situated in the middle of one of the longer walls. It was six months since Swift had paid it a visit and he hesitated for a moment before pressing the entry buzzer set to the side of the door. It made a fierce fizzing noise. After a few seconds there was a crackle from the intercom. 'Yes?'

He leaned forward to speak into the grille. 'DCI Swift.'

The door fell open, releasing a blast of chill air and an overpowering scent of lemon. The entrance was narrow and dimly lit. Swift put a finger over his nostrils and took in a few deep breaths before going downstairs to the basement where the main grisly business of the mortuary took place. Ahead of him were swing doors made from thick plastic sheeting. A yellow light showed behind them showing up the grains and scratches on the plastic. There was the low hum of a radio playing classical music. He placed a hand against each door and pushed them apart. The smell hit his nose like a vicious slap – the stench of rotting meat and the ghastly afterburn of alcohol.

The pathologist, Tanya Blake, was waiting for him. 'Are you all right?' she asked noticing Swift's pallor. She was small and slender, dressed in green scrubs with a face mask hanging from one ear.

'Give me a moment,' he said. 'I'll be fine.'

'We'll need to go into the storage room,' she said. 'Are you OK with that?'

Not really, he thought. 'Yes … lead on.'

'Sure?' she said.

At his nod, Blake used all her slight weight to heave the door open. A rush of frosty, alcohol-scented air shot out into the corridor. Brutal white lights flickered to life in the room beyond which was basically a giant fridge. 'Sorry, but I haven't had time to tidy him up much,' she said. 'We're even busier than usual, mainly because my new assistant took himself off mountain-biking last weekend and succeeded in breaking a wrist and an ankle bone.'

'I can see that might be rather a hindrance for someone in your line of work,' Swift said. Carrying out post-mortems involved a degree of stamina together with a dash of athleticism.

Swift watched as she slid a steel drawer open, noting the humps and valleys under the white sheet. There was a body under there, brutally damaged, forever stilled. He breathed in and the chilled air bit into the flesh of his throat.

Blake glanced at him, then pulled the sheet back.

The man was young, in his mid thirties, Swift guessed. His face was criss-crossed with lines of dried blood, but was otherwise unmarked. Strands of his thick brown hair lay across his forehead, slightly stained with blood.

'At the moment, I've concluded that death was caused by severe blows to the back of the head, consistent with a fall from a high place on to rock surfaces. I haven't been to the crime scene so far but I know the area anyway, and SOCO's sent me some photographs. It's not possible to be precise about which separate contact incident with sheer rock killed him, as the severity of each blow as he gathered speed probably made each subsequent impact more severe, but any one could have killed him outright. No major injuries to any of the internal organs, but there is significant bruising to both the trunk and limbs, as you would expect from a long descent down the side of a tall crag.'

'That seems to fit with what I've seen of the crime scene,' Swift said. 'Was he in good health; was there any alcohol in his blood, any trace of drugs?'

'Yes, in pretty good shape. No drugs or alcohol. He was carrying a little more fat than might have been good for him, but that's hardly unusual for a guy his age.'

They both looked at the body in solemn silence. Swift noticed amongst the bruising and burn scarring on the dead man's left upper arm was a faint BCG vaccination scar, a precaution from years before, which somehow made the body seem more vulnerable and pitiful than all the damage it had sustained just before death.

Blake stroked the dead man's cheek; Swift had noted before how tenderly she touched bodies once her necessarily brutal examinations had been completed. 'He was having an early morning walk,' she said softly. 'I wonder what he was thinking. Those last thoughts just seconds before the final heartbeat.'

Swift had a sudden thought of his late wife. What had she been thinking just before the train she was travelling in lurched off the rails? Before her heart gave its last beat? 'You treat your bodies with more consideration than some people give the living,' he told Blake, dryly.

She smiled an acknowledgement. 'I'm going to pull the sheet down further so you can see the main site of the burns,' she said. Slowly and gently she moved her hands. 'We've removed all the remnants of clothing and tested for traces of accelerant, blood samples have gone off for analysis and the body has been X-rayed for signs of gunshot wounds.'

'And?'

'As I said, there were no significant internal injuries. And all the other tests were negative, apart from the presence of an accelerant, which was brandy.'

Swift looked at the baked, cracked skin of the dead man's body and thighs.

'It seems likely that his sweatshirt and jeans were soaked in brandy and then set alight. The worst area of burning was on the chest, which is why the skin looks charred. The human body keeps on burning for some time after the fire goes out because of its subcutaneous fat.' She glanced across to him. 'Sorry, I'm probably telling you things you don't need or want to know.'

Swift had to admit to himself that he was now feeling queasy.

'However,' Blake continued, 'as you can see, the head and lower arms and legs have been less exposed to heat and that's why the skin is still pink.'

Swift forced himself to look carefully. Yes, the skin was pink, but disfigured with horrific mottling and blisters. He thought that he had seen enough. Moreover, in the midst of this observation and discussion of heat and fire, he was beginning to be affected by the coldness of the room. 'Can we talk some more in your office?' he asked Blake.

Back in the warmth of her office, safe from crushed, blackened cadavers, Swift was able to take a little pleasure in the hot, black coffee she prepared for him.

She made a steeple of her fingers and tapped it against her lips. 'If he had come in without the burns, I suppose the question would have been, did he fall or was he pushed?'

'Would you be prepared to make any comments at this stage?' Swift asked.

'It's hard to say when I haven't been to the spot from which he fell. But we might be able to tell you more when the forensic team have examined his clothes. There are certainly no identifiable traces on the body which we could test for DNA regarding a second person having touched him. But the burning and the smoke have complicated the issue. On the other hand, the cause of death was the direct result of the fall. If he had simply been set alight with the contents of a flask of brandy he would probably have survived with ready and appropriate care.'

Swift heard the doubt in her voice. 'I have been to the spot,' he said, 'and my current thinking is that he was most likely to have been pushed.' He gave her a brief run-down of his visit to the crag with Bernard Morrison.

'But the report from our SOCO team states that there was no useful evidence found at the site,' he continued. 'The place from which he fell is a narrow footpath which skirts around the highest reaches of the crag. It's a well-trodden earth path, which was dry on the morning of the incident, so that it would be unlikely to show up any useful impressions of footprints. Also, on public paths, footprints and any signs of a scuffle are easily destroyed by the walkers who come next.'

Blake nodded agreement.

They sat in silence for a few moments.

'And we still have no ID,' Swift said.

'We might just have something to help you with the ID when the report on the clothes comes back from forensics,' she said to him. 'And we could check dental records, take impressions and send them round to local dentists.'

'Have you a head-shot of our mystery man I could have for the file?' he asked.

She went to her filing cabinet, unlocked it and pulled a drawer out. 'There,' she said, handing him a white A4 envelope. 'Hope that might give you a lead.'

Swift smiled at her words of encouragement. 'One last thing,' he said as he got to his feet. 'Time of death? You mentioned earlier that our man was out for an early morning walk.'

'Indeed I did.' She consulted her draft report. 'Yes, time of death estimated somewhere between 2 a.m. and 8 a.m. on the day he was found. Sorry I can't be more precise than that. Owing to the burning, I was restricted in the areas of the body I could use to make an estimate of body temperature at the time of death.'

'That'll do fine,' Swift said, interested to note that her calculation and Bertrand Morrison's whilst not entirely consistent, did show some points of agreement. He thought Morrison had done rather well, given that his guess had been made solely on the basis of reasoning and common sense, with no help from measuring instruments and science. 'Thanks for all this, Tanya.'

'A pleasure,' she said, grinning.

'It's good to know that some people get true job satisfaction' he commented dryly.

'Oh, yeah, I do love my job,' Blake agreed. 'After all, not many professionals get to work with such docile clients.'

Swift gave a small grimace and left without delay.

On returning to his monastic cell of an office, he switched on his computer and keyed in notes on his interviews with Bertrand Morrison and Tanya Blake.

When that was done he sat for a time in front of the screen, running through the text, picking out the salient points.

Dead man found in woodland area at base of a crag – area well used by walkers, bikers etc

No ID. Nothing in pockets except cash
Likely that death caused by fall from high point of crag
Clothes set alight after death – burns mainly to torso area
? one perpetrator or two

He considered his next course of action. The primary consideration was the dead man's ID, but he would probably have to await
the report from the forensic team before he could move on with
that one.

He looked once again at the photograph of the dead man's face.
If he could only put a name to it then he and Cat could get cracking
on Monday morning.

Frustration bit into him. He'd planned to spend the weekend
painting his sitting room and repairing to the local pub for refreshment in the evening. And he could still do that, but he knew the
issue about the dead man's identity would needle him. He'd
checked the missing person lists but there were no matches there.

He tapped his fingers lightly against the black and white photograph for a few moments. He glanced at his watch. It was 4.30, a
time when many workers would be tidying their tools and clearing
their desks ready for the weekend ahead. But he knew someone
who would most likely still be at their desk. Someone who searched
and dug for information as eagerly as a squirrel seeks nuts.

He slipped on his jacket and picked up his car keys.

Craig sat across the table from his allocated probation officer. The
room in which they were meeting was small and rather dark,
having only one narrow window. The walls were beige and had
only one picture on them, that of a line of trees in a wood. Craig
decided that when he had a place of his own he would paint the
walls in a bright colour, maybe yellow. Yes, yellow would be good.
Like the yolk of an egg – he liked eggs. And he'd put up pictures of
people doing things; making stuff, cooking stew and baking pies.

The probationer was called Brian Norwood. He was something
of a disappointment to Craig, being a man in his fifties with a weary
manner, as though he was really too tired to think up anything that
would take the edge off Craig's terrified sense of being swamped by
confusion and fear as regards the outside world.

They talked about Craig's being temporarily booked into a nearby bedsit. They talked of Craig's chances of getting a job. Or rather Brian Norwood talked and Craig listened. Norwood consulted the thin pile of typed pages on his desk. There was a job going at an abattoir, something at a meat packing plant.

'Not very good wages,' Brian Norwood said. 'But it's a start.'

Craig could think of nothing worse for a released murderer than working with dead bodies. He looked at Norwood and said, 'All right then.' He was fagged out: he had no fight in him. The walk from his bedsit to the office had been so scary he had taken to counting his footsteps to try to steady himself down. The amount of open space between the cars and the buses, the sky and the ground, were frighteningly big. Everything was so far away he felt dizzy, as if there was nothing to cling to. He'd been in prison for eight years. Eight years when he had never been more than twenty feet away from a wall. The exercise yard had been just a narrow strip, and the high walls had protected him from the wind. Out here on the pavement it swirled around his face, jabbing and sharp, whipping his hair into his eyes. When a bus passed by he felt it might suddenly veer towards him, crushing him under its massive wheels. And who would be sorry to see him go. Him … a murdering bastard.

His toe hit a raised paving stone and he stumbled. He righted himself and stood very still for a moment, staring at the ground and wondering if he could bring himself to take even one more step. People walked past, not seeing the pain in his head, nor the fear in his gut.

'So, will you give one of these jobs a try?' Brian Norwood said, tapping his fingers on the papers in front of him.

'I'll have a think about it,' Craig muttered.

'Good man.' Norwood said. 'You can let me know next week.'

Craig stared at him.

'You're just out on licence,' Norwood explained. 'You've done your sentence and you're a free man, but we need to keep a check on you to make sure everything's going well.'

'Right.' Craig grasped the fingers of one hand in the other and twisted the joints so hard they hurt. He wondered about mentioning to Norwood that he was set on finding an old friend who might be able to help him. Maybe let him stay at their house for a bit. He glanced at Norwood's ted-up-looking face and kept his thoughts to himself.

Later on, he joined a queue at a bus stop. He wanted to ask the woman in front if the bus was going northwards, but every time he opened his mouth panic rose up in his chest. She was just an ordinary woman, not very tall, big arse on her, greasy hair. She started fiddling around in her bag and then her purse dropped out on to the ground. He bent to pick it up for her. He saw the bus coming, slowing down for the stop. 'Here,' he said, handing the purse over.

'Thanks,' she said, giving him a smile.

'Is it going north?' he asked in a rush, his voice coming out far too loud. 'The bus?'

She thought for a few moments. 'It's going to Otley,' she said. 'Yeah, that's north.'

'Thanks.' He couldn't believe he'd asked, just casual and normal. Couldn't believe she'd given him an answer, nice and friendly and easy. As if he was just an ordinary chap.

Swift observed Georgie Tyson's get-up as she got up from her desk to greet him. As usual, she was wearing black leather; not her usual biker's leathers but a bomber jacket paired with a short, tight skirt. Her heavy black bikers' boots completed the retro beatnik look, helped along with some bright pink tights and her spiky hair, currently black, streaked with burgundy.

'Hi, there!' she called out as he raised his hand in a welcoming wave from the doorway.

A few minutes later they were sitting on either side of the desk, hot coffee and biscuits on the desk top. Events seemed to drive on quickly when Georgie was around. Swift had known her for a couple of years. She was an ambitious newshound, hungry for advancement and the big time in journalism.

'How's the *Yorkshire Echo*?' Swift asked.

'Still nicely afloat and not able to do without me yet.' Georgie crunched hungrily on a chocolate biscuit and took another one.

'And you've been promoted to an office of your own,' he commented.

'Uh huh, and a column of my own. Don't you read the papers, DCI Swift?'

'It has been known,' he admitted. 'What sort of column?'

'Basically, it's all about me being on a bad-tempered rant and pulling people to bits. You know, writing about footballers' taste in casual clothes, and actors who speak at political rallies in support of causes they know fuck-all about.'

'Sounds just right for your talents,' Swift observed.

'Mmm, sometimes even *I* am a touch shame-faced about what I write, but the public seem to lap it up. And articulating the nation's annoyances pays a lot better than reporting on grubby dealings in the local council and so forth. And I've been able to buy my own place. I'm as chuffed with it as a little kid with a Wendy House.' She eyed him like a hawk considering its next swoop. 'So what can I do you for, Chief Inspector?'

'The body on the Fellbeck Crag,' he said.

'Ah, yes. Your press officer's being very cagey about that.' She didn't sound really interested. 'Some drunk staggering about and bumping his head on some inconvenient boulder, I'd have thought. All we know is that it's a man. Do you know who he is?'

'No,' said Swift. 'But I just thought you might.'

Her eyes widened. 'Me! Nah. I don't get out enough. Always got my nose to the grindstone.'

Swift took out the photograph Tanya Blake had given him and laid it on the desk in front of Georgie.

Her body stilled. 'Good God … that's Christian Hartwell.' She stared across at Swift, and he could tell that she was truly upset.

He was fairly unnerved himself. It had just been a shot in the dark to talk to Georgie Tyson. He had expected no more than a few ideas, possible leads. But this was something else.

'He's … he was … a journalist. He's been the top writer on our sports section for the past four or five years. God! I can't believe this. What happened to him?'

Swift gave a small smile. 'That is what I'm trying to find out.'

'Do you think he's been the victim of dirty work at the cross-roads?' Georgie asked, pulling herself back into professional mode. 'Murder? Assassination? It happens to journalists all the time.'

'Your words, not mine,' Swift said, 'so don't think you'll get away with going to press and putting your words in my mouth.'

'Wouldn't dream of it. You're far too nice a guy to play dirty tricks on.'

'And you are far too kind,' he said. 'Listen Georgie, I want to know more about Christian Hartwell, and if you'll keep quiet now, there are likely to be some goodies later. And, of course, if you don't keep quiet I'll be in the mire, and most definitely sent out to grass … in which case you'll get nothing. I give you my word as a decent guy.'

'Yeah. Fair dos, as my old granddad used to say. OK, Christian Hartwell, let's see. He joined the *Echo* around five years ago. He'd worked for local papers all over the place before that, and also done a spell of volunteer work in East Nepal and other places in the back arse of Africa. Which just shows he'd got a lot of guts. He was rather handsome in those days, solid, but not fat. He had really lovely dark eyes; you noticed his eyes because he was the kind of guy who really looked at people. And he had lovely thick brown hair.' She looked again at the photograph and gave a grimace of dismay.

'It sounds as though you had rather a fancy for him,' Swift commented.

'Does it?' She slanted a sly glance at him.

'OK, then. Did you have an affair with him?'

'Hey! That's off limits.'

'Fair enough … I apologize.'

'As a matter of fact,' she said, 'I didn't ever hop into bed with him. He'd had a steady girlfriend for a year or so before he joined our team. He told me that they'd been planning to get married, but she got killed in an accident. They were at a barbecue at some posh house with a swimming pool. She jumped off the diving board and it was faulty, not fixed properly. Her head was split open when she got hit by it, and that was that. What bloody awful bad luck. I think after that he was a bit wary of getting in deep with anyone else.' She stopped, chastened by her unthinking pun. 'Sorry.

'He always struck me as, kind of, rootless,' she continued. 'He didn't seem to have any family, which I used to consider was rather cool and made him gloriously free. But thinking it over, I'm not so sure.'

'What was he like at his job?'

'Well, I can only offer my own opinion,' she pointed out. 'But, in my book, he was almost too talented for our rag. He wrote some great articles based on his experiences in Africa. I mean, he'd witnessed some terrible brutality, women who were raped and murdered, children who were mutilated, whole villages set on fire. If you've witnessed those kind of scenes up close it inevitably shows through in your writing, and with Christian the power and pathos of what he had witnessed simply shone through in every line. The trouble was the readers could only take so much of it, and I think it got to be the same for him. In time, he got offered the sports section, strictly on the understanding that he left the misery issues behind and became more upbeat.'

'And did he succeed on the sports page?'

'Yeah. He had that canny ability to turn his hand to different styles of writing.' She helped herself to another biscuit, and munched as she cogitated further. 'His sports reporting was biting and witty and lots of fun,' she said, 'and it generated quite a bit of fan mail. I think that's probably what sparked off the idea of trying his hand at writing a novel. We used to tease him about it, of course. A very high proportion of journalists aspire to write a novel, but not nearly as high a proportion actually get around to it. However for the ones who do, the pickings can be pretty good, and so we were all both pleased and as jealous as hell when he got his advance cheque. Christian was tickled absolutely pink about the whole thing; it really perked him up a lot.'

'And when did all this happen?'

Georgie helped herself to another biscuit and ruffled the spikes of her hair as she tried to remember. 'He got his cheque around two months ago, and the book's due out in the spring of next year.'

'Have you read it?'

'Yes, I have. He was very secretive about it until his contract was signed and sealed. But after that he was happy to show a copy of his manuscript to anyone who was interested.'

'And what did you think of it?'

She grinned. 'It's one of those quirky, murky, foxy-poxy tales – full of sex, cute phraseology, snappy one-liners and a heap of improbabilities.'

'You wish you'd written it yourself?'

'Hah, don't I just? If he's lucky he'll make a packet.' She paused. 'Oh hell, he's dead.'

There was a short respectful pause. Swift broke the silence. 'So, despite a number of setbacks along the way, during his last months Christian appeared positive about his life. He was looking forward to the future, to the publication of his book and maybe a new career as a novelist.'

'Hang on there,' Georgie said. 'I should point out that nearly all journalists and writers are plagued with insecurity. If you do a dud piece you feel like crawling away into a hole. And if you do a fantastic piece, you have a nice gloat for a day or two and then the uncertainty comes rolling in. You can't quite believe that your masterpiece wasn't just a flash in the pan, you have a sneaky feeling that you'll never do another piece that equals it, and you can even get to a point where it's really hard to believe you did it at all.'

'You're telling me Christian could have been overcome by chronic insecurity?'

'It's possible.'

'And thrown himself off the side of a crag as a result.'

Georgie wrinkled her nose. 'Nah, I don't really believe that. I was just letting you into some trade secrets.'

'When did you last see him?'

'Ooh! Isn't that the standard sleuth's question on eyeing up a suspect and smelling a rat?'

'Yes,' he said.

She held up her hands. 'It wasn't me, gov.' He received another slicing glance. 'I'm not really a suspect, am I?' she asked, shaking her head in mock despair.

'I'm not smelling any rats just at this moment.'

'Phew.' She reached out towards the biscuits again, thought better of it and smacked the reaching hand away with her other hand.

'So when did you last see him?'

She frowned. 'Just remind me of the date he died?'

'Tuesday last. Three days ago.'

She leaned back, considering. 'It was the weekend before last, ten days ago. We were both on late afternoon shifts on the

Saturday. He was really looking forward to the next week. He was taking a fortnight's leave. He was planning to go down to London to have meetings with his editor and his literary agent. Maybe take in one or two parties. Possibly spend a few days in Cornwall – he often went there to relax and do a bit of photography. He was due back at work Monday of next week.' She fell silent.

'So, no one would have been likely to worry about his not being around?' he suggested. 'No family, girlfriend, or colleagues.'

'That's right. He was always a bit of a free spirit, as I mentioned before. He used to follow his instincts of the moment. I suppose he was quite an impulsive sort of guy.'

'Do you know if he had contacts in Cornwall? Did he stay at any particular place there?'

'No idea,' Georgie said. 'He just liked it there for the light and views.'

'For his photography?'

'Yep. He just did it for his own pleasure, but he was pretty good. The paper occasionally used some of his pictures.'

'Quite a talented guy, all round.'

'Yep.'

'Any enemies?'

'Not that I know of. He was pretty well liked.'

'Do you know anything about his family?'

She shook her head. 'Sorry, can't help you there. But I can ring down to personnel to give you details of his address, contact numbers and so on.' She eyed him from below her long black mascara-laden eyelashes. 'This is all too good to keep to myself. Sorry, but that's the way it is.'

He pointed a warning finger at her. 'No. You'll have to hold on until we've informed next of kin.'

She nodded. He heard a murmured, 'OK.'

'I mean it,' he told her, his tone uncompromising. 'That includes all your colleagues as well.'

'OK. Scout's honour,' she said. 'I'll phone your press officer tomorrow, see what's what.'

'Are you familiar with the geography of the crag?' he asked her. 'Any places where a person could fall and kill themselves? I speak hypothetically, of course.'

She stared at him. 'You're joking. Do I look like one of the world's outdoor girls?'

'There are one or two danger spots,' he told her. 'And a lot of people walk there, including little children and pet dogs. Apparently there have been appeals to the council to put up barriers or warning signs, but ...' He raised his eyebrows.

'But, no response?'

He gave a nod in the affirmative.

A smile curved Georgie's burgundy-tinted lips. 'Leave it with me. A bit of snapping at the heels of council officials is just my cup of tea. I can do a nice little piece on that.'

'I thought so,' he said. 'Don't ever let it be said that I don't offer you some juicy little bones to chew on from time to time.'

Back in his office he rang Cat Fallon on her mobile. It was now going on for 6 p.m. He wondered if she was at home yet, going on to imagine her in her little cottage, maybe pouring a glass of wine, or soaking in the bath. Getting ready to go out with Jeremy Howard.

She answered on the second ring. 'Cat Fallon.' Her voice somehow managed to sound both brisk and warm.

'It's Ed. It's work, is that OK?'

'Hi there. What have you got for me? I thought I didn't start until Monday.' She sounded perfectly unfazed, ready for anything.

'No, you don't ... and there's no pressure. Has Ravi Stratton sent you a copy of the initial notes on our murder case?'

'Yes, I'm up to speed.'

'I've got an ID. And I want to inform the next-of-kin as soon as possible. Maybe attend an identification at the morgue. I think it would be good to have a woman's touch on this one.'

'Right. You'd like me to come now then?'

'Yes. But if you have other arrangements....' He heard himself as hesitant and almost as shy as he had been as a teenager asking a girl out on a date for the first time. He reminded himself that this was a work assignment, and that his hesitant and shy days were long behind him.

'No problem. Nothing I can't get out of. Where shall I meet you?'

He gave her the address he had found in the personnel file at the *Echo*. He hung up and sat very still for a whole five minutes, hearing Cat's low voice resounding in his ears.

An hour later the two of them were standing outside the house where they were about to break their grim news. It was a crumbling villa set in a large rampant garden. Virginia creeper smothered most of the frontage of the house and there were one or two blue slates lying on the ground close to the front of the house, no doubt the results of the damage visited on untended old roofs by the recent gales.

The name *Old School House 1898* was painted on a wooden block just beside the front door, the lettering so faded by the weather that it was barely legible. As Swift pressed the brass bell a silvery tinkle sounded from the depths of the house.

'It's like something out of Dickens,' Cat said, looking up at the dark bulk of the house from which no sign of light or life emanated.

Swift thought that was an apt description. At the same time it struck him that this sudden and unplanned initiation of Cat into his team had been something of a bonus. The seriousness of the job of informing relatives of a death pushed aside such considerations as awkwardness and suppression of feelings regarding Cat, which might have bothered him at the more formal meeting planned for Monday. When they met she had offered him her hand and shaken it warmly as she joined him at the front door of the house, and her smile had been direct and frank as had always been the case in the past.

Swift had given her the brief details from Christian Hartwell's personnel file. And now they stood together, shoulder to shoulder, absorbed in the anticipation of the painful task ahead of them.

There was a long pause, the sound of a dog's bark, and then the glow of a bulb coming on in the hallway. 'I won't be long,' a voice reassured them. The door was thrown open to reveal an elderly woman with a mass of wiry silver hair which had been drawn up and piled into a loosely twisted knot.

On seeing the two officers, her face darkened with a sense of foreboding, although she barely glanced at their warrant cards. 'You don't look as though you're bringing good news,' she commented. 'But, please come in.'

She led them down a wide, dark hallway into a large, square kitchen. In contrast to the coolness of the hallway the kitchen was throbbing with warmth pulsing from a wood-burning stove which looked to Swift as if it had been manufactured in the 1950s. A small dog got up from its bed and greeted the officers with tail wags and kindly looks. It had a serious limp on one of its back legs and ears which didn't quite seem to match, one sticking up, the other curled over.

'That's Tamsin,' the woman said. 'Don't worry about her. She's lovely with people, terrible with other dogs. Please sit down,' she continued, gesturing to the assortment of ancient wooden chairs surrounding a large oak table.

Swift introduced himself and his colleague and then gestured to Cat to speak first.

'Are you Mrs Ruth Hartwell?' she asked, keeping her voice steady and gentle.

'Yes.' Ruth Hartwell sat down, placing herself behind a mound of books and a large lined writing pad with a pencil resting on it.

'I'm afraid we have some bad news,' Cat went on.

Ruth Hartwell raised her head and stared the officer straight in the eye. 'Just tell me what you have come to say.'

'A body was found this morning at Fellbeck Crag,' Cat said.

Ruth nodded. A picture of the crag came into her mind. It was the kind of healthy outdoors paradise currently recommended by government health advisors to counteract sloth and obesity. Ruth had walked there quite often in past years, but recently her worsening arthritis had made it more of a labour than a pleasure to walk over such rough and steep terrain. She looked across at the two officers who were watching her with grave, concerned expressions. 'Go on.'

There was a pause. 'We believe the body is that of Christian Hartwell – your son.'

Ruth froze, her eyes glazed and wide with shock. From a distance she heard the female officer offering soft words of regret. She noticed that through their obviously genuine concern they were watching her, assessing her reaction. She got up slowly from her chair and moved to the sink; a strange-looking figure swathed in long scarves over a thick wool sweater, beneath which was a flowing skirt which looked as though it might have been manufactured in the 1970s. She leaned over the sink, letting out a long moan.

Cat got up, and stood beside the stricken woman.

'Give me a minute; I shall be all right,' Ruth said.

'Would you like a drink of water?' Cat said. 'Or I could make some tea.'

'No, no. I'm not ill.' She straightened up and ran her hands over her unruly grey waves. 'I'm sorry,' she said, making her way back to her chair and staring down at the notebook on her table. 'How did it happen?'

'We think he fell from a high point on the crag,' Swift said. 'Some time last Tuesday.'

She nodded. 'I see.'

'We're sorry for the delay in telling you,' he went on. 'We've only just been able to identify him.'

She was sitting up very straight. 'I'd like some details, please. Don't be afraid to simply tell me the worst.'

Swift made a quick revision of the gentler, shorter description he had planned to give as a start off, guessing that this woman would not be satisfied. 'The body was concealed for some time amongst dense foliage and was eventually discovered by a dog.'

There was a silence. Cat and Swift watched her with concern. They were both aware that they had not yet completed the unenviable task they had come to do. Moreover, there was a lonely and stoical mournfulness about the bereaved mother which made it hard to proceed.

Cat took in a breath and leaned forward. 'Mrs Hartwell, would you feel able to identify your son's body?'

'Oh!' Her face took on a look of horror and distress which was painful to witness. 'But I am not his mother' she said, quietly.

Swift and Cat exchanged a glance. 'He had you down as next of kin in the personnel documents we were able to look at in his place of work,' Swift said, 'which is why we were able to find you at this address.'

'What?' she exclaimed. 'He had me down as next of kin.' She considered for a few moments. 'Yes, I can understand why he did that.'

The two detectives were temporarily at a loss.

'Perhaps you could explain the situation to us,' Swift said.

'Christian lived with us from the age of nine,' Ruth said. 'His mother used to be a friend of mine. She was a single parent, and she never told anyone who the father was. She used to bring him to stay with us in the school holidays, and on one of those occasions she left without him and didn't come back. And after that he lived with us.' She paused, looking reflective. 'I'd rather not say any more than that at present,' she stated.

Swift and Cat resisted the impulse for another glance, and allowed Ruth time to reflect on what had been said so far.

'Do you want me to come now?' Ruth asked. 'To look at him?'

'That would be very helpful, if you feel able to do it,' Cat said kindly. 'We'll take you and bring you back, of course.'

Ruth passed a hand over her forehead. 'Thank you.'

'Is there anyone you can contact to come with you?' Cat asked.

'No,' she said. 'I'm a widow and I don't want to disturb and upset my daughter.' She took some deep breaths to steady herself. 'Perhaps Tamsin could come with me,' she said.

It took a few moments for the penny to drop. 'Your dog?' Swift enquired.

'Yes. Would that be all right?'

'Yes, yes. Of course.' It struck him that Ruth Hartwell was a very lonely woman if the only creature she felt able to call on to accompany her to an ID was her dog.

Swift took the wheel, whilst Cat sat with Ruth Hartwell and her pet in the back seat. As they came into the town they slowed down to a halt at traffic lights. Ruth saw a rush of people crossing the road in front of the car. They were laughing and carefree, full of youth and hope. She recalled herself at that age, remembered the excitement about becoming an adult, the optimism of treading the path that lay ahead. And then her thoughts veered back instantly to Christian, reflecting on the loneliness of his early childhood. His mother had not been a cruel woman, simply not very interested in her child. And after all those troubled years of his early childhood, now his adulthood had been tragically cut short.

She held herself erect against the back of the car seat, her hand lightly resting on her dog's neck. She seemed to be shut into some parallel world, looking down on herself, as she wandered through her thoughts, seeing the dark world pass in front of her eyes beyond the car windows, but feeling very little at all.

She hardly registered the arrival at the morgue, the long walk down a cold corridor, the moment she was confronted with a table on which a body lay covered by a white cloth.

And yes, it was him, her Christian. She felt a rush of love and affection for him. And then, suddenly the lights above her were blinding her, making her unsteady. Salt water rushed into her mouth. She raised her gaze to connect with the pathologist as had been advised, but it seemed to slide away from the young woman's face and skidded up to the ceiling. Her legs were trembling and useless, ready to fall. There was an edge of darkness around her vision.

No, NO, I will not permit it, she told herself fiercely. I will not lose control, lose my dignity in front of these strangers. Dredging up every ounce of her will she lowered her head and thrust it as far down between her knees as she could. The woman officer was there instantly, placing a supporting arm around her waist. She wanted to bat it away, but her strength was required elsewhere, in the fight against black oblivion. Pulling all her reserves together she willed herself to return to a state of full awareness. Consciousness brought pain, but pain had to be felt in order to be defeated. Pain was preferable to the soft controlling pillow of darkness which would strip away every vestige of personal power and decision-making.

She straightened up and gently pushed away the woman detective's protective arm. She turned to the pathologist and the two officers who were looking on, quietly concerned. 'That is Christian,' she said. 'Known as Hartwell. And now, I want to go home, please.'

The two officers stood aside deferentially as she turned her back on the body and started to move towards the door. She supposed there were more questions that she should ask, but she was too drained and exhausted to think what. And what did it matter; Christian was dead, no amount of questions would bring him back.

The journey home passed in a blur.

'Are you sure we can't call anyone to come and stay with you?' the woman officer asked as the car drew to a halt outside the house.

'You have no need to worry about me,' Ruth said firmly. 'I'm used to being on my own.' Feeling that comment had been rather churlish, she added that they had both been very kind.

In the event, both officers insisted on seeing her safely into the house. Ruth half expected the man to patrol the entire building and ensure that there were no intruders or miscreants present. Which would have been a waste of time. Firstly, no one bothered with the *Old School House*, knowing there were no valuables to speak of within its crumbling walls. And secondly, a dog was a far better seeker-out of stowaways than any human searcher.

'Are you sure you don't want us to inform anyone else of Christian's death?' the woman asked. 'I was wondering about his mother … his birth mother. A girlfriend, perhaps?'

Ruth sighed internally. She was longing to lie down in her bed and sink into oblivion. 'His mother has been dead for some years now. And he never married; he was always something of a loner. As far as girlfriends go, I simply don't know.' She looked at the officers' concerned faces. 'I'll answer any further questions you have – but not now. I'm tired, and you must be also. You two go along,' she told the officers in the manner of a teacher dismissing children who were eager to be on their way home. 'Thank you very much for your concern. I'm free most times in the day if you want to talk again.'

Swift and Cat stepped out into the night. Both let out long deep breaths.

'Made of stern stuff,' Cat commented. 'I hope she'll be all right.'

'Yes.' Swift's deliberations turned to the crushing shock he had felt after Kate's sudden death. But he had had Naomi to share the grief with him. Ruth Hartwell looked so alone.

'I'm happy to come and see her again in the morning,' Cat said. 'Do a little digging.'

'No. You need to have your weekend to yourself, to do what you like.'

'Which probably means you want to talk to her by yourself,' she said, laughing. 'Come on, Ed. I know you, married to the job!'

He looked down at her and smiled. And you could be married to Jeremy Howard before too long, he thought with heavy regret.

DAY 5

Swift left it until 10.30 the next morning, then telephoned Ruth Hartwell and asked if he could call to see her later that morning. Within the hour he was following her down the dark oak-panelled hallway of the *Old School House* into her kitchen, shifting his thoughts from the morning's expedition to the crag to the interview ahead. The scent of cooking drifted from the kitchen, a roast or a casserole – comfort food.

Mrs Hartwell gestured to one of the oak chairs around the kitchen table and offered him a hot drink. He requested tea, noting that she seemed edgy and nervous at his arrival, and guessing that preparing tea would give her something to take the edge off her anxiety.

'Thank you for coming,' Ruth Hartwell said, pressing the switch on the kettle and reaching for a plain white china teapot. She turned to look at him as she spoke. Her gaze was direct and assessing, and there was something in her demeanour that spoke of insight and shrewdness.

As she poured the tea, he noted that her hands seemed quite steady and the emotional atmosphere in the room was now solemn, rather than tense. Mrs Hartwell struck him as a very self-composed person. He reflected on the extent to which women of Mrs Hartwell's generation, who opted to dress in old, dowdy clothes and wear their white hair long and piled up on top of their head in some kind of spiky tuft, easily became tarred with the brush of daft old bat, women to be ignored and patronized. 'I'm very sorry for the loss of your son,' he said.

She nodded. 'Thank you.' She gave him another of her long, appraising looks. 'Before you ask me any questions, I'd like to ask you some,' she told him.

'Go ahead.'

'You're a DCI and your colleague was a detective inspector. That means you think that Christian's death was not an accident – am I right?'

'Yes.' He leaned forward towards her. 'Mrs Hartwell, although we believe that Christian died as a result of injuries from a fall, we also have to take into account the fact that his clothes were set alight and that he suffered significant burns.'

She stared at him. 'Oh, no!'

'We're fairly confident he was already dead at the time his clothes started to burn,' he reassured her.

'So that means you think someone wanted to do him harm?'

'Yes, that could be the case. We also have to take into account the fact that he was carrying no wallet, no phone, no keys … all the usual things people carry around with them. Although he did have thirty or so pounds on him.'

He was about to elaborate further when she held up her hand to stop him. 'So, whoever set fire to him wasn't a petty thief?'

'That's the supposition we are currently working with.'

She shook her head in despair. 'I can't understand all this. I just can't imagine anyone wanting to harm him deliberately.'

'Mrs Hartwell, you mentioned yesterday that Christian was not actually your son,' Swift observed.

'That's right.' She pushed the teapot towards him and gestured to him to take a refill. 'Do you have children?' she asked.

'One daughter,' he said. 'She's just graduated.'

Ruth nodded, as though he passed some kind of test, as though having a child of his own would make him someone she could trust to talk to about her putative son. 'Would it help if I told you something of Christian's story?'

'Indeed, it would.'

'I first met him when he was four years old and living with his mother, Pamela Oldfied. She was looking after him on her own, which was not yet fashionable in those days. In fact, she was so feisty she declined to name Christian's father on the birth certificate, claiming he was just a one night stand at a drunken party and she didn't actually know who he was.'

'Do you believe that ... that she didn't know?'

Ruth shrugged. 'You never quite knew with Pamela; she'd tell you what it suited her to tell. She'd got herself into something of a dead-end situation: having an illegitimate baby to look after, getting the push from her parents and renting a flat in a little terrace house in Leeds city centre. It was one of those houses that made your heart sink into your boots when you opened the door and faced the gloom and the lingering smell of boiled cabbage.'

'How did you meet her?' Swift asked.

'She used to go to school with me. After that, we lost touch for a few years. I trained to be a social worker and she and Christian turned up on my case load. He was causing mayhem, both at home and at his nursery school, and I was called in to do a home visit and see what was what. Help and advise.' She gave a wry smile. 'It wasn't easy. Pamela was a pretty terrible mother. Her main strategy in coping with Christian was trying to pretend he wasn't there, or fobbing him off on to any other family who'd have him.' She shook her head, biting on her lip. 'What a job it was that I chose, like having your finger stuck permanently in the dike.'

'Is that a general remark or a specific reference to Pamela and Christian?'

'Both, probably. Anyway I became attached to both of them, and after I got married, had my family and stopped work, I made sure we kept in touch. Pamela and Christian used to come and stay in the school holidays. Christian loved being here, messing around in the garden, going out for walks in the country with the dogs. Visiting the farm up the road. Eating home-made food – all the usual things children like. He fitted in here like a duck takes to water. And Pamela! Well, she liked the freedom of not having to mind a child all the time. She'd go out a lot, have little flirtations at the local pub.'

'How did Christian react to that?' Swift asked.

'Oh, he didn't appear to mind at all. His mother had never been much of a companion for him, and, in fact, I think her frequent absences brought him a sense of relief, a freedom to do and think what he wanted.' She shook her head regretfully. 'I'm not trying to paint Pamela as a monster; it's just that she wasn't cut out for understanding children and enjoying their company. Anyway, in the summer when Christian was nine she asked if we'd look after him whilst she went for a weekend break with a new boyfriend.' She stopped and her eyes gleamed with tears. 'As I told you yesterday, she never came back, although she kept in touch by phone, and she wrote to him from time to time.'

'And Christian's reaction to this new situation?'

'He seemed to cope amazingly well. He'd sometimes ask about Pamela but he seemed happy just to carry on with his life here. He got on fine with our daughter; he settled in to the local school. Which, of course, was all well and good, and certainly very convenient and trouble-free for us. But desperately sad. And, of course, being rejected so heartlessly by his mother would have had a huge effect on him, even if he was not consciously aware of it.'

Swift thought of his daughter's childhood, and fully agreed. Naomi, of course, had had to cope with her mother's sudden death while she was still only in her teens. But she had never had to cope with indifference and outright parental rejection.

'And I have to say,' Ruth added, 'that he was a bit of a daredevil; impulsive and reckless, but then so are many young people.'

'Are you saying that he took life-threatening risks?' Swift asked.

'No, no. I believe that he loved life. And he certainly wouldn't have jumped off a crag, knowing he could kill himself.'

'Did you apply to foster him?'

'No. We simply took him into our home as a welcome addition to the family for however long he and his mother were happy for him to stay. I suppose that sounds shockingly informal and open-ended, but regulations weren't as tight then. And, in any case, Pamela still thought of him as her child, even though she was perfectly willing to put us in charge of his care and development.'

'And later on, Christian decided he wanted to take the name Hartwell?' Swift asked. 'When exactly was that?'

'Just after his mother died. He was eighteen then, and studying for his A levels.'

'I see.' Swift thought about it, guessing that once his birth mother was gone, Christian had felt free to take on the name of the family who had shown him most love. He was getting the impression that the dead man on the crag had had a number of major issues to deal with in his troubled youth.

'He didn't want to go to university,' Ruth continued. 'He opted for training as a journalist. He also did a photography course, and his pictures were remarkably good, in my view. In fact, I often thought he might have made more of a mark on the world with his photography rather than his writing.'

'He wanted to make a mark on the world?' Swift commented.

She smiled. 'Yes, I believe he was quite ambitious.' She stirred her tea. 'So what can I tell you next? Have we got to the point where you're going to ask me if he had any enemies, and if he'd been acting strangely recently?'

Swift agreed, wondering if Ruth Hartwell had some knowledge of police procedure or a liking for detective fiction. She seemed to have been one step ahead of him throughout the interview. Not because he was losing his grip, but because she seemed a strongly proactive person, in a quiet kind of way.

'I can't think of any current enemies,' Ruth said, 'and when I last saw him he seemed happy and positive. He was looking forward to the publication of his book and his aunt, Pamela's elder sister, had recently left him some money in her will. When he left, he gave me one of his half-embarrassed hugs, and he said, "Things are on the up." I keep remembering that.'

'When was it that you last saw him?' Swift prompted.

'About three weeks ago. In the past few years I haven't seen him very often at all. But he'd occasionally phone or send me a scribbled postcard.'

'Do you have a current address for him?' Swift asked.

'It's a flat in Burley-in-Wharfedale. I've never been there. He always visited here.' She reached for a battered handbag and rummaged through it, eventually coming up with a small hard-backed notebook which she leafed through and handed to Swift, indicating the information he had requested.

'We shall need to make a search of the flat,' he said gently.

'Yes. I understand.'

'Do you keep a key, here, Mrs Hartwell?'

'No. I think one of his neighbours has one.'

'Don't worry, we'll deal with it,' Swift reassured her.

As he spoke the last few words there was the sound of the front door opening. A voice called out. 'Hello! It's only me!' Footsteps progressed down the hallway. 'Hello!'

Ruth's face stilled. 'In here,' she called back.

A tall slender woman opened the door and walked purposefully into the room, stopping short on seeing Swift. 'Oh!' She glanced at Ruth, the question in her eyes almost an accusation.

Ruth got up, walked forward and put her arms around the woman, reaching up to kiss her cheek, but only managing to connect with air, as the woman turned away slightly in anticipation of the embrace.

'It's good of you to come, Harriet,' she said.

The woman gave a tight smile. 'You sounded a bit rough when you phoned last night.' She glanced once again at Swift.

'This is Detective Chief Inspector Swift,' Ruth told the visitor. She turned to Swift. 'My daughter, Harriet Brunswick,' she said.

Swift stood up in acknowledgement and held out his hand. Harriet Brunswick hesitated a moment before extending her own hand.

The dog had got up from its bed in a frenzy of prancing, barking welcome. 'Get down,' Harriet said, brushing the animal away with a firm hand.

Swift glanced across to Ruth and saw her give a tiny grimace. 'Go back to your bed,' she told the dog, with gentle command. 'Do you want tea?' she asked her daughter, preparing to get to her feet.

'Sit down, Mother,' Harriet said. 'I'll get it myself.' She took off her black coat and threw it over a chair before crossing to the kettle and switching it on.

Swift noticed that the label in the coat said Max Mara. And that Harriet Brunswick, in contrast to her mother, looked extremely polished and expensive. He also noticed a sea change in the atmosphere of the room. The calmness and openness of the previous minutes had now been overtaken by an air of tension and suspicion.

Harriet turned from the kettle and leaned up against the counter. 'I get the feeling I've interrupted something important. Would you like me to take my tea elsewhere?'

'We've been discussing Christian,' Ruth said. 'You've no need to go elsewhere, there are no secrets.'

'Good,' said Harriet, flashing a hard look at her mother.

'Do you think Christian had secrets?' Swift interposed, suddenly picking up the scent of an interesting line of enquiry. He addressed the question directly to Harriet.

'Doesn't everyone?' Harriet snapped back, immediately biting her lips. 'But as regards Christian I have no idea.' She turned back to the kettle. 'We were never close. We liked each other well enough, but he was just another visitor to the house. And I was quite used to that in my childhood.'

Swift noticed Ruth chew on her lip. 'My husband and I sometimes offered temporary accommodation to homeless people.'

'Lame ducks,' Harriet commented dryly. 'Or should I say dogs? I didn't really mind. I just determined to make quite a different sort of life for myself when I became an adult. It's a very common phenomenon.' She brought a cup of tea to the table and drew a chair out for herself. 'Are you all right, Mother?' she asked, her voice softening a little.

'Yes, but a sudden death is always a shock.' Ruth looked down at her hands.

Harriet nodded. 'Well, I'm here now, to help any way I can.'

Ruth gave a small smile. 'Where is Jake?' she asked, thinking wistfully that it was a long time since she had seen her grandson.

'Staying with his friend, Oliver. They'll have a great time together.'

Swift got up. 'I'll be on my way,' he said, appreciating that Ruth and her daughter needed the chance to resolve their personal difficulties in private. He considered staying on for a time, taking advantage of the edginess between them as a tool in the search for information. On balance, he doubted that he would achieve much in that direction at this stage and he had no intention of playing the role of voyeur and intruder.

Ruth jumped to her feet. 'I'll see you out.'

He smiled. 'No need.'

She followed him anyway. 'You will let me know of any developments, won't you?' she asked, her previous determination appearing to revive.

'Don't worry, Mrs Hartwell, I'll keep you in the picture.' He shook her hand with some warmth.

He had the feeling it would not be long before he was back at the *Old School House*.

Following Swift's departure, Ruth cleared the table and carried the cups and saucers to the sink. She ran water from the tap, squeezed out some liquid soap and picked up a dishcloth.

Harriet watched her, the old sensations of affection and irritation rising in equal amounts. 'I'll buy you a dishwasher for Christmas,' she said.

Ruth turned around, her smile wistful and wary. 'Thank you.'

'Would you use it?' Harriet asked. 'You're such a cheapskate you'd probably begrudge buying the detergent and squandering electricity.'

'I might use it,' Ruth countered mildly.

Harriet was looking around the kitchen: the old pine units, the ugly plastic worktops and the ancient wood-burning stove which must have been a relic of the 1950s. 'This place must be more eco-friendly than a bunny's burrow,' she commented.

'I'll take that as a compliment,' Ruth said, but her daughter's throwaway remarks were hurting.

'Why was a detective chief inspector here?'

Ruth dipped her hands into the warm sudsy water. 'It seems Christian's death wasn't an accident. The police aren't completely sure yet.'

Harriet pondered, but not for very long. 'Oh, God! That's not good news.'

Ruth didn't reply.

Harriet got up and leaned against the sink so that she could see her mother's face. 'So the police are involved? They think his death was suspicious … is that the terminology.'

'Yes.'

'And you're encouraging them in this belief?'

'I'm assisting them with their enquiries,' Ruth said firmly. 'Why would Christian simply fall off a cliff?'

'Because he was a madcap Hotspur who never really grew up.'

'He had a lot to look forward to,' Ruth said, resting her dripping hands on the edge of the sink, 'and he wasn't a suicidal type.'

'Sometimes people just have accidents,' Harriet pointed out.

Ruth nodded. 'The police are considering foul play, or even murder,' she said, keeping her voice steady. 'I can hardly instruct them to halt their enquiries.'

'So, what's in this for you, Mother?' Harriet demanded, appearing not to have registered her mother's mild protests. 'Are you concerned about Christian's good name? Is it vital to you that he must be shown to be neither suicidal nor careless enough to take a tumble on a country walk? Or are you doing this in some kind of sentimental homage to his dead mother?'

'Harriet, calm down,' Ruth said quietly, although she knew she was whistling in the wind.

'Or maybe you're just bored. You haven't exactly got a lot to do, have you?' Harriet flung at her.

Ruth began to dry her hands on a tea towel, noticing for the first time that it really was disgracefully ragged around the edges. 'If you mean shopping and travelling and socializing, no, I don't. But there are other things in life.'

'Is that a dig at me and Charles?'

'Of course not.' Ruth said evenly. 'I've got plenty of faults, but being critical of other people's choices isn't one of them.'

'OK, fair enough.' Harriet ruminated for a time. 'Mother, you do realize that if the police start digging, it'll all come out – the fiasco in Algeria.'

'Yes, and I'm sorry about that. But isn't it possible that what happened then could possibly be connected with Christian's death?'

'God! That was all sorted out years ago,' exclaimed Harriet with some force. 'We can really do without all this. Charles is up before the selection board next month, Director of Surgery. It's rather important.'

Ruth bowed her head. 'I'm sorry, Harriet.'

'No, you're not. You've no compunctions whatsoever about putting your concerns about Christian before Charles's career and thus my happiness. Me, your only child. And there's Jake to think of too.'

Ruth's face softened into a smile. Jake was her only grandchild. He was nine and she loved him unreservedly, and he was still young enough to love her back on the same terms. 'I personally don't think the Algeria incident has any bearing on Christian's death, but I do agree that Chief Inspector Swift might do some digging, as you call it. And I think that is justified.'

Harriet let out a snort of irritation.

'I also believe he'll keep quiet about anything he considers irrelevant to the case.'

'Aah!' Harriet was being driven to the very limits with her parent's possibly sound but infuriating line of reasoning. She took in a long breath and put up her hands in a gesture of truce. 'OK, OK. Have you got this Swift person's contact number?'

'Yes,' said Ruth. 'His card is on the table.'

'I'll go and see him and put *my* cards on the table,' said Harriet.

'Are you sure that's a good idea?' Ruth said.

'Well, it's better than lying low and giving him the impression that I'm harbouring information which has to be dragged out of me. And he's bound to follow up on me, given that I stupidly half spilled the beans by talking about secrets.'

'You have a point,' Ruth said, sensing a slight easing in the atmosphere now that her daughter had made a decision. 'There's wine in the fridge,' she said. 'Why don't you open it? We could do with a glass.'

'Good idea. What are you cooking?' Harriet asked, eyeing the Rayburn.

'Boeuf bourguignon. With dauphinoise potatoes.' Ruth shot her daughter a brief glance containing a degree of mischief and challenge.

'Wow!'

Harriet's look of amazement gave Ruth a stab of gratification. 'I thought it was time I expanded my cooking repertoire. I got a book from the library and I'm working my way through the recipes.'

Harriet laughed. 'I'll say this for you, Mother, you can never be accused of being boring.'

When Harriet Brunswick had called Swift later on to request a meeting with Swift he had not asked her what she wanted to talk about, even though it was seven in the evening and she would have a forty-five minute drive to reach his cottage. The urgency of her tone was enough to let him know that what she had to say was likely to have an interesting bearing on Christian Hartwell's death. He switched on the lights at the front of the house, to help her find her way down the long path. He saw the headlights of her car swing over the horizon and dissolve into the soft darkness as she swung the door open and shut. The stony nature of the path did not seem to impede her progress; she was very soon at the front door and tapping on the wood with firm knuckles.

Following his welcoming gesture, she moved purposefully through to the sitting room as though she had been to the cottage many times before.

'Tea? Coffee? Wine?' he asked.

'I'm fine thank you.' She tossed her coat on the sofa and sat down crossing her legs. She was wearing slim-fit black jeans and high-heeled shoes with bright scarlet soles. Diamonds twinkled in her ears and her shiny sable hair swung like a silk curtain as she moved her head. 'Thank you for seeing me,' she said. 'I'll get straight to the point, as the last thing I want to do is waste your time.'

She spoke as though she was chairing a conference, bringing the various participants to order so as to begin the proceedings promptly. She was tensed, wound like a spring.

'I've plenty of time,' he said.

'Obviously this has to do with Christian,' she said. 'I know my mother has told you about the way in which he came to be a part of our family – a rather unconventional arrangement to say the least.'

He gave a slight nod, made no comment.

'The whole set-up of our household was pretty unconventional,' she said. 'My father was a chaplain at Wentworth Prison and a great sympathizer with the criminal classes, the poor and the great unwashed.' She gave a rueful smile. 'Don't get me wrong, I'm not an evil fascist, but when you've shared your home with the odd child molester, alcoholic and thief in your tender years, you tend to become somewhat hardened and cynical. I didn't really mind it all that much when I was a child – I suppose I just accepted it as normal – but as I got to be a teenager, the time when you have a need and a duty to rebel from your parents' ideals, I really didn't like it much at all. Why couldn't we just have our tatty old house to ourselves? Why did we have to take in other people's rejects?'

'Yes, I can see that,' Swift said.

'I didn't mind about Christian being around, though. He was bright and engagingly naughty and altogether quite good fun. One day after he'd been in a spot of bother for pinching some apples from a neighbour's garden he climbed up on the roof of the house and refused to come down, sending my parents into a state of panic. In the end, my father suggested that my mother fry some onions. He said it always worked with prisoners who decided to take the same line as Christian. They just couldn't resist the lovely smell. My mother was never much of a cook, so it was rather a novelty to have this enticing smell wafting from the kitchen. Quite soon Christian gave in and came back down again, hungry enough to eat a horse.' She stopped. 'I'm sorry, I'm rattling on. This isn't really relevant, is it?'

'As regards any further investigation into Christian's death, any background information is useful,' Swift said, in neutral tones. And you've certainly conjured up an interesting picture, he thought.

'Yeah, well, you see, Christian had the ability to do that. I'll bet his forthcoming book will be quite an interesting read.'

'Do you think you'll make an appearance in it?' Swift enquired.

'God! I hope not.' She ran her fingers through her curtain of hair, and took in a long, determined breath. 'Right, I'll get to the point. When Christian and I were nineteen we went with some friends on a field trip to Algeria. There were four of us altogether, the other two being my future husband Charles and his friend Hugh. The trip was Hugh's brainchild: he was studying geography and he wanted to do some research on sand dunes for his PhD.'

'So Hugh was a postgraduate, older than you and Christian?' Swift asked.

'He was twenty-three, as was Charles. He was a final year medical student at that time.'

'Hugh fixed it all up and got approval from the Algerian government to do his research in a place called In Salah in the middle of the desert. He borrowed an old Land Rover from a relative and off we went. The trip was all to do with finding out what made sand dunes form and shift, which apparently no one had ever researched fully before. Just imagine, a gang of young people in a Land Rover in the middle of the Sahara, living in a tent and spending their days counting grains of sand.'

Swift thought it sounded like a vision of hell. 'Why did you go, then?'

'I went because Charles was going and we were already an item. And Christian went because it sounded like a totally off-the-wall project and therefore likely to be good fun. Oh, to be young and foolish again.' She gave a rueful smile and then the smile gradually faded.

'But it wasn't good fun?' Swift said.

'Too right. We got sick, we got diarrhoea, we got infestations in our hair and sand in our eyes. And we quarrelled. Christian and Charles didn't really get on. Christian was very laid back and all for letting things take their course, but Charles likes to be more proactive. Charles and Hugh clashed all the time. It got so bad they could hardly bear to speak to one another. And then Hugh got killed.'

'I see. And what did Charles and Hugh quarrel about?' Swift asked, beginning to have an understanding of Harriet's motivation in coming to see him.

'Just about everything; they were both very strong minded. But the main point of contention was about the rota Hugh devised for carrying out his research. He'd worked it out that we needed to make observations round the clock. We each had an allotted span of time out on the dunes. Charles argued that it was dangerous to go out there singly – especially for me as a woman on her own. And it was true that I attracted a good deal of attention from the Algerian men, with my pale skin and my habit of wearing shorts. Anyway, Hugh insisted that we went along with his plan, because if we doubled up it would take twice the amount of time to get the data we needed. Well, of course, we all gave in; the idea of being stuck in that arid, burning hell hole for a minute longer than neces-sary simply wasn't on. But, in the end, the worst happened. Hugh didn't come back from his shift one afternoon and when we found him he'd been beaten over the head with a stout stick and left to die out in the sun.' Her face screwed into a grimace of recalled pain as she spoke the words.

'Had anything been stolen from his body?' Swift asked, snapping into automatic investigative mode.

'His watch and his camera. The digital recording machine we'd used for collecting data was still present and correct.'

'Did the police become involved?'

'Yes. It was Charles who took charge of everything. He has that ability to shut his emotions down and simply get on with doing what needs to be done. I suppose that's a quality that has helped to make him such a successful surgeon. Anyway, he persuaded me and Christian that we should drive Hugh's body to the nearest *gendarmerie* ourselves and that we should contact the British Embassy in Algiers to advise us further. Which turned out to be a smart move. Without the consul, we'd most definitely all have ended up in jail as suspects. At least Charles and Christian would; the police didn't seem so suspicious of me – maybe as I was the one who dealt with all their questions in a mixture of halting schoolgirl French and English with gestures.'

'Or maybe their culture isn't happy to regard women as proactive enough to carry out a killing?'

'Possibly,' she agreed.

'Were you able to provide any relevant information about the killing?' Swift asked.

She nodded slowly. 'We had a very strange but true story about an irate Arab on a donkey. It's the crazy sort of story you'd tell at a dinner party, making the most of the exotic oddness of people in a foreign country in order to get a laugh. Except we never have told it, of course. The circumstances of Hugh's sudden death were so horrific the very thought of the furious Arab sends prickles across the back of my neck.'

'Will you tell me now?'

'A few days into working the rota, Hugh came back from the dunes one afternoon and told us that the figure of a man on a donkey suddenly came into view over the horizon. The man made straight for Hugh, and demanded that he pay a rent for parking the Land Rover under his palm tree in the square at In Salah the previous day. Given that Hugh didn't speak any Arabic except a few swear words he'd picked up on the way, and that the irate Arab had very little English, they couldn't have had much of a conversation. Hugh flatly refused to pay anything, and the guy started shouting, and Hugh tried a bit of Arabic swearing, and eventually the guy went away – still very irate.'

'So Hugh had effectively made himself an enemy.'

'Exactly.'

'What did the police do?'

'Shouted at us for moving Hugh's body and confiscated our passports. It was all very frightening.' She stopped for a few moments. 'After a day or so the guy from the embassy in Algiers arrived and he sorted it all out and we were able to come home. Charles insisted on arranging for Hugh's body to be flown home without delay to his parents, and he contacted them personally. I think he felt particularly bad about Hugh's death because they'd been so much at odds with each other.' She swallowed hard and shot Swift a quick glance, before turning away, her eyes glistening with tears.

'When we got back to the UK again, it was like being in heaven,' she said. 'I remember that when Charles drove the Land Rover off the boat at Calais, I felt like leaping out and kissing the tarmac. We went back to our former lives and gradually all the guilt and grief and angst died down. Christian enrolled for a course in journalism and Charles and I got married.' She hurried through the last details as though trying to give the impression that was the end of the story. That was that.

'Were either of the stolen items ever found?' Swift asked.

'No.' She thought for a few seconds 'And no one was ever brought to trial for the killing.'

'Were the UK police ever involved?'

'Not to my knowledge. There was certainly no follow-up after we came home.'

'Can you give me the date on which Hugh was killed?'

She grimaced. 'I'll never forget it. July 1989. The fifth.'

As Swift paused to make a few notes, Harriet fell silent. Her face was creased in uncertainty and anxiety and Swift was pretty sure she was already regretting having come to see him, and having possibly talked herself, and more importantly, her husband into a corner. He guessed that she was the kind of person who liked to have everything planned and under control. Uncertainty about what Swift might dig up if a full investigation ensued would be almost unbearable for her. He decided to go for brutal openness to what was on her mind. 'Why did you come to see me?' he asked. 'What are you worried about?'

She put her head in her hands. 'Oh, God, I've been such a fool.'

'Have you?'

'Telling you all this. Of course I have.'

'So why did you?'

'I'm sure you could answer that question without my help.' Her face had become angry and resentful.

'If I'd found out for myself, it would have looked rather worse,' he suggested.

'Charles is up for Director of Surgery at The Wentbridge in south London,' she said. 'He's tipped as hot favourite for the post and he's really keen to get it. If things came out about Algeria, it could ruin his chances.'

'I doubt it,' Swift said, 'not from what you've told me.' He waited, sensing the torment going on in her mind and emotions. 'So what is it that you didn't tell me?'

She shut her eyes tightly, opened them again. 'Charles was actually charged with Hugh's murder shortly after the police questioning was completed.'

'With what evidence and justification?'

'It was concerning alibis. Christian and I were in a café in the square when the killing took place, and there were plenty of people who could confirm that to the police. But Charles had gone off exploring, so he couldn't provide an alibi. He likes doing that occasionally, taking off on his own for some time out.' She looked at him with a pleading which somehow reminded him of his daughter, Naomi, when she got into difficulties. An appeal which was filled with both despair and challenge.

'Go on,' he said.

'The police dropped the charges after the embassy guy spoke with them. Don't ask me the ins and outs of it. I had the impression the legal system out there was complex and very different from ours.'

'It also sounds as if your "embassy guy" had commendably persuasive diplomatic skills,' Swift suggested.

She sighed. 'Yes, I suppose he did.' She was suddenly looking exhausted and defeated.

'Are you concerned that there will be a record of a charge having been made?' Swift asked. 'That it could come out in a security search if your husband is offered the job he is after?'

She looked at him, frowning. 'Well, yes, isn't that obvious?'

'But that would have been a risk quite aside from the issue of Christian's death,' he pointed out quietly.

'OK. But clearly any publicity could open up the whole thing again. Journalists digging for any juicy morsels and so on. Charles's name being in the papers.'

He allowed a silence to develop, allowing her mind to fully confront the most desperate fear which was torturing her.

'Had your husband any motive for killing Christian?' he asked.

'No,' she breathed, hardly disturbing the air as she spoke.

'Do you know where he was at the time Christian was killed?'

She shook her head, on the point of tears. 'No. I'm assuming he was going up and down some mountain for most of the day.'

Another death, another lack of alibi for Charles Brunswick, thought Swift. Which, of course, in no way compromised him in the absence of any supporting evidence or motive.

'My son, Jake, is the most precious thing in my life,' she said, with feeling. 'Charles *is* my life.' There was another pleading look.

'Where is Charles now?' Swift asked.

'He's a few miles away from here, in some pub up on the moors outside Pateley Bridge. He's on leave from work and doing some walking on the fells. By himself, with his phone switched off. It's something he likes to do occasionally, and I go along with it. He has a very responsible, stressful job; he deserves to have complete peace from time to time.' She stood up, tears now running down her face.

'When did he arrive in Yorkshire?' Swift asked.

'On Monday. He rang me in the afternoon to say he'd got there.' She snatched up her coat and began to move towards the door. 'I can't talk any more,' she said. 'Thinking of what I've already said is killing me.' She brushed past Swift. He followed.

'Are you going back to your mother's house?' he asked.

'Most probably,' she said, wiping fiercely at the wetness beneath her eyes. 'Don't worry about me. I'm tougher than you might think. And I've got a son to think about. I won't do anything stupid.' She rummaged in her bag and gave him her card. 'Just call if you want to speak to me again.' She had the front door open now and he watched her hurry up the path to her car.

He looked at her card. *Harriet Brunswick, B.A. LPC. Senior Consultant – personal injury claims. Stirrup and Samson Solicitors.*

And then he walked back into the cottage and picked up the phone.

Ruth found herself waiting in some anxiety for Harriet to return from her meeting with Swift. She tried to read, she tried to involve herself in a TV programme about a Victorian artist, but found she couldn't concentrate.

When the doorbell tinkled it was with massive relief that she walked to the front door. Harriet must have forgotten to take her key to the house with her.

Ruth swung open the door. And was then stabbed with surprise and disappointment to see a young man standing there. He was tall and broad-shouldered, a big slab of a lad with windblown hair and a hunted look in his eyes. Ruth felt no fear. She had a wealth of experience in dealing with strangers who simply turned up on the doorstep: she and her late husband had prided themselves on keeping an open house and always thinking the best of people unless they proved otherwise. Which sadly, had often happened. Behind her, Tamsin was standing quiet and watchful and the small dog's presence contributed further to Ruth's quiet trust that no harm would come to her from this young stranger.

'Hello,' Ruth said.

Craig felt himself trembling inside. He stood very still, willing her to delve back into her mind and retrieve some memory of him which would ease his total lack of confidence in proceeding any further. Having made it to her front door and dredged up the courage to ring the bell, he found himself now helpless and exhausted. 'It's Craig,' he said.

'Craig?' she murmured, staring hard at him. Her eyes sharpened with recognition. 'Craig Titmus!'

'Yeah.' He tried not to wince at the sound of his surname. The name of a murderer. 'I thought I would come to see you, Mrs Hartwell,' he said, to let her know that he knew her and he meant no harm.

'Craig.' she said, beginning to place him. 'I used to visit you when you were inside.'

'Aye,' he said. 'And you helped me learn to read.'

She smiled, remembering their sessions together. 'It was a long time ago,' she said. 'Come in.'

He hesitated. The little dog looked at him and wagged its tail. He stepped through the door and stared around him. A huge house, dark wood walls, a light that looked like an old-fashioned lantern sticking up from the end of the banister.

Words hammered inside him. *I want someone to love. I want someone to love me. I want to have a home and a family. I want to work in a kitchen and cook things.* His heart hammered in time with the words. He prayed that he could stop himself from shouting them out loud and frightening her.

She walked ahead of him and they ended up in a kitchen so big you could almost play a game of five-a-side football in it. The warmth of the room wrapped itself around him and he closed his eyes with the sudden pleasure of the heat. In the air there was a lovely smell of meat and potatoes.

'Sit down,' she told him. 'There, look, beside the stove.' Obediently he sat. He rubbed his hands on his knees. His hands looked too big and too red. He pulled them up to his chest and tucked them inside each other.

'Would you like something to eat?' Mrs Hartwell asked him. 'I've got some stew with beef in it, and some savoury potatoes.' She rested her hand briefly on his shoulder as she went towards the oven. He wanted her to leave it there; it was years since anyone had touched him. Touched him as a proper person.

'When were you released?' she asked, putting on some thick gloves and lifting a blue dish from the oven. She had her back to him, so he could look at her without feeling bad about it. He'd thought maybe she wouldn't be too put out to see him, but he'd never dared think she'd be like this – asking him in, giving him food, treating him like he was someone she could respect.

'A couple of days back.'

'Where have you been staying?' She was ladling out the stew

now, on to a plate with a pattern of flowers around the edge. It was good that she was busy, made him feel OK about talking.

'In a bedsit. Probation gave me the money.' He didn't mention the previous night when he'd slept in the bus station, wrapping his arms around his chest to keep warm. Watching her, he saw that she had got old-looking, more like a granny than a mum. When she'd come to the jail to teach reading, her hair had been dark brown, almost black, and she'd not had so many wrinkles on her face. He liked the idea of a granny – less scary than a mum.

She moved to a drawer, and started pulling out knives and forks. He jumped up. 'I'll do it.'

She turned to him, startled a little, then smiling.

'Am I shouting?' he asked, staring down at her, the cutlery in his fingers.

'No.' She let him set out the knife and fork, then placed the plate of food in front of him. He stared at it, before closing his eyes briefly and allowing the lovely smell to filter into his nostrils. He picked up his fork.

'You can stay here for the night, if you like, Craig,' she said, once he was filled with stew and potatoes and some tinned treacle pudding she'd found in the cupboard and smothered in cream.

He shot her a look, wondering if she was just winding him up. But no, her eyes were still kind.

'Would you like to do that?' she prompted.

'Yeah.' He couldn't believe it. He kept thinking she'd turn on him. Maybe turn into a female version of Blackwell. 'Thanks,' he said. He swallowed, not knowing what to say next.

'Craig is a nice name,' Ruth said. 'I remember you telling me how it came about that you got that name. It was your grandad who suggested it, because he was Scottish.'

He was astonished. 'How can you remember that?'

'Oh, I've always squirreled all kind of things into my memory.' She smiled at him.

'Aye,' said Craig, not believing his luck in having made this long journey and found Mrs Hartwell. But most of all that she still seemed to like him, even though he was a murderer. She knew that, he'd told her all those years ago when she taught him to read. Who else would have a murderer in their house?

The doorbell tinkled.

Ruth raised her head like a startled animal. She got up, giving Craig a reassuring smile. 'Oh, dear,' she murmured, as she walked towards the front door, seeing the shadowy figure of Harriet waiting behind it.

Craig started up as Harriet entered the kitchen.

'Hi,' she said to him, placing a paper bag with a bottle in it on the table and then shrugging off her coat.

'Who are you?'

'Craig,' he muttered.

'Right.' Harriet sat down at the table and drew a bottle of whisky from the paper bag. 'Who's for a nightcap?' she said, smiling at her two observers. Without waiting for a response she jumped up and rooted in one of the kitchen cupboards, producing three dusty-looking cut-glass tumblers.

Ruth had seen, as soon as she opened the door, that all was suddenly right with the world for Harriet. Which meant, first and foremost, that she'd had some positive phone contact with Charles, and that, presumably, all had gone well during her talk with Chief Inspector Swift. Maternal relief rolled through her. She took a swallow of whisky and water, enjoying the cold sensation as it rolled down her throat and tickled the lining of her stomach.

'Do you take water with it, Craig?' Harriet said with faint provocation, pushing a tumbler towards the young visitor.

He looked up at her. 'Don't know,' he said, his voice brittle, the lights in his eyes dancing with panic.

'If in doubt, I'd advise it,' she said, reaching forward and drowning the golden liquid in cold water drawn from the tap.

Ruth caught his eye. 'There's no need to drink it if you don't want, Craig. Just try a sip and see.'

Harriet swivelled a look of devilment at her parent. She raised her eyebrows. *Another of your lame ducks! Don't worry, I'm not going to make a fuss.*

Craig stood up, making the chair legs scrape against the flagged floor. 'I think I'd better be going.' His glance darted about, as though he were a cornered fox.

'It's too late to find a place for the night now,' Ruth said, drawing deep on her reserves of calm. She loved her daughter, she was happy for her new-found well-being, but she wasn't going to let this poor terrified young man be turned out of her house by Harriet's covert baiting. 'And, anyway, I want you to stay.'

Craig stood stock still. Then sat down and took a tentative sip of whisky.

Harriet turned her back on him and spoke to Ruth. 'I told the chief inspector the whole story. He didn't think the desert incident was relevant to Christian's death. Not at all.'

'Good.'

'And then on the way back here, Charles phoned, just to let me know how things were going at his end.' She took a large gulp of whisky and leaned back in her chair, closing her eyes and letting the fiery spirit soothe her.

Ruth recognized the signs. She knew that Harriet had undergone severe stress, had possibly reached a point where the strain had become unbearable, but that in some way the incidents of the evening had put things right. She understood too that Charles and Harriet's marriage was lived out on a knife-edge of passion, deep love and dangerous conflict. A dangerous mix of ingredients. But so far a heady brew which had worked for both of them.

All's well that ends well, Ruth thought. So far.

DAY 6

Swift set out at 8 a.m. next morning bound for the Black Sheep Inn, the only pub in a small hamlet accessed from the Dales village of Pateley Bridge.

If he had been travelling as the crow flies he could have made if from his cottage near Cracoe village to the Black Sheep Inn in probably less than twenty minutes. However, the lower slopes of Great Whernside were something of an obstacle, so he drove south to the small town of Pateley Bridge and then north again along a road which took him through the village of Ramsgill, after which the road became narrow and steep, ending just past the Black Sheep Inn. If you wanted to go further north at that point you had to get out of your car and walk.

The route was another tourists' gift of velvety hills, hedgerows crammed with wild flowers and in the distance glimpses of the river Nid curling through the valley with the sheen of a grey pearl. It was a clear morning with the expectant feel of a glorious sunny day just beginning. Now, in the middle of July, the foliage on the trees was beginning to darken, and in places looking a little tired, well past the dazzling acid green of May, and seeming to be just hanging on, waiting for the fiery beauty of autumn.

The pub's door was open when he arrived at 9.30 and one or two guests were taking advantage of the sunshine to breakfast outside on the wrought-iron tables set along the outside wall of the inn. He managed to squeeze his car into the one vacant space in the pub's tiny car park, fitting it in beside a gleaming red Audi RSS which, ten or so years before would have stabbed him with a tiny pang of envy. After a little searching inside the inn he eventually found a young waitress clearing a table in the oak-beamed dining room. 'I'm looking for Mr Charles Brunswick,' he told her.

'I'm sorry,' she said. 'I only work here on Sundays. I don't know all the customers' names.' She thought for a moment, and then shot him a worried glance.

'I'm from the North West Division of Bradford Police,' he told her, showing his warrant card.

'Oh!' She bit her lip.

'There's nothing to worry about,' Swift reassured her. 'But I would like to speak to him. Do you have a register of names here?'

Her face showed relief at being able to offer some help. 'Yes, we do. Would you like me to look at it?'

He followed her through to the bar where she took a leather diary from a drawer in an oak dresser. She placed it on the bar and opened it up to show the current week. 'There!' she said with some triumph, finding the name for him. 'They're in Room 6.'

Swift looked over her shoulder. Brunswick had signed in on the previous Monday. Mr and Mrs Brunswick, he had written, in barely legible script, consistent with a doctor's writing. It seemed clear what the scenario was. He felt a pang for the fiery Harriet.

He spoke again to the girl, who was waiting wide-eyed. 'Could you ring through to the room and ask him to come down to speak to me?'

She swallowed. 'Yes, of course.' She fiddled about a little with the small switchboard on the bar and eventually raised an answer from Room 6. 'He'll be with you in just a minute,' she told Swift.

'Would you like to sit in the snug?' she said gaining confidence now. 'It's nice and quiet in there at this time of day.'

Swift duly followed her and settled himself on a dark-red velvet sofa which was a paler dusky pink on the arms and cushions from the pressure of numerous hands and bottoms over the years. The girl offered him coffee and newspapers. 'I'm quite happy just to wait,' he told her, smiling.

'Right, I'll tell him where you are when he comes down,' she said, heading back to the dining room.

Charles Brunswick did not keep him waiting. Within a couple of minutes he was striding into the parlour, a sharp-featured, flame-haired man who had to duck his head in order to avoid the oak beam over the entry door. He homed in on Swift, extending his hand and greeting him with cheery camaraderie. 'Charles Brunswick. How can I help you?'

Swift shook the offered hand and showed his warrant card.

'A DCI, no less,' Brunswick exclaimed. He sat himself in a sofa opposite the one Swift had been sitting in and looked at him expectantly. 'I'm assuming this is about Christian Hartwell. I spoke to Harriet on the phone last night and she told me the sad news.'

And plenty more besides, Swift judged. 'What do you know so far, sir?' Swift asked, thinking that if Brunswick was in any way worried about this turn of events he was making a very good job of hiding it.

'Harriet said he had been found dead in some woodland area not too far away from here. Fallen off a crag, apparently. What a terrible thing to happen.'

'Yes,' Swift said.

'I can't pretend I'm devastated by the news,' Brunswick said. 'I hardly knew the guy. And when we did meet we'd very little in common.'

Swift thought of Harriet's desert story and noted that Brunswick was being economical with the truth.

'So why are you contacting me?' Brunswick followed up.

'We've reason to believe we shouldn't rule out foul play regarding Christian's death. We're treating it as murder.'

'Is that so?' He frowned. 'Well, I'm sorry to hear that. So, you're contacting all Christian's friends and enemies, eliminating them from your enquiries. Is that it?' His tone had become ironic and faintly patronizing.

'Yes,' said Swift, noting that he wasn't actually wielding the shining sword of truth himself.

'Are you on the search for alibis?'

'That could be helpful,' Swift said, noting the way Brunswick was trying to get the upper hand by taking it upon himself to ask the questions.

'What was the estimated time of death?' Brunswick asked, brisk and business-like.

'We don't have a very precise estimate, sir. However, it would be helpful if you could tell us where you were between 2 a.m. and 8 a.m. on Tuesday last?'

The answer came back almost immediately 'Right I was in bed from around 11 p.m. I got up around 7 a.m. I was planning to do Great Whernside that morning. I started out from here around just after 7.15.' He paused. 'I suppose you'll be wondering if anyone could confirm that?'

'It would be helpful,' Swift said, noting that Brunswick was still doing his job for him.

'Let's think. No, sorry, there wasn't anyone around.' A pause. And then a smile of triumph. 'But I stopped at a garage just down the road in Pateley Bridge as I needed to fill up. I bought some chocolate bars in the shop attached when I paid for the fuel. I'm pretty sure I've still got the receipt, and probably the number to call. He patted both back pockets of his jeans. 'Yes, wait a moment, it's here in my wallet. Westside Garage, 52 litres. Payment timed at 07.37. And here's the phone number. Got a pencil?' The words flowed out of him, presto and staccato.

Swift duly wrote down the contact number.

'They've probably got CCTV,' Brunswick said cheerfully. 'And I'll bet the guy who was on the till remembers me; most people do. There aren't a lot of guys six-four with bright red hair.'

No problem with self-image here, Swift thought. He wondered whether to press further. He'd need to check the alibi with the landlord and the garage, together with a consultation of an ordnance survey map. But even then he didn't think he'd got much to go on. The distances were probably too small and the time frame of the time of death too large to come to any conclusions. And there was something so deeply confident in Brunswick's manner and answer it led him to suspect he hadn't had anything to do with Christian Hartwell's murder. On the other hand, he wasn't going to rule him out entirely. Not yet. He might just be an ace bluffer. And if Harriet had filled him in fully on her conversation with him at his cottage yesterday evening, Charles had had a lot of time to get his story in order.

'Mr Brunswick … about the incident in Algiers?'

Brunswick raised his eyebrows, a gesture which almost seemed like a silent rebuke to the detective for bringing up such a distasteful matter. 'Oh, come on! That was nearly twenty years ago.'

'But you were there in a party including Christian Hartwell and you were charged with a murder.'

'Yes, and the charge was almost instantly dropped. The policing in Algiers twenty years back was somewhat primitive. Probably still is.'

Swift looked hard at him. 'Why did you say you hardly knew Christian Hartwell, when you spent a few weeks in his company in a lonely desert area? And he's been your brother-in-law for some years.'

Brunswick was in no way disconcerted. 'We didn't get on in Algiers,' he said. 'We just didn't click, and that's why I said I hardly knew him. We spent no quality time together, as the saying goes. You must have quite a few acquaintances from the past who don't count for anything in your life now,' he said to Swift, who refrained from commenting. 'And of course he wasn't my brother-in-law as you must know by now. No blood relationship to Harriet. And the three of us certainly didn't do get-togethers.'

Swift recognized that he wasn't going to get much further with Brunswick until he had done some further digging. He stood up. 'Thank you Mr Brunswick, you've been very helpful.'

Brunswick followed his lead. 'Not a problem, Chief Inspector.' He offered his hand again.

Swift shook it with professional politeness. As he walked to his car, Brunswick's voice echoed in his head, the rock-solid self-satisfaction grating like the buzzing of an insect in his ears.

DAY 7

Ravi Stratton welcomed Swift with a warm handshake and the offer of freshly brewed coffee. She had invited him and Cat Fallon for a review of the findings to date on the Hartwell case and his report lay on her desk, neatly stacked and, Swift guessed, already carefully considered. Cat had arrived at the station but was currently occupied in fielding an urgent phone call which had come in just before the review meeting began. She would join her colleagues as soon as possible.

Looking around Stratton's office, Swift noted that the stand-in superintendent was sensitive to the fact that the room was still the domain of its previous occupant, Damian Finch, as she had made no major changes in its arrangement or decor. There were just one or two small personal details that reflected her personal preferences – a family photograph on the desk together with fresh carnations in a slim glass vase. He noticed too that Finch's reproduction of the *Mona Lisa* painting, which had presided in a quietly judgemental way over the room, had been replaced by a gentle watercolour depicting a waterfall set against the slope of a hill and a pale-blue sky.

Having drunk her coffee, Stratton, formally dressed in a black suit, sat for a few moments with her hands laid on the desk in front of her, her face still and thoughtful. 'Thank you for this, Ed,' she said in formal, polite tones, tapping her fingers on the first page of the report. 'It's very clear and comprehensive. But I do have one or two questions.' She glanced at her watch. 'Shall we make a start?'

'Please go ahead,' he told her.

At this point there was a tap on the door and at Stratton's call to enter Cat Fallon slipped through looking apologetic and slightly harassed. 'I'm so sorry to be late, ma'am,' she told Stratton. 'A difficulty has cropped up on the case I was working on before I left Central.'

'We haven't quite started,' Stratton reassured her. 'I think you already know Chief Inspector Swift.'

Cat turned to him. 'Good morning, sir.'

He noted that her formality in addressing him was accompanied by a glint of irony in her eyes as she smiled at him. She was wearing a pale-green cotton dress printed with bright red flowers, bringing a touch of exotica to Stratton's mainly monochrome environment. He also noticed that she had dark rings beneath her eyes as though she had had one or two sleepless nights. He tried to put aside any theories as to why that might be, especially as regards her weekend activities with Jeremy.

Stratton handed Cat a copy Swift's report.

'I'll try to get up to speed as soon as possible,' Cat said, her eyes flying over the lines of print.

'I was about to ask Ed about his mention of there being sheep in the field close to the point from which Mr Hartwell fell,' Stratton explained.

He confirmed that sheep had been present in the field she mentioned.

'And deer, also?'

'That's correct.'

'And also that the netting separating these animals from the footpath was not wholly secure?'

'Yes.'

'Are you suggesting that one or more of these animals got loose and maybe ran into Mr Hartwell, causing him to fall?' Stratton enquired. 'It would seem to be a possibility.'

Cat was still busy skimming the report but Swift was aware that she would be taking in every detail he had mentioned, whilst at the same time attending to the verbal discussion and filing it all away with enviable accuracy.

'There is no forensic evidence to support a theory that contact with an animal could have caused Christian Hartwell's fall,' Swift said. 'But for the pathologist's and coroner's benefit I thought it was useful to give as full a picture of the nature of the locality in which Hartwell died.'

'Yes, yes, I see,' Stratton said, sounding doubtful. 'As regards Mr Brunswick,' she continued, 'can we rule him out, or not, from having had a part in Mr Hartwell's death?'

Swift noticed Cat smiling to herself, and looked forward to an explanation of why later, although he had a pretty good idea of what was entertaining her. He realized that his style of reporting was too even-handed for Ravi Stratton, as indeed it had been found to be by other bosses he had worked with. He belonged to the *on the one hand on the other hand camp*, resisting the temptation to come to clear-cut conclusions until he had all the necessary evidence to convince him. Others preferred the single-minded view.

'Clearly we can regard the dead man as closer than just a family friend. He did make the effort to change his name to Hartwell, which suggests some strong kind of bond with the family. And as we know, the majority of murder victims are killed by people they know, with family and friends at the top of the list. So as regards Brunswick, I think we should keep him in the frame. For a start, it's interesting that the alibi he gave doesn't quite add up. I didn't get anything from the CCTV at the garage he told me had visited – they wipe their tapes every day and re-record over them. And when I asked the cashier if he recalled serving a tall red-haired male early Tuesday morning, he seemed doubtful.'

'But when you asked what car the man had been driving he instantly remembered it,' Cat commented, having now caught up with her reading. 'What does Brunswick drive, as a matter of interest?'

'A red Audi RSS sports with registration CB 777. The cashier had looked out of the window and been very impressed. I'd noticed it in the car park at the Black Sheep Inn and been quite taken myself,' he added.

Cat raised her eyebrows. 'A bit flash for you, I would have thought,' she murmured.

Swift suppressed any response. As he glanced towards Stratton he noticed that she was frowning, concentrating hard on his words, her expression faintly sceptical.

'The alibi seems good until you look at the map and see that the petrol station is, in fact, four or five miles south of the Black Sheep Inn,' he continued. 'Brunswick told me that he was preparing to walk up to Great Whernside on Tuesday morning. If that were the case, he wouldn't have needed his car, as he could simply have walked. Moreover, the access to the east side of Whernside is only a few miles directly east from the Black Sheep Inn, and you can't actually get there by car; the road ends at the pub.'

'So why would Brunswick need to drive to Pateley for fuel if he couldn't use the car to get to Whernside?' Cat queried.

'Hard to say. Although he might have wanted to top the car up so that his companion could use it whilst he was off walking up a big hill.'

Cat raised her eyebrows. 'Companion?'

'He'd signed Mr and Mrs Brunswick in th ook.'

'Oh dear,' Cat sighed.

'And according to what Harriet suggested,' Swift continued, 'Charles was spending some time on his own. Moreover, she didn't drive up to Yorkshire until Saturday morning.'

Cat snorted. 'Men!'

'I didn't see his "companion".' Swift said. 'But I doubt it was Harriet Brunswick. She was talking to me on Saturday evening until around ten o'clock, as you'll see in the report. And she didn't seem to have very much idea of his precise whereabouts, or just what her husband was up to.' Swift had pondered for some time after he had realized the seriousness of Harriet's unspoken fears that her husband might be a dual murderer. And then had wondered what she would make of his being an adulterer.

'Right.' Again Stratton sounded doubtful. 'So could Mr Brunswick have had the opportunity to kill Christian Hartwell?' she asked.

Swift had the sudden thought that maybe Ravi Stratton wasn't the sharpest knife in the drawer, and instantly rejected the theory as unworthy and unjustified.

'Not if he was at a garage in Pateley Bridge at the time he claimed.'

'He could have got up in the night and driven to the crag,' Cat pointed out.

'Yes, I'd considered that. He'd have had to have been very quiet not to wake his companion and the other occupants of the pub. The car park is no more than a section of the pub's front terrace and the Audi has an engine that roars like a pride of lions. Someone would have heard him.'

'Should we check on it?' Stratton suggested.

Swift considered. He was not averse to another drive up to the scenically situated Black Sheep Inn and having a further talk with the pub staff. Moreover, he doubted if there would be much else for him to do unless they had a sudden new lead. Of course, if the 'companion' had already left, they would have difficulty tracing her, and even if they did she would probably simply support Brunswick's story – or deny any knowledge of him. But still. 'I'll go later today,' he told S'atton.

'What about the burning on Hartwell's clothes and body?' Cat said. 'I'm assuming we don't know if this was done by the person who pushed him off the crag, or by someone else.'

'Correct,' Swift confirmed. 'And neither Tanya Blake nor forensics have been able to help us on this so far. No DNA apart from Hartwell's own has been found on his body, or at the site.'

'Personal items were taken, but not money,' Cat mused. 'Which seems to rule out a random attack from passers-by. I see from Tanya's report that the money was found in a back pocket of Hartwell's jeans.'

Swift nodded, catching her drift and working on from there. 'And the missing items were likely to have been in his shirt and the front pockets of his trousers.'

'That suggests that the person who took them knew what they were looking for. And then burned relevant parts of his clothing to destroy any evidence he or she had left on Hartwell's body.'

Swift thought about it, and smiled at Cat. 'I'm happy to go with that theory, for the moment,' he said, glancing at Stratton for a response, but she made no comment, and moved on to a new topic.

'Turning to the episode in the desert,' she said, 'do you think that was relevant in regard to Hartwell's death?'

'I certainly think it's worth investigating that further,' Swift said. 'Although I suspect the effort and time involved might simply involve us in getting entangled in the jaws of a red herring.'

Ravi Stratton stared at him, her large brown eyes puzzled. 'I see,' she said politely.

No more attempts at jokes, Swift reminded himself.

'I'll handle that,' Cat offered. 'Talk to the police in Algiers. Polish up my French.'

'You speak French?' Swift enquired, not aware that this was one of Cat's talents.

'*Mais oui, bien sur.*'

Stratton bent her head, reviewing the last section of his report. 'So is there anything further we should be doing to move this case along?'

At this point Swift was personally concerned that this case could drag on and get nowhere very fast. There were still no witnesses who could throw light on what had happened to Hartwell, no useful forensics, no vital DNA.

'We'll go and speak to Ruth Hartwell and Brunswick again,' he told Stratton. 'And we need to check with uniform to see if they've got anything yet on Hartwell's flat. And get updates from SOCO and forensics on the off chance some new evidence has come to light.' He injected the maximum determination and optimism into his voice.

Stratton regarded him solemnly for a few moments. 'Thank you, Ed,' she said, 'for all your work and advice. It has been most helpful.'

The genuine appreciation in the superintendent's tone made Swift feel ashamed of himself for his previous doubts about her competence. Am I turning into a condescending bastard, he asked himself, as he and Cat left the superintendent to her own private deliberations.

Cat sat down on the one spare chair in Swift's office and blew out a long breath. 'Ravi Stratton is a very pleasant and conscientious colleague, but she is a bit hard going.' She glanced at Swift. 'Sorry – that was a touch bitchy of me.'

'You've simply mentioned something I've thought myself,' he admitted. 'So does that make me a bitch too?'

She smiled. 'You mentioned seeing Ruth Hartwell again. 'Would you like me to do that? We could have a woman to woman heart to heart.'

He thought about it. 'Yes, sounds a good idea.'

'You've already promised Ravi Stratton you'll go dashing off to check on Brunswick's alibi,' she reminded him, her tone dry. 'I think you should be setting off now, Boss,' she added with another glint.

Her dark eyes were vivid with humour and insight. The colours of her dress seemed to glow in Swift's small bare office.

He thought of the song *Nice work if you can get it*, and predicted that working with Cat would fall nicely into that category.

Craig had got up early that morning, left his bedroom and crept across the landing to the bathroom. He listened for any sounds coming from the other rooms, praying he could leave the house without anyone seeing or hearing him go. He wanted to have a shave, but it was too risky. He needed to go as soon as possible. It had been wrong to come. Mrs Hartwell didn't really know him and it was wrong to expect her to help him. He hadn't expected that was what she would do when he had decided to turn up on her doorstep. All he'd thought about was not being on his own and terrified of every little new thing that confronted him wherever he looked. But as soon as she'd spoken to him and urged him to come in through her door, he knew she was the sort of person who felt she should help him. But then her daughter had turned up and she didn't like him at all, he could tell. And all of that was causing trouble for Mrs Hartwell.

I have to leave this house, he told himself. He felt so shaky that it was as much as he could do to hold one thought in his mind. Letting any other in would do for him. I have to leave this house. Hold on to that.

He tip-toed into the kitchen to find his jacket. The dog heard him. She got out of her basket, took a long stretch and approached him tentatively. He had a sudden memory of the dog he and his mum had when he was a kid; a big fluffy Alsatian called Beauty. He used to walk with her down the fields behind their house in the morning. Then Barry Jackson came along and parked himself in his mum's life, and Beauty got banished to a kennel in the backyard. A hatred for Jackson rose up in his chest. He was glad that he'd stuck a knife in the fucker and killed him. Glad, glad, glad! He'd told the police that. And that was why the judge had him banged up for life.

He found himself breathing hard. Looking down at the dog, he saw her back away. His heart contracted. He made his voice calm and soft. 'Here, lass. Come here. There's nowt to be frightened of.' He squatted down on his haunches and the dog came slowly up to him and sniffed his fingers. He reached out to stroke her and the feel of her solid warmth under his fingers steadied him. 'I have to leave now, lass,' he told her.

Carrying his plastic bag in one hand he stole down the hallway. The door was on a simple latch, no chains or keys needed to open it. He slipped through and pulled the door shut so gently that it made only the tiniest scratching click. He walked down the long path leading to the road. There were squares of lawn on either side of it, one of them still containing a child's wood-framed swing. Keep walking, he told himself, wincing at the thought of getting to the main road and the busy pavements.

It was not yet 7.30, so there were not many people about. There was drizzle in the air and the people he passed kept their heads bowed, concentrating on withstanding the morning chill and dampness. He kept his own head well down, walked close to the wall and counted his steps under his breath.

He came to a shop. People were walking in, so he followed on. He walked down the rows of newspapers and magazines and birthday cards. On past the pencils and exercise books; they were like they'd had in the prison when they went for reading and writing lessons.

He kept looking around, but no one was taking any notice of him. Maybe he wasn't as famous as Blackwell had said. He came to a row of shelves stacked with little bars wrapped in shiny paper – red and blue and silver. Rows and rows of them. He stared at them, recalling memories from long ago. They had sweet stuff in prison, but not these rows and rows stretching on and on. He reached out and took one in his hand, turning it over, screwing his eyes up.

A voice called out. 'Can I help you?'

His nerves screeched. He turned towards the voice. There was a woman behind the serving counter. She was tiny with bright sharp eyes. She was smiling, but he wasn't sure if she meant it.

'Do you want to buy one?' she asked.

He looked at her, dumb and helpless. She came out from behind the counter and moved towards him. Instinctively he moved back and stood very still, the bar still in his hand.

'Did you want to buy that one?' Her eyes bored into him.

He shook his head. 'Dunno.'

'That one's coconut,' she said. 'But if you wanted you could have one with biscuit in it, or toffee cream. Or just a plain bar of chocolate.'

She wasn't mad at him. She was helping him. He broke into a smile.

She smiled back. She took the bar in his hand and put it back on the shelf. 'Here,' she said, offering one in a red and silver wrapper. 'A Kit-Kat. Everyone loves a Kit-Kat.'

He got out the money in his pocket and felt the panic rising again. 'Have I got enough?'

She reached out and took some coins from his hand. 'Come to the till and I'll give you change,' she said. When she'd given him the change, she said, 'Bye then.' And smiled at him.

Outside the shop he unwrapped the bar and bit into it. He smiled again.

There were notices pinned to a board at the side of the shop door. He started reading them. Stuff for sale: computers and bikes and lawn-mowers. All sorts. Nearly all of them had a picture to show what you were getting.

And then there were jobs. Child-minder wanted for two days a week. Cleaner wanted, must have references and own car. Kitchen worker needed for busy pub – apply to the manager at the Coach and Horses. He stared, concentrating so hard that the letters began to glow and shiver.

Ruth walked Harriet to her car. Harriet threw her leather holdall into the boot and pushed the lid down. She smiled at her mother. 'Mum, are you going to be all right?'

'Why shouldn't I be?' Ruth asked.

'Well, Christian's death has been a real shock for you. And I'm sorry if I wasn't as sympathetic as I should have been.'

Ruth smiled. This was always the pattern. She and Harriet

maintained a suspenseful truce when they were together, moments of peace punctuated by outbursts of irritation from Harriet and the occasional spark of retaliation from Ruth. And then as they said their farewells, Harriet would relent. And yet Ruth knew that if they went back into the house, there would be yet another round of mother/daughter fencing and her daughter's hidden resentment would start up all over again. 'I know. And I'm so pleased there was no fallout for you and Charles to worry about. Truly, I am.'

Harriet offered herself for a brief hug and Ruth managed to land a kiss on her cheek.

'And don't fret about Craig,' Harriet said, settling into the driving seat and clicking her seat belt into the plastic receptacle. 'He's not your responsibility. And he'll cope.'

Ruth nodded. As she went back into the house, duly fretting about Craig's sudden departure, she picked up the mail which had arrived earlier. There was a gas bill, a flier from a recently opened Chinese takeaway and a letter from her firm of solicitors asking her to contact them as soon as possible. Informing her that they wished to speak to her on a matter of some urgency concerning the issue of Mr Christian Hartwell's estate following his recent death. It was like some kind of summons, and a few hours later she was climbing the steps to Barley and Knight Solicitors, the firm who had advised both her and her husband for the past forty years. Not that they had been troubled much by the Hartwells, who had inherited the *Old School House* from Ruth's father-in-law and lived there happily ever after, thus never requiring the services of the conveyance department. In fact, the only major contact Ruth had had with the firm had been following her husband's death when she had sought their advice about his oversight in making a will. She recalled the courteous, elderly man who had helped her, but the name she had been given to ask for at reception today was Emma Varley, and clearly not him.

Barley and Knight's offices were situated on the second and third floors of an old Victorian house which would once have required a fleet of servants to clean and run it. The décor was reminiscent of the seventies, with much beige and brown in evidence. The receptionist was a plump motherly person with a wavy perm.

Her apparel fitted in nicely with the décor – a knee-length brown skirt and a beige cardigan with mother-of-pearl buttons. Ruth smiled at her, feeling rather raffish in her swirling ankle-length skirt, with her silver hair piled on her head. She introduced herself. 'I've come to see Emma Varley.'

'Ah, yes, Mrs Hartwell,' said the receptionist, smiling kindly. 'Just go through the door on your left. She's waiting for you.'

Ruth had the impression the receptionist was watching her as she walked towards the flush dark-wood door, that there was some kind of concern in her whole manner. Maybe she was like that with all the clients.

Emma Varley was standing rather stiffly beside her desk, a young woman neat in a navy skirt and a pale cream sweater. Ruth heard the same concern in Emma Varley's voice as she had heard from the receptionist.

'Mrs Hartwell, do come in and sit down.' Emma Varley sat down behind her desk. 'I'm one of the trainee solicitors here,' she said, with a faint tinge of apology in her voice.

She was about to continue but Ruth made a soft interjection. 'You sound as though I might object to your junior status.'

Emma glanced down at her desk and cleared her throat. 'I have to make it clear. Some of our clients prefer to deal with the partners.'

'Ah, yes. The top man syndrome,' said Ruth. 'Well, so far I'm very happy to be advised by you.' As she spoke, Ruth noticed tiny sparkling earrings shaped like butterflies beneath the sweep of Emma's hair. She found herself warming to the young lawyer.

'First of all, Mrs Hartwell, I'd like to offer you my sincere condolences on your recent loss.' She opened the file lying on her desk. 'I've invited you here on the instructions of Christian Hartwell. The late Christian Hartwell.'

Ruth stiffened, experiencing a stabbing chill of surprise and shock. 'Go on.'

'He made an appointment to see me the week before last. He wanted to make a will. He also gave me a packet for you, asking that, in the event of his death, we should make contact with you and give you it in person.' She pushed a padded envelope across the desk.

Ruth looked at it, recognizing Christian's spiky handwriting on the front. The envelope was firmly stuck down and as a further precaution sealed with a tiny piece of melted red wax. She glanced across the desk to Emma Varley. 'I'm assuming you don't know the contents of this envelope?'

'No. It has been left unopened, as he instructed. You don't need to open it now, Mrs Hartwell,' she added, kindly.

'Right.' Ruth stared down at the envelope. 'This is completely unexpected.' She was uncertain whether to open the letter immediately and ease the tension which was rising within her, or wait until she was alone.

Emma Varley was speaking again. 'I also have to tell you that Mr Hartwell named you as his next of kin. And he's left you his apartment, some money, and all his effects – books, papers, photographs.'

'His apartment!' Ruth exclaimed, thinking of Christian's dull little flat in a purpose-built block on the outskirts of Burley-in-Wharfedale.

'Yes.' Emma consulted the file again. She looked across at Ruth. 'Mrs Hartwell, he's left you everything; there is no one else named as a beneficiary.'

Ruth closed her eyes for a moment. 'Why would he do that? It's crazy – I'm thirty years his senior.'

The solicitor nodded sympathetically.

'Are you aware of the relationship between me and Christian?' Ruth asked. 'You do understand that he is not my son, nor any blood relation of mine.'

'Yes, he mentioned that he had lived with you and your family for some years and that you had been a mother figure for him. And I did point out that he needed to take the age difference between himself and you into consideration when making a will. But he insisted there was no one else he wanted to have his possessions and money.'

'Oh! This is just so sad,' Ruth exclaimed, rubbing the back of her neck in consternation and loosening some long silver strands from their anchorage in her topknot.

Emma left a tactful silence.

'I mean, to have no family to whom he could leave his estate,' Ruth elaborated.

'He was clearly very fond of you, Mrs Hartwell,' the solicitor offered.

Ruth nodded. Tears welled up. 'Oh, Christian!' She thought of him, so alone, with no wife or partner, no children. Seemingly no family or close friends at all.

'Regarding Mr Hartwell's apartment,' Emma Varley said, her voice once again tinged with apology. 'His effects need to be gone through and cleared. The landlords are pressing to have the apartment emptied. So they can re-let it.'

'His effects! Are they my responsibility?' Ruth asked, her heart sinking at the thought of going through Christian's things. Anybody's things for that matter.

'Well, unless you want the landlords to do it.'

Ruth sighed. 'I'll do it.'

'There isn't very much, from what we can gather.'

'It's OK,' Ruth said. 'It's the least I can do for Christian.' She suddenly felt like crying, blinked a few times and swiftly put a stop to it.

Emma Varley opened the top drawer of her desk and pulled out some keys on a round of hairy string with a paper tag attached. 'Flat 3, 56 Calverley Street.' She handed over the keys to Ruth who accepted them with a marked lack of eagerness.

'There is quite a lot of money,' Emma Varley mentioned gently, sensitive to her client's unusual reticence in accepting the property and guessing a windfall of money might be equally problematic for her. 'His aunt died recently and left him a gift of two hundred thousand pounds.'

Ruth shook her head in disbelief. 'I'll think about that later,' she said, putting the keys to the flat in her bag, but feeling the need to clutch the white envelope in her hand. She stood up. 'Thank you for your help, Emma. I think I need to go away and try to digest all you've told me.'

The solicitor gave a small sad smile. 'I think you do, Mrs Hartwell.'

When Ruth got home there was still no sign of Craig. She placed the unopened envelope on the kitchen table and laid the keys to Christian's flat on top. She made herself a cup of hot, strong coffee, then took Tamsin for a walk in the park at the end of the road. It was a bright summer day, with a pleasing tinge of freshness in the air. Little children sat in the kiddies' swings, shouting to their parents or carers to push them higher and higher. The wind lifted the leaves of the trees, and the full-blown roses glowed with ruby colour.

On arriving back home, she heated up some soup and debated whether to open the envelope without delay and get whatever surprise was waiting for her over and done with. Her hand hovered over the small red seal. On impulse she stuffed both envelope and keys into a kitchen drawer and pushed it firmly shut. She got out cleaning materials, put on her rubber gloves and set about cleaning the oven with a will, a task which occurred at less and less frequent intervals as she got older.

A polite rapping on the front door was a welcome interruption. It's Craig, she thought and a spark of happiness sprang up. She peeled off her gloves and walked lightly to the front door.

Her visitor was about as different from Craig as could be imagined. He was a small, slightly built man, wearing neatly pressed grey trousers and a dark-green sweater over a white T-shirt. He had well-trimmed mousy hair and rimless glasses. She instantly assumed that he was a local, with some petition about street parking or the cutting down of trees.

'Hello,' she said, her voice light and friendly. She was about to make a further welcoming remark when she stopped. There was something about his eyes which pulled her up short. They were cold eyes, empty and without sympathy.

'Mrs Ruth Hartwell?' His voice was soft, with no hint of a regional accent.

She had a sudden desire to deny it, to let him believe she was the cleaner, that Mrs Hartwell was on a six-month cruise in the Caribbean. 'Yes,' she said. She felt a pricking sensation around the back of her neck, and then a hot trembling feeling spreading to her arms and her throat. She guessed it would be because she was tired and stressed as a result of the recent events. She heard Tamsin come up behind her. The dog looked at the visitor but made no attempt to greet him. She placed herself beside Ruth, who felt the animal's support and tried to get a better grip on herself.

'You're Christian Hartwell's mother, aren't you?' the man asked, his voice perfectly steady and polite.

Ruth told herself to stop thinking wildly about women who got assaulted or murdered on their doorsteps. She had never been fearful about people coming to the house. Well, it would be a different story if they were pointing a gun at her. But this man was outwardly mild-mannered and as far as she could see without the company of a gun. And she would not be intimidated. 'You want to talk about Christian, is that it?'

He nodded.

'Come in, then.' She took him through to the kitchen. 'Do you want coffee?' she asked with her automatic politeness.

'Yes, that would be nice.' He sat down at the table and folded his hands in front of him. The dog got into her basket and sat bolt upright, regarding the visitor with disapproval.

Ruth switched on the kettle. 'What's your name?' she asked, schooling herself to sound unruffled and polite.

'Mac.' He spun the word out, laying emphasis on the last letter which sent out a loud clicking sound. His eyes, whilst cool and expressionless, seemed to challenge her.

Ruth felt the chill in the atmosphere. Was this man trying to tell her something very unpleasant?

'Look,' she said, shrewd enough to know when she was on the sharp end of menace, 'just tell me how I can help you. I'm rather busy, I've got a doctor's appointment in half an hour.'

'Oh, dear. Are you not well?' he asked. He smiled a chilly smile.

'Flu jab for the over sixties,' she lied.

'Better safe than sorry,' he said. 'OK, I won't trouble you more than I need. I used to work with Christian. On the *Echo*. It's a long while ago, now. We got together recently and he talked about his ideas for a new book and I talked about my own ideas. We decided it might be a smart move to collaborate. He'd do the text and I'd do the photos.'

'I see,' Ruth said, ignoring the kettle's coming up to boil. She'd changed her mind about giving this man refreshment. She couldn't wait to get rid of him. And yet, quite why, she couldn't say.

'The idea was for one of those books where you capture people in certain settings, then think up snappy captions. I'd already done the photos, sent them on to Christian.'

'But?' her voice was meant to be steely, but came out weary.

'I've lost the originals, made a mistake and deleted them from my camera.' He stared right at her, his eyes like those of a deadly snake. 'So I'd be grateful to have the copies back.'

'I haven't got them,' she said, wondering if that was the very worst thing she could have said. As pathetic as pleading a doctor's appointment.

He spread his hands in a gesture of disappointment. His eyes were suddenly drawn to the kitchen window. 'You have got a visitor,' he said.

Ruth followed his gaze. Craig stood outside the kitchen window, peering in with anxious eyes. She could not have been more pleased to see him if he had been the Angel Gabriel. She went to the kitchen door and unlocked it. 'Craig!' she exclaimed, 'come in.'

Craig's bulk filled the doorway; the sheer size of him equally as menacing as Mac's snake eyes, in Ruth's book. 'Go sit down,' she told him, her voice warm with welcome and affection.

Mac looked from Ruth to Craig then held out his hand. 'Pleased to meet you, Craig,' he said. 'How are you?'

'Good,' Craig muttered.

'I'm Mac,' he said. 'Mac the Knife,' he added, as though it were a joke. He began to hum the famous tune from *The Threepenny Opera*.

Ruth froze. She noted that Craig didn't appear to register either the tune or the song title; she assumed because he was too young. 'Mac was just leaving,' she told Craig with a sideways glance at the unwelcome visitor.

'I thought you were going to give me some coffee,' said Mac, shooting her a look that made her feel like rushing to the phone in the hall and dialling 999.

Getting no response from Ruth, Mac turned to Craig. 'Are you one of Mrs Hartwell's family?' he asked.

'Aye.' Craig stared hard at Mac, then turned away. 'I've got a job,' he told Ruth. 'At the pub down the road. The boss said I had to go on Friday for a trial.'

'Well done!' said Ruth. 'Look, Craig, I have to go the doctor. I won't be long.' She looked meaningfully at Mac. 'I'll see you to the door,' she said.

He followed her down the hall. 'Chill, Mrs Hartwell. I only wanted to talk to you.'

'I can't tell you anything about Christian,' she insisted. 'I've not been much involved with him for a long time now.'

'But you're his mother, aren't you? His next of kin?'

She bit on her lip, judging that silence was best.

'And his sister is called Harriet, is that right? He used to talk about her.'

Ruth swallowed.

'I really must get to my appointment,' she said, unlocking her old Ford Escort and praying it would start.

He shut the driver's door for her. His eyes bored into her. A smile slithered over his face as she let in the clutch.

She drove down the road, not knowing where she was heading, her hands shaking. She knew that he knew she had been lying.

And he knew that she had a daughter, he knew her name. And if things didn't work out with Mrs Hartwell she could be the next lever.

As soon as he heard Ruth's car start up Craig, who had been standing behind the door listening carefully to the final exchanges between her and the man who called himself Mac the Knife, moved softly down the hallway. Mac the Knife was sauntering down the path. He glanced back once, but Craig had hidden himself in the shadow behind the door. He stepped out of the door as the creepy guy rounded the gate post. He pushed at the latch to click it in open position, but drew the door against the frame so that the dog would not get out, and he would be able to get back in.

When he reached the road he kept well back, watching every step Mac the Knife took as he walked along the road. Quite soon he paused at a bus stop just as a bus approached, hopped on and was swallowed up into the bus within seconds.

Craig stood still, waiting until the bus was out of sight. 'Smart move,' he muttered in grudging admiration of the creepy guy's efforts to render himself untraceable.

He looked up and down the road, hoping he would see Ruth's car. She'd been upset by the guy, he could tell. And she was an old lady. He hoped she wouldn't do anything daft. He made his way back to the house and sat on the kitchen floor, dipping his head and resting his hands between his knees. The dog came out of her basket and sat beside him, leaning her weight against his ribs. And then he waited.

Swift found the landlord of the Black Sheep Inn serving at the bar and joking with a small, all male, clientele. He was a man in his fifties, of a chunky build, and with gnarled weather beaten features. He immediately broke off his banter with his customers on seeing Swift. 'Now sir, what can I get you?'

Swift looked at the array of bitters on offer and pushed away the temptation of ordering half a pint of ale. The current zero tolerance on drinking was not to be taken lightly. Instead, he showed his warrant card and was instantly rewarded by the landlord's suggestion that they should go and sit somewhere quieter to talk. 'Aye, Tom,' he called out to one of his customers, 'just take over serving on for a few minutes while I go and persuade this gentleman I've no wicked deeds to answer for.'

He led Swift through to the parlour where he had spoken with Charles Brunswick the previous day.

'Albert Smart, licensee of this hostelry,' the landlord said. 'How can I help you, Detective Chief Inspector? Was it you that came yesterday?'

'It was. I spoke to one of your residents, Mr Charles Brunswick.'

'Oh, aye. And now you've come again; one of the top brasses. Which makes me think something important must be up?'

'I've come in connection with a murder enquiry,' Swift told him. 'We were hoping Mr Brunswick would be able to help us further.'

'Well now, you're going to be disappointed. Mr Brunswick left earlier this morning, with his lady wife. You'll have to catch up with him elsewhere. Probably down in the capital.'

'I was hoping you might be able to help me, Mr Smart.'

'Were you now? I'll do me best.'

'We're interested to know where Mr Brunswick was on Tuesday last between the hours of 2 and 8 a.m.'

Smart laughed. 'You don't go for the easy questions, do you Chief Inspector? The fact of the matter is I sleep like the dead between those hours you mention. However, my wife wakes at the sound of a feather dropping so why don't I go get her and see if she can throw any light on the matter.'

He went off and very soon returned with a plump, attractive blonde woman dressed in a navy and white summer frock, its neat belt accentuating her curves.

'This is Iris,' the landlord said. 'The lady of the house.'

Iris smiled at Swift. 'You're asking about last Tuesday night,' she said. 'What do you want to know?'

Being accustomed to a good deal of ducking and diving when being questioned, Swift was impressed by the couple's directness. 'I'd like to know if Mr Charles Brunswick, one of your residents, was here during those hours?'

'Monday,' she said thoughtfully. 'That's the day they arrived.'

'Did they have dinner here, love?' her husband asked.

She held up her hand. 'Don't interrupt, I'm just trying to get the pictures in my mind. Monday. Right, Monday is one of my days for serving in the dining room. And, yes, they had dinner here that night. I could check it in the book, but I'm totally sure. We had roast duck on the menu that evening and she was very complimentary about it, which was nice of her. They had coffee and then they ordered a second bottle of wine and sat talking. They didn't come into the bar and they went to bed around 10.15.'

Albert shook his head. 'I don't know how she remembers all this stuff. I can hardly remember what happened this morning. But she's invariably spot on, even going back years.'

Iris shrugged. 'It's just a knack.'

'Where was Mr Brunswick's car parked?' Swift asked.

'Oh, out on the front,' Iris said, straightaway. 'I kept eyeing it up; it was a real swanky motor. Fancy number plate too.'

'And was it there all night – between Monday and Tuesday morning?' Swift asked.

'Oh, yes. I'd have heard if it had started up. I'm a very light sleeper. But Mr Brunswick would have had a job on if he'd wanted to use it in the night. Our son got in late on Monday and parked behind it and blocked him in. He sometimes does that if every-where else is parked up. If there's an emergency he'll move it right away, or we will. But most customers here sleep like babies, it's so quiet and the air's very enervating for people not used to the country-side.'

'You sound pretty sure of your details, Mrs Smart,' Swift remarked.

'I am, yes,' she said.

Swift believed her. She struck him as all capability and common sense and blunt straightforwardness.

'What time did your son move the car the next morning?' he asked.

'About a quarter past seven. That's his usual time to set off to work. It was just as well, because Mr Brunswick came down a few minutes later and went out in the car. He wasn't gone long, came back with some newspapers. They ordered breakfast in bed and I didn't see either or them till lunchtime.'

'They seemed a very happily married couple,' Albert Smart remarked with meaning, giving Swift a man-to-man glance. 'Iris had quite a job most days finding a slot to get in the room to tidy up.'

Iris's lips tightened. 'That's true. But you have to live and let live. It's none of our business.'

'No, love,' Albert agreed, slightly chastened. 'Does that fit the bill, Chief Inspector?' he asked.

'Thank you both; it was very useful.'

'Are you investigating the death of this man Christian Hartwell who was found at Fellbeck Crag?' Mrs Smart asked. 'I saw a report in the *Echo*.'

'You see,' her husband exclaimed, 'she knows everything.'

'I used to know Mrs Hartwell just after she had Harriet,' Mrs Smart said. 'We were both members of the Mother's Union. She was one of those people who would help anyone in trouble, and, do you know, I never heard her say an unkind word about anyone. I used to wish I had it in me to be such a genuinely good person. I'd never have had the courage to take on someone else's child like she did. Christian was a bit wild in his teens. Well, that's what I thought, but Ruth and her husband simply accepted him for what he was and dealt with whatever came up.'

'Did you know him personally?'

'No, only what Mrs Hartwell told me. But Albert and I moved

away from the area when he was about sixteen and I lost touch then. I'm presuming he opted to take the Hartwell's name.'

Swift nodded.

'Well, you can't get a bigger compliment than that, can you.' She sighed. 'Poor Ruth, this death will have hit her hard.' She paused. 'Do you really think Mr Brunswick might have had something to do with Christian's death?'

'We're simply eliminating people from our enquiries, Mrs Smart.'

She smiled. 'I've heard that one before.'

Albert cleared his throat. 'Well, I hope Mr Brunswick is off the hook, he seemed a nice bloke. Are you sure you won't have one for the road?' he asked Swift as they moved back into the bar. 'On the house, of course. Our Black Sheep bitter is like nectar.'

Swift smiled. 'Not in the rule book,' he said. 'I'll come another time when I'm not on duty.'

'Bring the wife,' Albert said. 'We keep a very nice Chardonnay for the ladies.'

Swift manoeuvred his car out of the tiny parking area, thinking that Charles Brunswick had a lot for which to thank Iris Smart and her careful observation of her residents.

Craig heard Ruth's footsteps in the hallway and jumped to his feet.

'Are you OK?' he asked her.

'I've just been driving around. I'm fine.' She sank down on a chair and unwound the long scarf she was wearing round her neck.

Craig watched her with concern. 'I was worried about you.' She gave him a grateful smile.

He sat down at the table opposite her, having no clue of what he might say next. He just wanted her to be all right.

'Tell me about this new job,' she said.

'It's at the pub down the road. Clearing up in the kitchen, washing up and the mopping the floors and stuff.'

'That sounds good.'

'I've to go in on Friday. Eight o'clock sharp, the boss said. The weekend is when they're busy.'

'Did they ask for references?'

'What?'

She looked at him, knowing the answer. 'Never mind.'

He heard weariness and sadness in her voice.

She got up slowly and went across to one of the drawers in the kitchen cupboards. Craig watched as she pulled out a white envelope and a bunch of keys. She took a small glinting instrument from the midst of a bunch of pens crammed into a mug on the unit top and began to slit the envelope open. Then suddenly changed her mind and dropped both the envelope and the opener on to the table.

'Is that blade sharp?' Craig asked, alarmed to see what looked like a small dagger which had made a good job of slicing its way half way through a few inches of the thick white paper.

She smiled. 'It's a paper-opener. I don't think it would be much good for doing any serious damage.'

Craig stared at her, not sure whether she was joking or not. 'You don't want to do anyone any serious damage, do you?'

'No,' she reassured him. 'I don't want to do any serious damage of any kind,' she said dryly.

He watched her with concern on his face. 'If you're in trouble with someone, I'll sort them out for you.'

'No, no,' she said hurriedly.

He was not mollified. 'That guy who was here before. The creepy one with the piggy eyes. It's him you're in trouble with, isn't it?'

Ruth frowned, not quite sure what or how much to say.

'I followed him,' Craig said.

Ruth gazed at him. 'Good heavens!'

'He got on a bus, so there's no knowing where he was off to. I thought if he got in a car I could have got the reg number.'

'Yes,' said Ruth, faintly. 'Listen,' she went on, her voice firmer, 'I don't fully understand what that man who called himself Mac was talking about. But it seems to me that he thinks I've got something he wants. Some photographs.'

'Well, have you?'

She shook her head. 'Not that I know of, that's the worrying thing.'

'The bastard,' hissed Craig. 'I hate him.' But hate was too soft a word. In his head he thought he would like to kill him.

*

Cat had tried to make an appointment to see Ruth talk to her about the team's investigations and their conclusions, but she seemed to be often out, or maybe she didn't bother to answer the phone every time it rang. She decided to simply drive to the *Old School House* and see if Ruth was in.

Reaching the house, she parked the car and killed the engine. Pulling the bell, she anticipated its quirky tinkle, which did not disappoint her.

Ruth answered promptly, her dog trotting behind like Mary's little lamb. 'Oh! Inspector Fallon!' Cat saw surprise, then a fleeting relief cross her face, to be finally replaced with a hunted look of anxiety.

'Is it convenient to have a word?' she asked.

'Yes, of course. Come in.'

The young man sitting at the kitchen table was still and wary-looking, his eyes lighting on Cat and staying there.

'This is Craig,' Ruth told Swift. 'He's staying here for a while.' She seemed to be on the point of saying something further and then decided against it.

Cat smiled at the young man, whose dark hair almost obscured his eyes, making it difficult to assess his mood. Another of Ruth's lame ducks, she assumed. 'Hello,' she said. 'I'm Inspector Cat Fallon.'

There was a definite spasm of alarm on the young man's face as he grunted an acknowledgement.

'Craig,' said Ruth, brightly. 'Would you mind popping down to the shops and getting some milk, we're running a bit short?' She dug out her purse from a battered handbag, and handed the young man a two-pound coin.

He looked at her warm smile of encouragement and got to his feet. 'Aye, sure.'

After the door had closed behind him, Ruth looked Cat straight in the eye. 'He's just served a long prison sentence. I used to do prison visiting some years ago, and Craig was one of my regulars. In time he was moved to a unit up in the north-east, so I lost touch. He was released a few days ago.'

'And he simply turned up on your doorstep?' Cat suggested, a note of wryness in her voice.

Ruth smiled. 'Yes. Right out of the blue.'

'You obviously inspire trust,' Cat said.

'My daughter says I'm just a soft touch,' Ruth observed. 'He's staying here for a while to find his feet.' she added, with a hint of defensiveness.'

'You've no need to justify your hospitable tendencies to me,' Cat said, gently.

'Ah, well, there's good and bad in this world. And there's brave and there's foolish. You just have to work out what seems to be the right path for you, as an individual, to follow. I know many people would say I'm a sentimental fool for letting an ex-convict into my home. But I believe I can help him, and … I like him here. I'm sometimes far more lonely than I allow my family to know.'

Ruth got up and switched on the kettle. Cat watched her take a full carton of milk from the fridge and then calmly pour it down the sink. 'There, I knew I was running out,' she said. 'He'll be back in no time with the fresh milk. He's learning to be a good shopper.' She fussed about at the counter, dropping tea bags into her white china teapot, and rattling spoons. She said nothing more, simply brought mugs of tea to the table and sat down again. Cat had the impression the issue of Craig and his current residence in the Hartwell household was temporarily closed, and she decided not to push further.

'Chief Inspector Swift has completed a report regarding Christian's death,' Cat told her. She explained what he had discovered during his investigations and sketched out the recommendations in his report to his superior officer. 'Unfortunately we still don't have any witnesses who have come forward to help us. However, I've just had information from our Scene of Crime Officers team to say that they found traces of blood on the stones over which we believe Christian fell, and they match the samples we had taken from his body, so at least we have precise knowledge of where he fell from.'

Ruth listened carefully. 'Does that help you?'

'Not very much, I'm afraid. Is there anything you have thought of, Mrs Hartwell, since we last talked? Anything at all which could have a bearing on Christian's death?'

Ruth hesitated for a few moments. 'I was invited in to see my solicitor earlier on today. Christian has made a will in my favour. He's left me everything – his apartment, all his personal belongings and his money. It's unbelievable, and also very sad. I can't quite get to grips with it.'

Cat's expression sharpened. 'Do you know when the will was made?'

'About ten days ago. Of course I'm aware that the making of the will so soon before Christian's death must mean something.'

'As though he had some inkling of what was coming?'

'Possibly. And yet again, maybe it was sheer coincidence. After all, he had recently received a large legacy from an aunt, and he also had the expectation of further money from his book if it was a success. All reasons to make a will.' Her mind surged on to the packet she had not opened. And the arrival of the unwanted visitor. The urge to confide in Cat Fallon regarding Mac the Knife was overwhelming, and yet she couldn't bring herself to do it. Somehow, telling her would make the covert menace of the man worse, make it more real.

Cat, watching the older woman, was well aware that she was grappling with some internal struggle. Everyone in the police had seen this kind of conflict when interviewing people in the course of their work. People trying to shield loved ones, people afraid of revealing information which could wreck someone else's life, people wondering how they could cover their own backs with a lie. People terrified of the repercussions if they spoke out.

Cat waited. As she sat, looking down at her hands, she was already thinking through the discussion she would have with Ed on the developments which had emerged during this interview. And it suddenly occurred to her how glad she was that she had made the decision to join his team.

She looked up and saw Ruth staring back into her face, her eyes now burning with her need to share her desperate inner worries. Cat held still, knowing the critical point of revelation was near.

At that moment Ruth's young protégé came back with the milk. And the moment of unburdening was gone.

*

Later on, Ruth sat at the kitchen table, the padded envelope once again in front of her. She was on her own as Craig had gone up to his room. She supposed that after all those years of imprisonment he sometimes found the strain of being in the outside world overwhelming and felt safer sitting on his bed with the door closed and his thoughts free to swirl in his head, trying to make sense of his new life.

She picked at the red sealing wax and gradually worked the flap of the envelope free. Inside was a mobile phone and a further envelope, also sealed.

Ruth stared at the shiny black phone. She was well aware of being a Luddite as far as the use of new technology went. Having been a prison chaplain's wife for thirty-odd years and having shared the burden of answering phone calls on his behalf for much of the day and some of the night, she had always considered the ownership of a mobile phone to be a terrible intrusion into one's life. To be constantly available at the end of one of those little gadgets seemed to her like a kind of hell. She smiled to herself, recalling that her grandson Jake liked to tease her about her ancient two-tone grey bakelite phone with its push-around dial being a museum piece, and to marvel at the diminutive size of her television.

She turned the little phone around in her hands, then hesitantly ran her fingers over its blank grey screen. Nothing happened. She had no idea whether it required turning on or not. And maybe its battery was flat, an inconvenience which was a constant source of frustration for Harriet.

She guessed Craig would know what to do to bring it to life. But did she want that? What revelations might the little phone be hiding? And the envelope. Were the photographs Mac the Knife was wanting inside that envelope? Fear made its spider-legged way down her spine. Could she face finding out? She heard Craig coming down from his self-imposed sole confinement and thrust both the phone and the envelope back into the drawer.

She smiled at him. 'Would you like a trip out in the car?'

Instantly he was wary, but excited at the same time. 'Where do you want to go?'

Ruth smiled at him, wondering how long it would take him to build up the personal self-esteem which would enable him to consider that he had a right to be a party in making a decision regarding the destination of a trip out.

'To a little place called Burley-in-Wharfedale,' she told him. 'It's about twenty minutes drive from here. I need to check on an apartment there. For … a friend of mine.'

He thought about it. 'OK.'

Ruth got out a map. It was so old it had torn along the creases. But it had Calverley Street clearly marked on its southern side. She took the countryside route, driving close to the bank of the River Wharfe and past farming estates that once used to rely wholly on farming for their livelihood but now were more centred around the catering and tourist industries.

Craig looked out of the window, entranced with the views. The ground and the hills were so vividly green, and the sky above enormous. Ruth pointed out the river and suggested that he might see some interesting birds: herons, perhaps, or woodpeckers. He didn't manage to make out any birds, but the river itself fascinated him – a broad motorway of water, sometimes gently sliding, sometimes flowing fast and choppy, all the time gleaming blue/black in its banks.

Once in Burley, they drove along broad residential streets bordered by tall trees and big stone houses. At the end of the street Ruth was looking for there was a small two-storey block of flats built of red brick. A band of grass and some scratchy-looking green bushes formed a communal garden. More tall, old trees bordered the garden and when they got out of the car they had to be careful not to trip over the roots which had burst up through the paving stones like the knuckles of giant fingers.

Craig looked up at the flats. 'Why do you need to come here?'

'I need to sort through my friend's things,' she said.

'Why?' he asked, childlike in needing explanations of things a person of his age who hadn't spent years in prison wouldn't have thought twice about.

'I promised I would,' she said calmly, and that seemed to satisfy him. Inside herself, she felt a strong reluctance to go on with this mission and would have liked to run back to the safety of the car and go home. She was afraid of what she might find in Christian's flat, fearful of getting more embroiled in whatever had been going on during Christian's last days. And then there was the here and now, the fear that somehow Mac the Knife was watching her, knowing every move she made.

Christian's flat was on the ground floor. The July sun was shining on the windows, picking out the grime and highlighting the cheap, flimsy curtains.

'Has your friend gone away somewhere?' Craig asked, watching her fit the key into the lock.

'Yes,' she said, brisk and terse at the notion of being on the brink of an awful revelation.

Which was, to some extent, the case.

As they walked into the living room they could see that the place had been ransacked. The coffee table had been upended. A single mug lay on the floor, its contents having spilled out, making a dark stain on the small beige rug on which the table stood. The sofa had been overturned and the covering fabric slashed in several places. All the drawers had been pulled from a CD cabinet which stood against the back wall.

A large slimline TV seemed intact, its red standby light glowing. Craig went across to it and pressed a switch. A superlatively clear picture came up on the screen: a herd of elephants walked across a desert under a cobalt blue sky. 'Digital,' said Craig. 'The buggers who came in here must have been mad not to take it.'

Quite apart from the havoc created by the intruders, Ruth was taken aback at the dismalness of the flat. The wood plank floorboards had been painted black, the varnish chipped and dusty. The wallpaper was faded and torn, showing islands of dark red paint underneath. The furniture was an assortment of cheap tat, the kind of thing you might take out of a skip, or buy from a junk shop, devoid of any pretence to be stylish. Worn out, shabby items no one would ever have bothered to love and look after.

The kitchen was small and bore little sign of any cooking having taken place in it for a very long time. The contents of the waste bin were strewn on the floor – empty takeaway boxes of Indian food and pizza, empty cans of lager.

Ruth sighed, thinking of Christian coming home to this soulless, brutal place.

In the bedroom the bed had been stripped and the mattress

pulled out to rest at a crazy angle against the base. It had been savagely ripped open in several places.

'Wonder if they got what they were looking for,' Craig said, leaning against the door frame.

'What makes you ask that?' Ruth asked, with a degree of sharpness.

'Because if they left that telly behind they were either blind, cretins, or looking for summat else.'

That was the longest speech Ruth had heard him make. He was coming on.

There was a knock on the entrance door.

Ruth froze. A picture of Mac the Knife leapt into her head.

'I'll get it,' Craig ambled to the door and opened it.

A man in a stripy T-shirt and dark-blue jeans peered expectantly at Craig, then seeing Ruth hovering in the background ventured a tentative smile. 'I'm from the flat across the hallway,' he said, jerking his head in the direction of a half open door. 'Can I help you?'

'Oh! Come in,' said Ruth, highly relieved to see anyone who was not the snake-eyed Mac. 'We're looking through Christian's things. I'm Mrs Hartwell … a relative.'

'I see. I heard noises and I wondered if everything was all right.' He looked around the room, suddenly realizing that it had been gone through by someone with no regard for the well-being of the contents. 'Bloody hell. What's been going on here?'

'We don't really know,' said Ruth.

'I'd no idea about all this lot,' the neighbour said. 'I mean, if I'd heard anything I'd have been in here like a shot.' He looked down at his hands which were covered in flour, then wiped them vigorously on a tea towel tucked into the waste band of his jeans. 'I'm a bit messy.' he apologized, 'I'm making bread.'

Ruth was looking around the room again, thinking that Christian had made very little attempt to make it a comfortable and welcoming place. Even before his yellowed and battered paperback books had been strewn around the floor, and his duffle bag tossed into a corner of the room with its contents of worn shirts and underpants scattered over it, the place must have been hollow and unwelcoming. Maybe he'd been staying somewhere else in recent months, maybe there had been a girlfriend, or boyfriend for that matter, and he had been staying with them.

'I'm really sorry about Christian,' the neighbour said. 'I didn't know him well. I've only been here a few months. But he seemed a nice guy.'

'Yes,' Ruth said. 'He was.'

'I wonder how they got in?' the neighbour said, rubbing his forehead and leaving little white grains of flour in his shaggy dark fringe. 'Mind you, the main door's not much stronger than paper. It must be dead easy to get in this place. We've asked the landlord to get us a new door. It's promised for next month. We can but hope.'

'It'd be no bother getting in here,' Craig said, grasping the light-weight entry door to the flat and swinging it to and fro. 'I mean, any burglar with a bit of savvy could pick that lock. It's pathetic.'

'Thanks for the free advice,' the neighbour said, grinning. 'I'll take heed.'

'Did you say you were making bread?' Craig asked him.

'Yeah.'

'Can you really do that? On your own?'

The neighbour smiled. 'Sure, I've done it loads of times. Do you want to come and watch? The dough should be risen by now.'

They went off together, Craig smiling like a small boy who'd been unexpectedly invited to a party.

Ruth hung back, going through the place again, picking up the mug from the floor, rubbing at the dark stain of coffee and wondering if there were cleaning materials in the kitchen she could use to try and get it out, make the place look more ordered and homelike. She stood at the bedroom door and imagined Christian sitting in his bed in the mornings, drinking his instant coffee and contemplating his day. In her mind, she went back through the years, seeing him as small and alone as he had been when his mother abandoned him, just a speck of humanity, as helpless as the dust in the atmosphere, blown about by all the invisible currents. Gently, she shut the door, sensing that reviving memories of Christian was like running the tip of your tongue around a trou-blesome tooth – poking at the tender and painful flesh and making the pain worse.

She looked into the small bathroom, which was surprisingly clean and fresh-smelling. She noticed a pine-scented air freshener on the windowsill and smiled.

Returning to the living room, she took a last look around, resolving to find a reliable house clearing firm to take everything away and dispose of it. Christian's effects. She couldn't bear to look at them ever again.

She shut the entry door to the flat behind her, locked it carefully and went in search of Craig. A glorious smell of baking filled the hallway and guided her to the door of the neighbour's flat. The door was ajar and she went straight in, heading for the kitchen. Craig was watching transfixed as the neighbour pulled a batch of golden bread rolls from the oven. 'Wow!' he said.

'I think we should go now,' Ruth said to him.

Craig looked about to protest, then thought better of it.

'Here,' said the neighbour, 'I'll put a few in a bag for you.'

Ruth told the friendly neighbour. 'I think I'll get some house clearers to deal with the rest of the things.' She wanted to explain why she had chosen this seemingly heartless attitude towards Christian's belongings, but couldn't quite think how to phrase it.

'Aye, you do right. There's nothing much of value to take away with you,' the neighbour said, consolingly. 'Are you going to contact the police ... about the break in? It would help our case about the new front door.' His tone was both apologetic and urging.

'Yes, I understand,' Ruth said. 'Leave it with me.' Damn, she thought. And then it suddenly dawned on her that, of course, she must contact the police. Specifically Chief Inspector Swift. This was surely no routine break-in. She thought of Mac the Knife, and once again fear swirled inside her.

Craig accepted the rolls from the neighbour with a smile of thanks. He looked at Ruth, seeming rooted to the spot. She guessed he could hardly bear to tear himself away from the baking session.

'You're not going to leave the TV are you?' he asked.

'What?'

'The telly in your friend's flat?'

'Oh!'

'He's right,' the neighbour said. 'It's a nice one. I'm sure Christian would have wanted you to have it.'

'Oh, I don't know' Ruth protested. She supposed it was all legal and above board to take away any item of Christian's, bearing in mind she was the sole beneficiary of his will. But it didn't seem right to do so soon after his death. And she hated being cast in the role of greedy relative.

Ruth looked at Craig's eager face and capitulated. 'OK, then. But won't it be very heavy?'

'Nah, no problem.' He drew himself up and flexed his shoulders and biceps.

'Nah,' said the neighbour, grinning up at Craig, 'A piece of piss, if you'll pardon my French.'

Swift and Cat met up in his office around 5.30. Having exchanged details of their findings of the day, they sat in reflective silence for a time.

'Slow progress?' Cat suggested, optimistically.

'You could put it that way. I've contacted the Burley-in-Wharfedale team. They've had all hands on deck chasing a bunch of rampaging truants from the local school but they're going to send a couple of officers to look at the flat in Calverley Street and get back to us as soon as possible.'

Cat nodded. 'So after your follow up visit to The Black Sheep Inn it looks like there's no need for me to polish up my French in order to make a call to the police in Algiers about whatever it was Brunswick got up to there twenty years ago,' she said with a degree of regret.

'Afraid not. I can see no way Brunswick could have got himself to Fellbeck Crag, tracked Hartwell, pushed him off the crag and then set fire to him, even if he had known Hartwell's whereabouts.'

'And if he didn't know, he'd have had to have spent time finding him and tracking him,' Cat said.

'Exactly.'

'We need to get Ruth Hartwell to spill the beans on what's bothering her,' Cat said. 'And I don't think she'll do that when big-boy ex-con Craig is around.'

'We could invite her in to talk to us here,' Swift suggested.

Cat looked around. 'It's a bit of a monk's cell.'

'I could ask Ravi Stratton for another chair and a plant to make things look more welcoming,' Swift said, attempting to keep a straight face.

Cat grinned. 'Good thinking,' she said. Then, 'Do you think Ruth is frightened of Craig?'

'No, I don't think she is. According to her daughter, Ruth is a serial rescuer of people in need. She was married to a prison chaplain and was herself a social worker and a prison visitor. My take on it is that Ruth has a very clear idea of the risks she takes with her lame ducks, she knows what she's doing and she's basically a very confident woman.'

'But something has rattled the bars of her cage,' Cat pointed out. 'Or, more likely, someone.'

Swift was in full agreement, but would Ruth be persuaded to tell them who? Because if not, he doubted once again that they were going to move this case on. He dialled the number of the *Old School House* but, as Cat had found before, there was no reply, and Ruth Hartwell didn't use an answering service.

'I'll call her in the morning and invite her in,' he decided. 'No point in trying again to get her now and having her fret all night about it.'

'Agreed.'

'And possibly using the time to cook up some tale to satisfy us,' he added, reflecting on Ruth Hartwell's shrewdness. He shut down his computer, and said to Cat, 'Time to knock off. And I haven't had anything to eat since breakfast.' He was about to invite her to join him for a bite to eat, then remembered that she had Jeremy to think about as regards a dinner companion.

'Fancy a quick drink?' Cat said cheerily.

'Sure.' He glanced at her, the faint surprise clearly showing in his face.

'Jeremy and I are going out to dinner this evening,' she told him. 'But that doesn't mean I can't have a glass of wine with you first.'

Swift took her to a nearby French bistro. Cat sipped at her wine, washing it down with a glass of mineral water so there was no risk of driving over the limit. They fell back into the easy friendship they had shared over the years. And when it came for her to leave he was dismayed to discover how much he wanted her to forget about Jeremy Howard and come home with him instead.

*

At the *Old School House* Craig had spent some time fiddling with the television which had once belonged to Christian Hartwell and eventually got a picture up on the screen. He felt elation. This TV was the most fantastic piece of equipment he had ever had in his hands and under his control. It had numerous digital channels and a remote with tiny black buttons which responded instantly to the touch of his fingers. He pointed it at the screen and channel-hopped until he was dizzy.

Ruth, meanwhile, had retired to the bathroom, locked the door and run a hot bath. Before undressing and getting in to the water she sat on the Lloyd Loom chair which had once belonged to her mother and finally opened the flat envelope which she had found nestling inside the larger padded one which Emma Varley had given her.

As she had both feared and yet somehow hoped, it contained a number of photographs.

She began to go through them. There were old photographs of Christian and his mother. One of them showed him as a baby kicking on rug wearing just a vest and a nappy. Another was a portrait of an eight- or nine-year-old Christian standing under an apple tree on a bright, sunny day, quite possibly in the garden of the *Old School House*. And there was one of Pamela, glamorous in a low-cut sundress, sporting long dangling earrings in the shape of parrots. The surfaces of the pictures were grainy and scratched and the colours had faded to orange and yellow. They seemed to be pictures from another life, another world.

She dug around amongst the other photos, sadness and a growing anxiety stirring within. But it was impossible to stop now. And then she found some pictures which were quite different from the family snaps. The images were in black and white, glossy and new-looking. Looking at two or three was enough to make her wince at the images of a number of half naked women writhing around poles: a group of men sprawled in their chairs watching them, their faces drunken and vulpine. Ruth was no aficionado of lap-dancing clubs but she had a strong feeling this was no seedy back-street club. The décor looked expensive – marble walls, velvet drapes at the windows, sparkling chrome furniture. The whole scene was anathema to her. What was Christian doing in a place like that? Was it for professional reasons or personal pleasure? And then she came to a photograph which made the colour drain from her face. What she saw was bad enough, but the knowledge that she must share it with Chief Inspector Swift and his colleague made things even worse.

DAY 8

Ruth rose early and took Tamsin for a walk in the nearby park. There was a tingling crispness in the air and the sky on the horizon was patched with dark tongues of cloud standing out from a gleaming background of pale, buttery light.

She walked around the boating lake, through the regimented ranks of pom-pom dahlias, and up the stone steps leading to a high terrace which was the home of ranks of stone statues, depicting departed grandees from the Victorian era.

Tamsin hopped along briskly on her three good legs, the smaller, withered limb swaying cheerily, her long curly tail waving with the joy of being out in the open air and free to run.

Ruth loved this time of the day, when the town and countryside were just waking to welcome a new day. She quite often had the park to herself, although the occasional early morning runner would break the solitude.

She walked with her head down, her thoughts occupied with the issue of Christian's envelope of photographs and the shiny mobile phone. 'Do I, or do I not, show the photographs to Chief Inspector Swift?' she asked herself, speaking the words very softly. 'That is the question.' Her mind couldn't focus, couldn't sort out the right way from the wrong, and possibly disastrous, way.

As she reached the end of the terrace a figure walked out from behind the last statue.

It was Mac the Knife.

He fell into step with her, his manner easy and relaxed. 'Good morning, Mrs Hartwell. Nice morning for a walk, eh?'

He might as well have been holding a gun to her temple for the cold terror Ruth experienced. 'What do you want?' she demanded, hearing her voice sound in her head; the quavering voice of a panic-stricken old woman.

'Just those photos, the ones I told you about.'

She thought about the cardboard box filled with pictures which she had taken from Christian's flat. She had placed them under the sideboard in her dining room, a draughty cold room she hadn't used for years and treated as a temporary storage place for items she didn't quite know what to do with. Her mouth went dry. She couldn't speak. Wouldn't speak. Wouldn't bloody just cave in to his demands. Her heart was hitting her breast bone so hard she thought it would break a rib.

'Come on, love, just tell me where they are.'

She stayed silent. She felt a prickle of sensation move over her scalp. She tried to speak but her lips wouldn't work.

Tamsin had come close, was sitting at her feet, watchful and afraid.

Moments went by.

Mac the Knife took a pair of shiny surgical scissors from his pocket, then grasped Tamsin by the collar. The dog sprang up, trying to shake herself free. Ruth saw the flash of the blades, saw his fingers move to encase the flap of Tamsin's left ear.

There was a drilling feeling inside her skull. And then it seemed as though a huge plastic tube was lowering itself on to her, enclosing her. Her vision and her hearing seemed to have left her and become swallowed up in a blur of cloud. She found herself cut off from the outside world.

And then there was nothing. Just darkness and silence.

It was around three hours later that Swift rang the bell at the *Old School House*. Having failed to get Ruth to answer the phone on the several occasions he had called between 9.30 and 10 o'clock, he had got into his car and driven around to her place, a faint anxiety about her welfare stirring within him. He was disappointed that Cat was not able to be in on the visit, but she had phoned in with heartfelt apologies to say she that she had suffered a migraine in the early hours of the morning and was reluctant to drive until the disturbances to her vision had settled.

The door to the Hartwell house was opened by Ruth's young protégé, Craig. Seeing him standing framed in the doorway, Swift was impressed by the young man's sheer physical presence: his tallness and his sheer mass, the shoulders those of a rugby prop-forward. Craig regarded Swift with wary dark eyes under heavy black eyebrows.

'Hello,' Swift said. 'I was hoping to see Mrs Hartwell.'

'She's not here.' His tone was uncompromising.

'Do you think she'll be back soon?' Swift kept his tone calm and pleasant.

'Yeah. Guess so.'

'Could I come in and wait?' Swift said.

The young man's deep forehead contracted into folds. 'Yeah, OK.'

He opened the door just wide enough to allow Swift to pass through, closing it as Swift walked into the hallway and overtaking him to lead the way down the hall into the kitchen.

Glancing through the doorway into the front room Swift could see a large TV set tuned to a cartoon show which played out to an accompaniment of lively music and loud whoops.

The young man went through into the kitchen and stood beside the table, his head bent away from the visitor.

'May I sit down?' Swift asked.

The young man nodded.

'Would you like to sit down too?' Swift suggested.

He followed, sitting as far from the policeman as possible. There was a long silence.

'Do you know where Mrs Hartwell has gone?' Swift asked gently.

'Taken the dog for a walk.'

'Right.' He allowed another silence to fall. 'Perhaps we could have some coffee?' he suggested eventually, guessing that might free up the young man to talk whilst diverted with a practical task.

'OK.' The young man got up. He was wearing a pair of new denims, and a pristine grey sweatshirt with North Bay written on it. There was a crease down the middle, indicating that the shirt had only recently come out of the packet. The sleeves were slightly too short, revealing the young man's large wrist bones. On his feet were spotless grey trainers with silver stripes. Swift saw that everything was new, giving a strangely self-conscious look, as though he were wearing a costume put together by someone else. Which, given the clothes would be prison issue on discharge, was in fact the case.

'Have you known Mrs Hartwell long?' Swift asked, as the young man busied himself with the kettle and the coffee jar.

'Aye, quite a few years.' He spooned grounds into two mugs. 'She helped me learn to read and write.'

'Did you ever meet Christian Hartwell, Craig?'

There was another pause, and more frowning.

'Do you mind me calling you Craig?' Swift asked. 'I'm afraid I don't know your surname.'

There was a beat of silence. 'I don't mind.'

'And did you know Christian Hartwell?' Swift persevered.

'No. I never came to this house before. I only ever saw Mrs Hartwell ...' He jerked himself straight and shot Swift a look of blazing defiance. 'I met her in prison. I've been in prison for eight years. Just got out of Wentworth.'

'That's a long time to serve,' Swift said.

'Yeah.' His Adam's apple dipped and bobbed.

'It's all behind you now,' Swift said, accepting a mug of steaming black coffee which scalded his lips when he took a sip.

'Do you want milk?' the young man said.

'This is fine.'

The young man sat down again. There was a lessening of tension in the air now that the topic of prison had been opened and closed. He looked across at Swift, his eyes clearly holding some information which he was afraid to reveal. Swift guessed he was experiencing the same kind of conflict which Cat had reported seeing in Ruth Hartwell's eyes the day before.

Swift took a further sip of his coffee, this time with a degree of caution. 'I expect Mrs Hartwell will be back any minute,' he remarked, casually.

The pleading in the young man's eyes transformed itself into sudden desperation. 'I'm worried about her,' he said. 'She's been out for going on three hours.'

'Perhaps she's taking the dog a long walk – it's a fine morning for walking.'

'No!' He shook his head vigorously. 'She only takes it twenty minutes or so at a time. It's disabled, you see. Its mum lay on it when it were a tiny pup and made its bones go out of shape. Mrs Hartwell told me all about it.' He sank into silence after this long speech, his forehead heavily creased.

'What do you think has happened to her?' Swift said.

'Dunno.' His breathing harsh and jagged.

Swift leaned forward, trying to ease the boy's anxiety. 'Tell me what you think has happened to Mrs Hartwell,' he repeated.

'She's in some sort of trouble.'

'Can you tell me about it?'

He swallowed hard, his eyes flicking from one side to the other. 'There was a man here yesterday. He was up to no good.'

Ah – now we're going somewhere. 'Did he come to see you or to see Mrs Hartwell?'

'Mrs Hartwell,' he said, grasping on to a question which required a plain, simple answer. 'He came to see her.'

'Were you here when he arrived?' Swift asked, beginning to build a picture of the scene, having a keen sense that it was one of significance.

'No, I was out.' He sliced a brief glance at Swift. 'Seeing if I could get some work at the local pub.'

'Did you get it?'

'Yeah.'

'Well done.' Swift drank some more black coffee.

The young man ploughed on. 'He was all puffed up with himself. He said his name was Mac the Knife. I didn't like the sound of that.' He drew in a long breath, steeling himself for the next speech.

'No, neither would I,' Swift commented.

'Mrs Hartwell … was like … getting a bit worked up. She said she had to go to the doctor's. She tried to get away from him, but he kept following her.'

'Did you follow them?' Swift asked, keeping steadfastly neutral.

'Oh, aye.'

'And did you hear anything?'

'He said, "Chill. I only wanted to talk to you about Christian". And she said that she couldn't tell him nothing, she hadn't been in touch ...' He took another restorative breath.

Swift was impressed. 'Did he say anything else?'

'He kept going on at her. Something about this Christian being her next of kin.' He looked again at Swift. 'That means she was important to him, doesn't it? Like me and my mum.'

'Exactly.' Swift waited a few moments.

Craig frowned, seeming to have become exhausted with the effort of volunteering so much information. He began gnawing at his knuckles, leaving teeth marks in the skin. 'He was certainly after scaring her,' he burst out. 'He was a slimy, bullying bastard. And I've met a fair few of those.' The irises of his eyes shivered as he flicked yet another glance at Swift, who guessed that most of the bullies the young man had in mind had been policemen or screws, people whom he would see as basically on Swift's side.

'Anything else?' Swift prompted, impressed with the young man's account, and sensing that it was a pretty accurate recollection of what he had seen and heard. If only all informants were as clear and straightforward.

The young man was scratching at a patch of eczema on his right palm, picking at the skin and making it bleed. He gave a long slow shake of the head. 'What have I to do? Have I to go looking for her? Yeah, that's it.' He got to his feet, swallowing hard, panic showing in his eyes. 'I don't know where to go....'

Swift could feel the young man's fear and his despair at being unable to formulate some kind of plan to help Mrs Hartwell, his friend, perhaps the only person he could trust at the moment. 'Why don't I phone in to the station and see if there have been any reports of her whereabouts?'

'Aye, yes.' He sat slumped in his chair, his head hanging down, his hands lying loosely between his legs.

Swift spoke quietly and crisply into his phone. After he cut the connection he stood up and put his hand lightly on the other man's shoulder. 'She's been taken to the local hospital. The A and E staff are assessing her now. She doesn't appear injured, but she's unconscious.' He felt the younger man's broad shoulder bones sag. A low groan of misery resonated in his chest.

As Swift reached for his car keys he contemplated offering to drive the distressed young man to the hospital to see how Ruth Hartwell was faring. Instantly he dismissed the idea as inappropriate and intrusive. Ex-convict Craig was not related to Ruth, and, given that he had still been in prison at the time Christian Hartwell was killed, he had no clear role to play in the drama surrounding the current events in Ruth's life. His first task here was to check with Ruth's doctor at the hospital and to ensure that Harriet Brunswick was informed as soon as possible.

Giving the stricken young man a card with his contact number on, and a reassuring smile, he walked quickly from the house and slid behind the wheel of his car.

Larry McBride walked away from Ruth Hartwell's huddled, collapsed body and headed towards the gates of the park. His steps were regular and purposeful, his heart rate only minimally above its normal level. He had wanted to scare the old lady, make her aware of how seriously he wanted those photographs. He had not expected her to capitulate in quite the way she had done. She was not looking at all good, and that did slightly disturb him. If she died, his main lever was gone.

He would have to make a thorough search of her house, cross his fingers that she had not already disposed of the pictures or lodged them in a safe place with either the police or her solicitor. He knew the whereabouts of her solicitor's office, but the knowledge was of little use, getting into the safe of a law firm being somewhat more problematical than frightening a decent, law-abiding woman like Ruth Hartwell. Not impossible to arrange, but risky.

This job was turning out to be unnervingly complex. He thought he'd cracked it when he broke into Hartwell's flat and found his state-of-the-art Nikon camera flung into a corner of the sofa. Quite a number of jobs were like that; you thought you were going to have to get into a real sweat finding what you were looking for, and then it just dropped into your lap like a ripe plum. He'd run the camera through its paces. The bugger had deleted everything and then taken shots over the deletions just to make sure the erased stuff wasn't found by a special retrieving process. He'd had to look through fifty shots of Hartwell's kitchen sink to find that out.

And then he'd come up with Mrs Hartwell, her great big house, her giant-sized, well-muscled relative and her bloody dog. Not the best scenario in which to institute a search. Or an assassination.

Having left the park, he walked through the streets, planning his next move. A grey drizzle was coming from the sky, turning to sludgy grease underfoot as it hit the pavements. A whining, punishing wind whipped around the blackened stone buildings.

He hated Yorkshire; the pasty-faced women with their flat vowels and ugly bulk, the aggressively jesting blokes in the pubs, the chummy shopkeepers who asked impertinent personal questions. At least in London people mainly left you alone as you churned through the packed, anonymous streets. Biddy didn't like London. She wanted to go back to Huddersfield where they both had been born. But he had always wanted excitement and change. The entry into a profession, the dearest wish of many of the parents of his generation, repelled him. The mere thought of years of studying followed by even more years of routine, safety and dullness made him feel suffocated before he had even started. He left school at fifteen and drifted into a life of hazard and chance: a couple of years working on an assembly line a factory making tools, then a stint in a betting shop, a spot of taxi-driving, a few years as a debt collector's assistant. And then the big break came – being taken on as a bodyguard to a guy he met in a pub in Leeds. The guy turned out to be a fraudster and a thug, with fingers in pies in London, New York and Bangkok. McBride had got to see the world. The work was exciting and dangerous, and the money was fantastic. Until the fraudster was caught and banged up, and everything stopped.

But the experience he had gained working as a tough man and manipulator opened up an opportunity he would never have dreamed of. He'd landed a plum, reached the peak of his ambitions. But there was always an edge of fear when you were at the top, that dread of plummeting down. He had a sudden uneasy image of Christian Hartwell's body dizzily twisting over the jagged lumps of rock on its way down to certain death. He slowed to a halt, his thoughts temporarily paralyzing him, making any kind of physical action impossible.

He'd made such a bungle of this killing. The thought of his ineptitude brought out a wave of heat which lay on the skin beneath his shirt like a slimy grey membrane. He'd been given the perfect means to do the deed: a superb knife, a state-of-the-art shooter if push came to shove. He'd tracked the guy for five whole days, ending up eventually in Yorkshire and to this craggy place where he had seen the opportunity to take out his target without any physical contact – a beautiful, clean kill. On the first sighting of the place where he could carry out the plan, he had rejected it. He needed a swift and foolproof dispatch – a knife in the kidneys and that was that. But though he was a hard man, knifing still took a lot of bottle, and he had had a trembling thought that he might not have quite the bottle he used to. Twenty-four hours had passed and he was once again tracking his target up the endless stone steps. And when the target reached that critical point, he had suddenly just needed to do it. There and then: a hard poke with the tips of his fingers. And the guy was gone. And he was filled with relief – until he remembered that he still had to make a search of the guy's pockets. If he was carrying those photographs on him, the murder would have been in vain. There had been moments of indecision and then the relief of the plan to use his lighter and the brandy he always carried in his hip flask. And in the event, he'd found nothing of any use to the boss. He'd made a bollocks of the whole thing.

His heart gave a warning kick of fear. He resumed his walk, refusing to be intimidated by his own terror.

He passed a row of phone boxes, barely noticing them through the hurry and urgency of his thoughts. But something had registered subliminally. He slowed to a halt, then turned back and stepped into one of the empty boxes. Having dialled 999, he altered his voice to a higher pitch, then gave details for the need of an ambulance. He gave clear and accurate details of the whereabouts of the woman in need and, when asked for his own details, supplied a plausible-sounding name and address for their records and hung up.

He walked on, pondering his next move. The image of the big, sad lad who was some kind of relative of the old lady's crept into his mind. The *Old School House* would have been ripe for a spot of breaking in and searching if it weren't for him. He could probably handle him, as long as he was not carrying a knife of his own, but extra deaths always created extra risks, something else the boss would not like. Still not at the point where he could fix on the next plan of action, he reflected that calling the ambulance had surely been a good move. Maybe with quick discovery and care, the old girl might be as right as rain before too long. And he reassured himself that if he got his act together she would be no problem to manipulate. An old girl with a daughter and maybe the added bonus of grandchildren. Putty in his hands.

Craig waited until Swift's car was out of sight. He stood in the doorway of the *Old School House* at a loss as to what to do next. Eventually, he went into the sitting room and – with much reluctance – switched off the big shiny television. He knew that he needed all his wits about him, now that he was on his own, entirely alone with the terrifying knowledge that he had only himself to rely on when deciding what to do next. He reached into his pocket and pulled out the slim black mobile phone which he had found in Mrs Hartwell's drawer. He had been through all of her drawers and cupboards in the spare available moments since he came to the house. Not from a wish to steal anything, simply to get a sense of the place and of Mrs Hartwell's life. And because it was impossible to resist the temptation when there was no one to stop him or find out. In one of the food cupboards he had found an old treacle tin containing a rolled bundle of twenty-pound notes. He stared at the bundle for some time; the largest amount of cash he had ever held in his hands in the whole of his life. Carefully, reluctantly, he replaced the tin in its hiding place.

The phone he simply couldn't resist. Mobile phones were like gold in prison. Men would knife each other to get their hands on one that was smuggled in. It wasn't as if he was taking the phone, he was simply looking after it for Mrs Hartwell. When she came home he would put it back in the drawer. He'd had no problem switching it on, but the battery was flat and he couldn't find a charger. He told himself it was not an unsolvable problem; he'd work something out.

The sudden sound of the doorbell sent needles of alarm through his nerves. He stood very still, willing whoever was standing outside the house to go away. But they kept ringing. He tiptoed down the hallway. He felt the familiar terror of confronting the unknown.

'Anyone at home?' a woman's voice called. 'I've got your dog.'

Craig swallowed down the saliva which was pouring into his mouth. Someone had found Mrs Hartwell's dog! He had to open the door, he had to take care of Mrs Hartwell's dog.

As he cautiously pulled the door open, Tamsin gave a short bark which seemed to signal pleasure in seeing him. She leapt forward and put her paws up against his knees.

'You can tell someone's glad to get home,' the woman said, cheerily.

Craig bent to caress the dog. Preoccupied by the panic and anxiety which had gripped him when Ruth failed to return to the house, he had forgotten about the dog. He squatted down on his heels and hugged the dog to him. She was part of Ruth's family, the creature she probably spent more time with than anyone else, now that she was on her own. And her dog was safe now, and he would look after it. He glanced up at the woman. 'Thank you,' he said. 'Thank you.'

The woman looked startled and then gratified to hear the note of deep sincerity in his voice. 'I found her sitting under a bush in the park.' She chattered on, but Craig wasn't listening. He just wanted her to go away and leave him to wrestle with his bewilderment regarding what to do next.

Eventually the woman sensed that he was not going to enter into any kind of conversation with her. As she talked and tried to engage with him she gradually sensed that there was something strange about him, something potentially scary. I wouldn't like to meet him alone on a dark night, she told herself, before bending to give Tamsin a farewell pat and departing.

Craig shut the door firmly and returned to the kitchen. 'I don't know what to fucking do,' he told the dog. Tamsin heard him out, then took herself off to her basket, curled up and went to sleep.

*

Back at the station Swift fielded an anxious telephone call from Harriet Brunswick in London. She had just been informed of her mother's admission to hospital by the ward sister.

'Of course, they won't tell me a bloody thing that's any use,' she fumed. 'Just that's she's "stable", although she hasn't woken up properly or spoken yet. She's had a CT scan and they're awaiting the results. Useless.'

Swift realized that beneath the irritability and anger in Harriet's voice was frustration and guilt at not being able to do anything to help from such a distance.

'If I could get hold of Charles, I'd get him to speak to Mother's consultant and find out just what's what. But he's in theatre and I haven't managed to contact him yet.'

Swift offered her information regarding the time of her mother's collapse and its whereabouts.

There was a long silence, followed by a long sigh. 'I knew something like this would happen,' she protested. 'She doesn't take enough care of herself, always wrapped up in thinking about the needs of other people.'

Swift made no comment.

Harriet instantly came back at him. 'And you say she was simply walking the dog in the park when she collapsed in the park?'

'Yes. The police and emergency services were alerted by an anonymous caller.'

'God! You make it sound a bit suspicious.'

'There was no evidence that she was attacked or had anything stolen,' he volunteered, frustrated to be having this conversation on the phone, when he needed to see her face to face to gauge her reactions fully.

'This is a bloody nightmare,' she said.

He could imagine her, furiously balancing all her responsibilities – child, sick mother, job, husband – although hopefully the latter would be a support rather than a cause for anxiety. Recalling his interview with Charles Brunswick, he was not convinced that would be the case.

'Is that boy still around?' she asked. 'Craig whatever his name is?'

'He was in the house when I visited earlier.'

'Wonderful! He could have the whole place full of dossers and tossers by now.'

Again Swift didn't comment, being sure Ruth Hartwell would prefer the house to be occupied by Craig 'whatever-his-name-was' than to be empty and the young man on the streets.

'Would you get someone to check?' Harriet asked, softening her tone. 'Not heavy-handed stuff, just a PC walking up the drive to make sure the old place isn't being trashed.'

'Yes, sure thing. And I'll go and see your mother as soon as she's fit to talk to me. Will you be travelling up to see her?'

'Of course. Just give me time to sort things out,' she snapped. 'I don't think I can get away today but I'll be on my way tomorrow – unless the hospital tell me otherwise.'

Swift heard the connection click off. He sat for a few moments, thinking over the conversation. He wondered if Harriet had any idea of the potential hornet's nest she might be walking into when she arrived in Yorkshire.

He phoned Cat's mobile and enquired after her health.

'I'm doing fine,' she told him. 'I'll be in tomorrow, no problem. Any developments with the Hartwell case?'

Swift heard fatigue in her voice. His wife Kate had occasionally suffered a bad migraine and it could easily take twenty-four hours until she was fully recovered. 'I'll e-mail my notes to you. Reading them is optional. Just relax and get well.'

And after that he reached for the phone again and put in a call to the governor of Wentworth Prison.

Craig went into the sitting room and turned the volume up on the TV. He sat cross-legged on the floor, grasping the remote and pointing it at the set with stabbing gestures, channel-hopping in the hope of finding something to distract him from the problem of getting to the hospital.

Hours went by and eventually the room grew dark. He went into the kitchen and found cheese and bread in the fridge. He made coffee. He let Tamsin go out into the back garden to relieve herself.

He made sure the house was securely locked. And then he took his supper into the front room and curled up on the sofa, letting the flickering patterns of light from the screen glide across his vision until gradually they soothed him to sleep.

DAY 9

Superintendent Ravi Stratton called into Swift's office for an update on the Hartwell case. It was only 7.30 on a cool July morning and the station was quiet, most personnel on daytime shifts having not yet arrived.

Stratton was looking good in a closely fitting navy suit and a cream silk blouse. Her long hair was loose, framing her face and lying on her shoulders. There was an air of steely determination about her, a quality which had not been nearly so much in evidence on the last occasion they had spoken.

'I've just had information from the Burley-in-Wharfedale team,' she told him. 'They've had a look at Christian Hartwell's flat. It's been broken into.'

'Right. Any further information?'

'The forensic team are going in to see what they can come up with. The report from the uniform PCs who went in mentions that there was a TV stand in the living room, but no TV.'

'That sounds like a break-in with intent to steal,' Swift said. 'Or a clever way to make it look like one.' The sudden thought of the big new TV in Mrs Hartwell's sitting room came into his mind – something to ponder on later. 'Ravi,' he said, 'was there a camera found in Hartwell's flat?'

She glanced through the list in front of her. 'There's no mention of it.' She looked up. 'Is that significant?'

'Maybe.' He gave her an outline of his findings from the previous day: Charles Brunswick appearing to be out of the frame, as also did the young man currently lodging at Ruth Hartwell's house. 'I checked with the prison governor. Craig Titmus was still behind bars when Hartwell was killed.'

Stratton leaned forward as Swift went on to tell her about Craig's account of a threatening visitor who had demanded to be given some photographs which he believed to be in Ruth's possession. And then of Ruth's admission to hospital and the preceding circumstances.

Stratton raised her eyebrows. 'Do we know if she showed any signs of being attacked?'

'No obvious signs. I spoke with the ward sister earlier on this morning. Mrs Hartwell is said to be doing well. She's conscious again but still sleepy. They initially thought she might have had a stroke, but are now wondering if she simply had some kind of blackout. The sister commented that everyone is allowed one blackout without being considered brain damaged or in need of medical intervention. But they're still waiting for the results of the CT scan,' Swift concluded.

Stratton looked thoughtful.

'I think we should do a search of the *Old School House*,' Swift said. 'And I think we need a warrant, just to be on the safe side. There's young Craig to contend with and also Harriet Brunswick, who is something of a force to be reckoned with. We don't want to waste time being sent on our way.'

'I'll get one.' Stratton was so quick and sharp this morning, Swift kept glancing at her to try to put his finger on exactly why she seemed so different from how she had been in their last case discussion.

'And I'll go and talk to Ruth Hartwell as soon as she's fully conscious,' he concluded.

Stratton had been watching him carefully. 'I get the impression you're concerned we're not making significant progress,' she remarked, 'but I think we are gradually building up a picture. We've certainly got more pieces of information to work with, even though they are not fitting into any format yet. But they will. I have every confidence in you and Inspector Fallon.' She shook her hair back in a small gesture of assertion and Swift had the briefest glance of the shiny glint of beige plastic in her left ear. With a leap of insight he understood the reason behind her hesitations during the last discussion and the new sharpness now. Not to mention the new way of wearing her hair.

There was something about this knowledge that made him warm to her. And as they watched each other with silent assessment over the desk, he could feel the atmosphere soften.

'How are you getting on with Inspector Fallon?' she asked.

'Very well,' he said simply.

'Good,' she said. 'And good luck.' She smiled. 'I think we need a little of that.'

Craig needed to see Ruth, needed to see with his own eyes that she was still alive. Which meant he needed to find the hospital. He decided to fall back on the strategy he had used when making his way from the prison release gate to the *Old School House*. He would go out into the street and even if he felt the need to count every footstep he would make his way to the bus stop where the snake-eyed man had disappeared into a passing bus. He would stay until someone came to wait at the stop, someone whom he felt he could speak to. And he would ask them which bus he needed to get to the hospital. It didn't matter how long it took, the one thing to focus on was getting there.

He counted the change he had from his prison release money, wondering if that was enough for the bus fare to the hospital. And then it dawned on him that Mac the Knife could well pay another visit to the house and carry out a similar search of his own. He took the treacle tin from the kitchen cupboard, pulled the notes from it and folded them as flat as he could make them before putting them in the pocket of his jeans along with his own money. He vowed that he would tell her he had taken it to keep it safe. That was the very first thing he would tell her. And the next thing he would do was to ask her what he should do with the envelope of photographs in her dining room: the ones he had seen her place earlier in the kitchen drawer. It hadn't taken him long to work out that the photos in the box could be the ones Mac the Knife was looking for. He had had a quick look through them, but they meant nothing to him. He slid the envelope into the laundry basket which stood beside the washer and tucked it underneath the clothes.

The journey did not take as long as Craig had thought. But it was harrowing. Getting up the courage to speak to strangers and ask them questions did not seem to be getting any easier. The first man he had spoken to, who was one ahead of him in the queue at the bus stop, had been both dismissive and faintly hostile. 'Can't help. Don't live round here, pal,' he'd said. But his eyes had been cold and he hadn't sounded pally at all. Craig felt panic rise in his throat. He stepped back from the queue and looked up and down the street, having the sudden feeling that he was about to be ambushed and a stabbing fear that his old enemy Blackwell might materialize out of nowhere and shatter his attempts to fit into the new world which he had chosen for himself. A world that could easily be torn away from him.

The man who had been standing behind him, a pensioner sporting unruly tufts of grey hair crammed beneath a flat cap, turned in his direction and smiled. 'You want the number 89, son,' he said. 'It'll take you right to the hospital.' He gestured to the space Craig had left in the queue. 'Get yourself back in line. It'll be coming any minute.'

This act of kindness lifted Craig's spirits. The old man sat down two seats in front of him and Craig hardly took his eyes off him, having the sense of having found a temporary anchor in a turbulent sea. When the old man got up, made his way to the central exit door and then cautiously down the steps to the street, Craig followed him and trailed him to the hospital entrance, keeping his distance so as not to cause the man alarm. He wanted to catch him up and ask him how he would find Mrs Hartwell in this vast building which reared above him, its windows reflecting the cold grey light of this chilly summer day. But by the time he reached the inside of the hospital the man had vanished into the throng of people crowding the reception area.

Looking around him, Craig found himself instinctively shrinking from the clamour and bustle. He was on the point of turning around and walking straight out when he reminded himself of the purpose of this visit, and of how important Mrs Hartwell had become to him, and how he longed to help her in whatever way he could.

He noticed two women dressed in navy suits sitting behind big round desks which sat like islands in this big sea of people.

Guessing they were hospital officials, he joined one of the queues. His heart thrashed in his chest as he eventually got to the front of the queue and found himself face to face with the business-like woman sitting behind the desk. 'Mrs Ruth Hartwell,' he said. 'I need to see her.' He held himself rigid, waiting for a brush off, a put down, a rebuke. Rejection had been the norm for so much of his life.

'When was she admitted?' the woman asked, her face and voice flat and neutral.

'This morning.'

She tapped the keys of her lap top. 'She's in Wharfedale Ward.' She pointed down the long corridor stretching away to his left. 'Follow the signs.'

He wiped his hands nervously over his denim-clad hips, automatically waiting for a spoken dismissal.

She raised her eyebrows, nodding in the direction she had previously indicated. *Go on*, her eyes told him.

'Right!' he said, snapping to attention. 'Thanks.'

As he turned, he heard her murmur, 'You're welcome,' and another tiny flame of warmth flickered inside him.

Finding the ward was not a problem, but when he tried the twin entry doors he found they were locked. He stood, staring around him, at a loss, instinctively swamped with feelings of guilt. A woman came up behind him and pressed a button on the wall adjacent to the doors. There was a crackling sound from a small loudspeaker just above the button and a clipped, robotic-sounding voice said, 'Wharfedale Ward.'

'I've come to attend a case review on Mrs Turner. I'm her daughter.'

'Come through,' the robot said.

The woman pushed at the doors which miraculously opened. She went through and politely held the door for Craig. He glowed with triumph; he was beginning to get the hang of things.

But then the row of beds he had expected to see as the door closed behind him turned out to be a corridor. Uncertain what to do, he followed the woman who had helped him. She marched forward confidently, knowing the ropes, pausing at a large desk and smiling at the two people who were sitting behind it, bidding them, good morning.

Craig followed suit, but didn't get as far as saying good morning.

'Excuse me!' One of the people sitting behind the desk was speaking to him in a sharp, questioning voice, making his skin prickle with agitation.

He turned. The woman was dressed in a green uniform and was eyeing him with suspicion.

'Who are you?'

He swallowed. 'I want to see Mrs Hartwell.' He heard his words in his head. They sounded too loud and too pushy.

'Are you family or a friend?'

His mind raced. 'Next of kin,' he said.

'Her son?' The woman's face had become more friendly.

'Yeah.'

'Oh, right. She'll be glad you've come. It's not visiting hours now, you know,' she said. 'But it's all right to speak to her, just for a few minutes.'

He nodded. He looked through to the room where Mrs Turner's daughter had gone. 'Is she in there?'

'Yes.' She looked at him curiously. 'Have you spoken to anyone yet about how she is?'

'No.'

'We had thought she might have had a mild stroke, but now we think she simply suffered a temporary blackout. She's recovered consciousness and she's doing well. But we'd like to keep her under observation for another 24 hours to ensure that she's stable.'

'Oh.' He couldn't take it all in. He wanted to ask more questions, but was not sure what exactly he should say.

'First bed on the right,' she said. The phone on the desk rang, claiming the woman's attention, and he could tell she had already lost interest in him.

He walked through into the ward, fearful of what he might find, hardly daring to look at the figure in the bed.

It was coming up to ten o'clock and Cat had still not turned up at the station. Swift was beginning to be concerned and was highly relieved to hear her at the other end of the phone some minutes later.

'Hi!' she said. 'You've every right to say, *what time do you call this?*'

'Are you OK?' he asked, hearing a bright brittleness in her voice which was uncharacteristic.

'Yes.' A pause. 'I'm having an espresso in the café just across the road. Would you like to join me?'

Frowning in concern, he shrugged on his jacket. 'I'll be right there.' He ran quickly down the steps and out into the street.

She was sitting at a table by the window and waved as she saw him. As he spotted her, his nerves tingled. She stood up as he joined her at the small round table. An electric thrill of shock went through him. Instinctively he put his arms around her and hugged her to him for a few seconds.

'Sorry to drag you out of the office,' she said as they sat down facing each other. 'I needed a good strong coffee, and maybe a little tea and sympathy as well.' She smiled, her soft generous mouth curving into a grin filled with irony.

She crossed her long legs and took a sip of her thick, dark coffee. Despite the sulky July weather, she was wearing yet another summery dress, this one sporting dramatic black swirls on a cream background. A bright-green cardigan was slung over her shoulders and her chestnut hair swung around her face, the ends curving around her chin.

Swift felt a lurch of the heart he had not experienced for a long while. His eyes kept resting on her lips, he didn't seem to be able to pull them away. He took in a breath and made himself bite the bullet. 'Are you going to tell me that you walked into a door?' he said. 'Or to mind my own business?'

Cat didn't hesitate. 'Jeremy did it,' she said. 'A great thumping backhander. He really meant it.' She touched the bloody split in her lip, tentatively patted the bruising all around the left side of her mouth. 'I fell back against the bathroom basin, so I guess I'll have a black eye as well before too long.'

Swift looked at the bruised looking area around her left cheekbone. 'It's already coming on quite nicely,' he said, rage and frustration building up at the thought of Cat's being abused in this way.

'I picked myself up and considered thumping him back,' she said. 'And then I knew that was the very last thing to do.'

'So what *did* you do?' Swift tried not to imagine the scene of Jeremy swinging a crashing blow across Cat's beautiful mouth, tried not to imagine seeking Jeremy out and beating him up good and proper as Richard, his landlord, would say.

'I packed a few things and went back to my flat, which mercifully hasn't sold yet. Saved by the credit crunch, can you believe that? It's an ill wind that blows nobody any good,' she joked.

He shook his head in disbelief.

'I'm up for talking about it,' she said, softly.

He opened his hands. 'Go on.'

'There's been quite a bit of pressure from Jeremy in the past few weeks for me to give up my job.' She let out a hiss of self-reproach, flung her arms out in frustrated disbelief of what she had to tell. 'No, let's be honest, it's been there right from the start. I suppose I just assumed he was half joking, I mean even in the police force most men seemed to have cottoned on that it's OK for a woman to hold down a serious job.'

'Oh, we blokes are getting to be quite an enlightened bunch,' Swift agreed.

'In the last few days since I moved area and got involved in this case, he's become quite pushy about it. And, of course, I became rather more determined not to start composing my resignation letter without giving the matter a lot of thought.'

'Why did he want you to resign? I'd have thought having a high-ranking police officer for a girlfriend might have been something to feel proud about.'

She shook her head. 'Ed, Ed!' She chided. 'Those are the thoughts of a reasonable, unprejudiced modern-thinking man. In no way does Jeremy fit into that category. And I suppose before the penny dropped I was automatically placing him in it, because he was so charming and seemingly thoughtful. Wrong! He's the sort of man who wants a wife who is under his control, her life defined by him, his money and his business contacts.' She put down her cup of espresso and he saw her hands shaking with feeling.

'The dinner party we went to the night before last night was given by one of his business colleagues. There was quite a lot of interest in my job. Lots of questions, you know the kind of thing. And plenty of suggestions that the police were too soft on criminals nowadays, buried in bureaucracy, too few bobbies on the beat. I don't think the words riff-raff or bloody immigrants were actually used, but I got the drift. I had rather more to drink than I should have, and I noticed that Jeremy was … monitoring it, if you like. Which, of course, made me worse. When we got back to his place he did a little gentle chiding about the drinking. And I more or less told him to piss off.' She stopped. 'No, I actually *told* him to piss off. He went rather quiet then, and I apologized for swearing at him. And then the job thing came up. He wants me to go away with him to Thailand. He'd actually booked a flight for next week. I said no way was I going, certainly not until this case is wound up and that, in any case, I wouldn't leave the service without working out my notice. He said there was no need; I didn't need to be scraping around, grubbing to make a living now I was with him. I was on the point of telling him to stuff his money and that I had my loyalty to my colleagues to think about. And that I rather valued my job.'

'But, you didn't.'

'No. I just very quietly told him that I wasn't going to Thailand with him next week.'

Swift knew what Cat was like when she told you something very quietly. Not many people would mess with her when she really meant something.

'And suddenly I was aware of a sound like a shot. And falling. And then a very sore face and a split lip. It all happened so quickly …' She stared at him, wretched and re-living the shock.

Swift reached out and touched her hand.

'Oh God, Ed,' she burst out. 'I feel so stupid. At my age, with all my experience, not to have seen it coming. To have made such an abysmal assessment of his character. To have fallen for a bullying, chauvinistic bastard. I feel so … ashamed.'

'Isn't that what abused women often say?

She looked at him, shaking her head in self reproach. 'Yeah. Textbook stuff. I've joined the ranks.'

'No. You took it once because it came out of the blue. And then you cleared out. That's not shameful. Totally the opposite.'

'Thank God I didn't marry him. It was on the cards.'

Yes, thank God, he thought. 'What's going to happen now?'

'I don't want to go back to my place,' she said, and he could see she had worked things out, made some sort of plan.

'You can stay at the cottage with me,' he said. 'No strings attached, of course.'

'Bless you,' she said softly. Her shoulders relaxed. 'It's not just that I know Jeremy will come to the flat to find me, try to persuade me to go back to him. I want to get away, to be in a completely different atmosphere.'

He smiled. 'It's very simple and rural out there in the National Park.'

'That sounds just the ticket.' She took in some deep breaths and he could see that the shock of an assault from someone you know well kept returning to strike her afresh with its horror. Spotting a passing waitress, Cat got herself together and ordered more coffees. 'And by the way,' she said, 'the migraine wasn't a fantasy. It hit me around three in the morning, just to make my day.'

When the fresh coffee arrived she heaped brown sugar into her cup. 'I am up for doing some work,' she told him. 'I read your e-mails. I'm up to speed.'

He told her about his early morning meeting with Ravi Stratton. 'We'll have to wait for a warrant if we want to search Ruth Hartwell's place. But I thought we should visit the house anyway, see how young Craig is getting on by himself, if you take my drift.'

'See if Ruth has any belongings left,' Cat remarked, grinning and then wincing and touching her bruised eye.

'I don't want to prejudge him,' Swift told her, 'but he's been inside a very long time, he's missed most of his growing up period behind bars and has very little knowledge of the wicked ways of the modern world. It's hard to expect him to behave like an angel.'

'Right,' she said, draining her coffee. She worked her fingers gently around her face. 'Will I frighten the horses?' she asked.

'What police officer worth their salt never got a few battle scars?' he said, settling up the bill, and tucking some coins under his saucer for the waitress to find.

'Are you sure you feel up to this?' he asked, as they got into his car.

'Work,' she said, 'best medicine I can think of.'

*

Ruth was a tolerant and patient woman, but not patient enough to sit doing nothing in a hospital ward. She wanted out. She had reached the stage of having mainly recovered from the shock of her collapse, although she had a faintly woolly feeling in her head and a pain in her hip from her fall on to the concrete path in the park. But she judged she had not come to much harm and her main consideration was to get back home as soon as possible. She needed to give her family the reassurance she was not an invalid, she needed to be there for Craig, and she had to talk to the police frankly and openly about the events of the last two days, and the serious threat she and her family were under regarding Mac the Knife.

She was simply waiting for her doctor to do his ward round and agree to her discharge. She had breakfasted at 7 a.m. and the hours seemed to be dragging before any real life started up on the ward. She was spending her time deliberating on all that had to be done, interspersed with an occasional doze.

On seeing Craig walk into the ward, looking enormous, some-what wild and utterly bewildered, she felt a spark of delight and relief that he had not run away in fright following her disappearance.

She held out a hand to welcome him. He stood, looking down at her, deep rings of worry under his eyes. 'Are you all right?'

'I'm very well,' she told him, making her voice bright and cheery, although the effort to speak was exhausting. 'I had breakfast in bed today for the first time in decades.' She kept smiling, trying to reassure him. 'Did Tamsin get herself home?' she asked, suddenly remembering her dog.

He nodded. 'A woman brought her back. I've given her some food. She's all right.'

Ruth smiled. 'She's clever, that dog, if no one had found her she'd have made her way home on her own. She's done it before.'

'Yeah,' said Craig. He remembered that he had something to tell Mrs Hartwell. His mind had gone blank with the effort of getting to the hospital and surmounting the hurdles to find where she was. 'How long do you have to stay in here?' he asked her.

Ruth smiled. He made it sound like a prison sentence, which in a way it was. 'Not long, I hope.'

Craig saw someone moving to stand close to the bed. A shadow fell across Ruth's white bed cover. He looked around, startled and then dismayed to see that it was Mrs Hartwell's daughter. And that she wasn't looking at all pleased.

'What the hell are you doing here?' she hissed at him, brushing past him to place her fingers briefly on her mother's arm. 'Mum! We've all been so worried about you.' It sounded like an accusation.

'I'm doing fine,' Ruth said, her voice faint and laced with anxiety. She looked from her daughter to Craig, who sat in a miserable huddled lump on his chair. 'Craig, will you get my daughter a chair?' she asked, pointing to a small stack of chairs near the entry to the ward.

'Oh, for Christ's sake,' Harriet exclaimed. She rounded on Craig. 'Don't bother about getting a chair. I'll have yours. Just get out. You shouldn't be here anyway, and I want to talk to my mother in private. Just push off.'

'Harriet!' Ruth protested, knowing it was no use.

Craig leapt up from his chair and disappeared like lightning down the corridor leading to the exit doors.

Ruth sighed.

'I'd like you to myself,' Harriet said. 'Without any of your lame ducks and dogs. Just for once.'

McBride was keeping a watch on the *Old School House*, being pretty sure the goods he wanted were somewhere in that rambling place. He recognized that the old lady might have been sharp enough to hide them elsewhere: with a neighbour, or a friend, or, God forbid, the police. He tried to dismiss such notions; those were the tactics of a canny criminal, not a law-abiding old woman. No, he judged the pictures were most likely to be in Ruth's domain, why else had she looked so alarmed when he had mentioned them?

The problem was the big lad was still around all the time in the house. And the dog as well. Not good. And worse still, feelings of frustration and helplessness were now his constant enemies. His old bravado seemed to be seeping away from him. He had been so well briefed on this assignment: the boss's foot soldiers had done all the research any action man could wish for. And still he hadn't done what was required of him. He should be ashamed of himself. Moreover, time was running out and he was beginning to be worried, not an emotion which had usually seized him before.

His considerations regarding his next tactical move were suddenly jolted into decision-making by a call from his boss. It was almost unheard of for the boss to make a call personally to his minions. That task was usually delegated to the second-in-command, a bully-boy from the boss's past who had been to school with him, apparently. Whilst bully-boy used a hectoring, threatening approach, the boss was softly spoken and excessively polite, a style which elicited instant shuddering tension in his hirelings.

'Mac,' he said, leaving his voice and its tone to act as his sole introduction. 'I want those photographs. I want this matter dealt with. I want it dealt with within the next twelve hours.'

The connection clicked off, leaving McBride dry mouthed and shocked as though a bolt of electricity had passed through him. Without those photographs, he could well end up a dead man very soon.

He ran through the possibilities yet again. OK – there was no way he could work further on Mrs Hartwell, not with her in the security of a hospital ward. All he could do was simply go on waiting, keeping a watchful eye on the front door of the *Old School House*. He had been watching for twenty-four hours now without any sleep and he was feeling rough. He tried to squeeze new inspiration from his weary brain. He supposed he would have to steel himself: break in and disable or kill the lad if he was at home. Then deal with the dog.

But, joy of joy, as in answer to a prayer, at that very moment the young guy opened the front door and walked away down the path. Mac watched him turn into the road, walk down towards the bus stop and join the queue. Hallelujah! Now, at last, he could get going.

Without a break in his stride, he went up the driveway and peeled off to the side of the house, rounding the corner where the bins were kept at the back of the house. He schooled the muscles of his face to relax whilst he pulled on his latex gloves. He looked up at the side of the house next door. There appeared to be only one window and it had a pane of thick frosted glass, so not much danger of being overlooked from there. Stepping up to the dividing fence he checked that there was no one in the garden. Looking down Ruth's garden, he noted a small wooden gate leading out to a narrow track which ran alongside the back of the row of houses, giving ample opportunity to make a quick getaway if necessary. He reached into his pocket and felt for his old trusty skeleton key, turning its cold firm shank in his fingers. It had been a while since he had used it, and most modern locks were complex now. But he'd eyed up this one on his last visit and it was pretty old and would cause no problem at all. He spat on the bit of the key, rubbing the saliva over it so as to muffle any sound from his entry. He crept up to the door and looked through the glass of its upper section. He saw the dog sleeping in her basket. Damn! Well, he'd dealt with dogs before. What needed to be done in that quarter, he would do. As he inserted his key into the lock, he heard the front doorbell chime. Once, twice. And then some pretty heavy knocking. The dog woke up.

And then, oh, Jesus God! There were footsteps sounding along the front, a shadow growing on the pathway at the corner of the house. It didn't take him long to decide what to do. He bolted like lightning down the garden, pushed open the rotting wooden gate and was gone.

As Ruth watched Craig being banished from the ward by Harriet's rejecting words, her pent-up patience in dealing with her daughter's selfish and bullying behaviour through the years welled up inside and broke through like an explosion.

'Have you any idea what that boy has been through?' she demanded of Harriet. 'What it's like being in prison for all those years? The suffocation of the spirit, the taking away of all the things ordinary people take for granted. That boy's mother's co-habitee used to abuse his mother, and she couldn't stand up for herself. And eventually he put a stop to her misery by sticking a kitchen knife in the man. A crime to which Craig freely confessed. He was twelve years old at the time. He was in custodial care during the formative years of his young adulthood. He had no proper schooling. No peer friends. No family to love him and take him to the seaside. He was locked away, jeered at and bullied by prison officers. Made to feel he was nothing, of no human worth. And then when he gets out it is to a world completely changed from the one he knew. His mother had disowned him. He has no friends, no family. Considering the deprivation he has suffered, he has done rather well, in my view. And you have sent him away, rejected him, put the fear of God into him.'

Harriet opened her mouth to protest, but Ruth was not to be stopped.

'How dare you, Harriet?' Ruth spat at her. 'How dare you judge me on the way I run my life and what I choose to do? When did I ever make any demands on you? Have I not helped you out when you needed me? Remember the times I dropped everything to travel to your house and look after Jake when he was ill, or listened to you and comforted you when Charles was causing you anxiety. Does all that count for nothing?' She sat forward, her face flushed with rage and frustration. 'And how dare you not give me the respect I deserve as a mother? How dare you rampage around my life and spoil things for me?'

By this time the five other women in the ward were completely transfixed by Ruth's dramatic outburst, listening intently, wanting more.

Harriet was stunned. 'For goodness sake, Mum, keep your voice down.' She glanced around the ward, seeing only approval for Ruth's performance in the other patients' eyes. Any minute now they would be applauding.

The ward sister came hurrying in and looked at Ruth with concern. 'Are you all right, Mrs Hartwell?'

Ruth slumped back against the pillows. 'No,' she said. 'I don't think I am. But it's nothing you can help with.'

When the ward sister had left, she turned to Harriet. 'It's good of you to come to see me,' she said formally. 'I'm feeling tired now, I'd like to rest.' She crossed her arms over her chest and closed her eyes, leaving Harriet with the problem of wondering what on earth to do next.

*

Swift and Cat stood outside the *Old School House*, once again waiting for a reply to the tinkle of the bell. They tried it twice. Swift pushed at the door, but it was locked. They spent some time knocking.

'Let's have a look round the back.' Cat suggested.

The house had a narrow flagged path which led around its eastern side to the north-facing back wall. They made their way along, taking care not to slip on the stones which were slippery following the drizzle and damp of the previous days. The back door was of solid pine, with a large window forming its top half. Swift peered through, seeing that the kitchen was empty, except for Ruth Hartwell's small dog who had heard strangers approaching and leapt up from her basket barking furiously.

Cat turned the brass knob on the door and pushed slightly. 'It's not locked,' she said. 'What now?' They looked at each other, having the same thought.

'What about the dog?' Cat wondered.

'She's OK when Ruth is around,' Swift said. 'My guess is that if we seem confident enough she'll accept us.'

'On your head be it,' said Cat.

Swift went in first, speaking softly to the dog as he did so. 'Here, Tamsin, good girl.'

Tamsin stopped barking and looked at him. 'Good girl,' he said again, keeping his voice very calm and reassuring. Tamsin gave a low growl of uncertainty.

'Hey, Tamsin,' said Cat, stepping forward. 'How about a taste of Cadbury's Flaky Bar.' She held a chunk of milk chocolate in the flat of her palm and bent down offering it to the dog. Tamsin hesitated. Cautiously she took the chocolate, allowed Cat to pat and stroke her before moving back to her bed and observing the two visitors with alert consideration.

'Why don't I have a quick look round, see if I can spot Craig, or anything else of interest?' Swift volunteered.

'Sure. I'll guard the dog,' said Cat. 'And field any callers who might turn up.'

As Swift prepared to leave the kitchen the dog jumped up, her hackles rising. Cat stepped in, dug more Cadbury's Flaky Bar from her pocket and lured the dog to come back to her basket. Sensing that the situation of keeping the dog sweet was of some importance, Cat sat down on the floor and talked to the animal whilst she surveyed the kitchen. There was nothing of immediate interest on the table or the tired-looking kitchen units. She decided to leave the drawers and cupboards until Swift came back.

'Hey, there, girl,' she told the dog. 'I'll bet you'd be a useful informant about a few things if you could only talk.' The dog put her ears back and gave some indications of approving of the new visitor. Cat put out a hand to stroke her again. She noticed the plastic laundry holder on the floor a few yards away. There were items of underwear, some towels and dishcloths piled in it. The tip of a large white envelope poked through the plastic mesh at the bottom of the holder. Keeping one hand gently stroking the dog she reached out the other and pulled the envelope out of the holder. The flap was not sealed and as she pulled the envelope towards her a pile of photographs slithered out.

'What have we here?' she asked the dog, gently removing her caressing hand, so as to have two pairs of fingers in order to scoop up the shiny sheets from the floor. She had a quick glance through, stopping to stare more closely at the pictures of the lap-dancers and their audience. 'Well, well!'

She called out to Swift as she heard him coming down the stairs. 'Anyone at home?'

He came through the kitchen doors. 'Well, if there is, they're very well hidden.'

'No big-boy Craig?'

'Nope.' He looked down at her hands. 'Anything of interest there?'

'Photographs. Could they be the ones Mrs Hartwell's unwelcome visitor was after?' She handed them to Swift who had a rifle through.

'I'd say the child photographs are of a young Christian Hartwell. As for the shots in the night club—'

'Good-looking girls, aren't they?' Cat suggested.

'Certainly are.' He handed Cat a photograph of one of the men who was ogling the half-naked girls. 'And that guy is our friend Charles Brunswick.'

'Have we struck gold?'

The dog suddenly cocked her head and jumped out of her basket. At the same time there was the sound of a key in the lock of the front door. Swift and Cat glanced at each other.

'Caught in the act,' Swift said wryly. He got up and took out his warrant card.

A tall thin woman in her fifties was coming down the hallway. Swift stepped forward. 'Police!' he said, calmly. 'Nothing to be alarmed about.'

The woman drew in a sharp breath. 'Oh, heavens! You gave me such a shock.'

Swift apologized and introduced himself and Cat. 'And you are?'

'Cassandra Mortimer. I live next door. Ruth phoned me a few minutes ago and asked me to come in and get the dog and look after her until she gets back home.'

'Right. We've been checking on the house to make sure it's secure,' Swift said, in response to her doubtful expression.

Cassandra Mortimer looked at the two officers with frowning curiosity. 'With titles like yours, you must be the organ grinders. I thought they sent the uniform monkeys to do little jobs like securing houses.'

'That's often the case,' Cat admitted.

'Are you on the Christian Hartwell case?' the woman asked abruptly.

'Yes.'

'Poor Ruth, she doesn't seem to have much luck. Her surrogate son killed and her daughter a harpy.' She bent to pat Tamsin who was jumping up at her in welcome. 'I'm afraid I can't help you in your enquiries. Christian had left home by the time we moved in next door.' She straightened up. 'I would like to ask, though, if you could tell me something about this glowering young giant who seems to have appeared on Ruth's scene. My husband's bound to ask me when I get back in.'

'He's a friend of Ruth's,' Swift told her. 'She used to teach him at one time.'

Cassandra's eyes narrowed with scepticism. 'All above board, is it?'

'Mrs Hartwell told me that she had invited him to stay of her own free will,' Swift said.

'Oh well, as long as we don't have a murderer or a rapist lodging with our next-door neighbour I suppose we should be grateful,' said the long, tall Cassandra. She looked hard at Cat. 'Been in a spot of trouble, have you Inspector?'

Cat kept a straight face. 'You could say so.'

Cassandra picked up Tamsin's lead, which was hanging over the back of one of the kitchen chairs. 'Come on, little one. You come and stay with me until your mum gets back.' She turned to the two watching officers. 'You'll make sure to lock up when you go, won't you? Not that Ruth ever bothers. Just drop the latch.'

'Surely.' Swift then stopped her in her tracks to the door by asking her if she had seen any other visitors to the house whom she didn't recognize.

She turned. 'Sorry, can't help. I've got more things to do than twitch the curtains all day.' And then she was gone.

Cat looked at Swift. 'I rather think that puts us in our place.'

'We've been thoroughly Cassandra-ed,' he agreed, picking up the photographs and slotting them back in the envelope. 'We'll take these to the station for safe-keeping. I'll let Ruth Hartwell know.' He took a quick last look around and then they left – ensuring, of course, that the latch clicked firmly behind them.

Craig flew out of the hospital, his heart beating so strongly he felt that there were stretched guitar strings twanging in his chest. When he looked around him the sky and the buildings seemed out of focus, blurred and yet dazzling in their brightness. For a few moments he wondered if he was going to be struck down, if this was it, death coming for him. It seemed that he had lost his chance with Ruth now. It was all over. He saw a bus drawing in to the kerb and stumbled on to it.

Swift cleared space on his desk and laid out the photographs which had been lodging in Ruth's laundry holder. Together, he and Cat embarked on a careful appraisal of each picture.

They placed the older photographs of a young Christian Hartwell and a woman they assumed was his mother together in one pile and the more recent pictures of the nightclub in another.

As they were sorting through, Swift reminded himself that both

Ruth and his journalist pal Georgie Tyson had reported that Hartwell was a keen photographer.

'So, what he's given to the solicitor falls into two categories, family pictures from the past, and then these recent ones. Presumably, the family photos were taken by Ruth herself, or other members of the family, but the more recent ones by Christian.'

'I'd think it's safe to assume he was the photographer,' Swift commented, 'and that for some reason he wanted her to have them.'

'I wonder when the more recent photos were taken?' Cat wondered.

Swift looked again at the shots taken in the lap-dancing club. 'Brunswick looks very much as he does now, so I'd guess quite recently. Maybe on Hartwell's last visit to the capital a couple of weeks ago.'

'So why did Christian want Ruth to have them, I wonder?'

'Maybe he just didn't want them to be found in his flat.'

'He could have destroyed them, burned them.'

'Perhaps he was trying to tell Ruth some kind of story, send a message.'

Cat looked through the pile once again. She lifted one photo out on its own looked at it closely.

'What?' Swift asked.

'This guy here,' she said, tapping the print with the tip of her pencil, indicating a man in the lap-dancer's audience who had his face partly turned away from the camera. 'I'm pretty sure that's Julian Roseborough.' She handed the picture to Swift. 'Look.'

Swift took a few moments to register the face and the mane of blond hair. Memory stirred. 'He was at Jeremy's birthday gathering.'

'That's right. I think they've known each other for some years, collaborated on some property development ventures. I'm not really sure exactly when and where they met, but what I can tell you is that Julian is the son and heir of the guy who owns Roseborough Supermarkets – and is reputedly worth zillions.'

'Impressive credentials.' Swift smiled at her. 'You've been moving in exalted circles, Cat,' he said in wry tones.

She grimaced. 'And look where it's got me.'

They looked once again through the pictures. 'And where do these get us?' Swift wondered.

Craig sat on the bus, his body frozen into stillness, random thoughts scratching at his emotions. He heard Harriet's voice in his head, her hissing words, 'What the hell are *you* doing here?' The words kept on playing – over and over again.

Getting on the bus had been a snap decision. On leaving the hospital, he had had no idea what he should do or where he should go. He had seen the bus draw up at the stop outside the hospital and the decision to get on it seemed to have been made through some mental process he had not been aware of. He was suddenly aware he was mounting the step and then coming face to face with the driver who was doling out tickets. He had run out of change and had given the driver a five-pound note. There had been a prickly little scene when the driver wanted to know where Craig was going and Craig couldn't think of anywhere.

'We go as far as Thirsk,' the driver told him with barely concealed irritation.

'Right, then, I'll go there,' Craig said.

The driver sighed, dug in his leather bag and got out the change. Craig took it and started to lumber down the body of the bus. 'Hey! Don't you want your ticket?' the driver shouted.

Craig flinched at the anger and scorn in the man's voice. When he was eventually seated, he found himself trembling with humiliation and uncertainty.

Looking out of the window now, he saw a patchwork of fields and hedges, and sometimes a few little houses beside the road. For some time now the bus had not made any stops, but gradually the landscape began to change. There were more houses and fewer fields. The bus made more stops, allowing people to get off through the big door situated in the centre of the bus whilst new passengers got on at the front, handing their passes to the driver or buying new tickets. Watching the driver, Craig thought of him as rather like a prison guard, except he was stopping anyone getting into his bus without paying the price, whilst POs were stopping people getting out of their prison before paying the price. He watched the people who were climbing in, wondering where they had come from and where they were going. He envied them, people who had homes to go to and jobs to do and people to care about them.

The bus eventually drew up in a large square, bordered with shops and cafés and hotels. Everybody got off and Craig followed on.

He wandered along the pavements, looking mainly into the cafés. He hadn't eaten since the day before and his stomach was hollow and growling with hunger. The cafés seemed to be full of women and children: old ladies talking together and eating scones and cakes, young mums trying desperately to talk to their friends whilst keeping an eye on their kids at the same time. He knew he would stick out like a sore thumb amongst them. But at least he had money in his pocket and that was something to be grateful for.

He walked around the square three times until eventually he steeled himself to walk into the doorway of a small friendly looking pub. He went to the toilet first and washed his face and hands, then smoothed his hair down. Staring at himself in the mirror; he didn't think he looked too bad. True, there was a shadow of stubble beginning to show on his face, but there was nothing to be done about that. Anyway, he'd noticed plenty of young guys around who didn't seem that fussed about shaving.

Nobody took much notice of him settled at a small table in a corner of the bar, as he sipped a half pint of lager and ate a cheese-burger and chips he had ordered at the bar. It was warm and cosy in the pub and after he'd finished his food he started to feel better about his situation. The lager had given him a little boost of confi-dence and he went up to the bar and bought a packet of cigarettes and a slim folder of matches which bore the name of the pub. The woman at the bar was plump and pretty and friendly. 'Are you a student, love?' she asked him.

He shook his head. 'No.' He could see she was curious about him, and he'd have liked to have been able to tell her about what job he had. Not the clearing-up job in the pub back near Mrs Hartwell's place, which he'd no chance of getting now. He'd prob-ably never dare show his face again in that part of the world. He couldn't go back to Mrs Hartwell, not with her daughter hating him so much and wanting rid of him. The thought saddened him.

'Hey, cheer up,' the bar lady said. 'It may never happen.'

Oh, but it has happened, he thought. I murdered a guy and got thrown in prison. Not too many people could say that. But then, not too many people would want to. He gave her a little smile. 'No, that's right,' he said.

He went back to his table and lit a cigarette, the first one he'd had in a long time. Pulling the acrid smoke into his lungs made him relax further. Heaven.

But when the cigarette and the lager were finished, he started to wonder what to do next. He tried to organize his thoughts, factoring in all the things which had happened since he arrived at the *Old School House*. Mrs Hartwell being so kind, and then getting so worried about that bloke Mac the Knife turning up. And then there was this puzzle about the man called Christian who had died: her next of kin, Mac the Knife had said. And was he the same person whose flat they had been to see? Mrs Hartwell had said it had belonged to a friend of hers. He didn't quite understand it all. But one thing he knew for certain, he trusted Mrs Hartwell, he knew she liked him and that he liked her. And that had she wanted to help him and now it was all spoiled.

Someone had stopped by his table, looking down at him. He jerked his head up. The woman he saw was wearing one of the lowest cut dresses he'd seen, outside of lasses he'd seen on TV. Her boobs were the size of grapefruits, almost falling out of her dress as she bent towards him. 'Can I cadge a match?' she asked, glancing at his little cardboard wallet.

Craig recalled watching films where men offered to light a lady's cigarette, holding the match whilst the lady inhaled. 'Sure.' He tore a match from the folder and struck it against the lighting strip. He noticed his hand shaking slightly as he held out the match and she bent her head. She was wearing a spicy perfume which tickled his nostrils. She smiled at him and slid on to the stool next to him. 'Do you mind if I sit here?' she said, placing her large glass of white wine on the table.

'No,' Craig said, slightly alarmed at this turn of events.

'I'm Alma,' she said, looking at him expectantly.

'Oh, aye.' He took in her long auburn waves, her dangling earrings, and her heavy make-up. He tried to keep his glance from her breasts which were both alarming and exciting.

She smiled. 'And what's your name?'

'Craig.'

'Ooh. That's a nice name. Is it Scotch?'

'Scottish,' he corrected her, remembering what his granddad used to tell him.

'Really.' She took a draw on her cigarette. 'You know your stuff, don't you?'

He made no comment. Her presence seemed to envelop him: the look of her, the smell of her, the sense that she wanted something from him.

'So what's a big handsome lad like you doing in a place like this?' she asked, causing him to wonder if she was being friendly or sending him up.

'Just having summat to eat,' he said.

'Haven't seen you round here before.' She was eyeing him with close interest, sizing him up.

'No,' he agreed.

'Strong silent type, aren't you?' she said, laughing and blowing out a plume of smoke from her glistening fuchsia-pink lips.

He couldn't think of an answer.

'Like another lager?' she asked, pointing to his empty glass. 'I'm buying.'

He hesitated. He wished she would go away, leave him alone to think. 'All right,' he said.

She got up and went to the bar. A few moments later she was back at the table. 'Craig, love, I'm really sorry but I'm a bit short for paying. Could you lend me a quid?'

Craig searched in his pockets, his hand going to his back pocket and lifting out the wad of notes he'd taken from Ruth Hartwell's teapot, then quickly shoving it back again as he remembered that the bus driver had given him some loose change, which he'd put in his other pocket. He got out two pound coins and gave them to the woman.

'Thanks love, I only need the one,' she said, giving him back the coin she didn't require and sashaying back to the bar.

'There,' she said on her return. 'Cheers.'

She'd bought him a pint and he knew he had to be careful; the half had already made him a little woozy. He sipped it cautiously and answered the woman in monosyllables as she asked him questions about himself. Where did he work? Where were his family? Did he have a girlfriend? What sort of music did he like?

After a while, she suggested that they move on to another bar, somewhere where they laid on a bit of entertainment.

'OK,' he said, planning to give her the slip once they were outside.

He followed her out of the exit door which led to the car park behind the pub. She took his hand and led the way to a Range Rover which stood in a far corner. For a moment he thought she was going to open it up and invite him to take a ride with her. His mind whirled, and spun even faster when she pushed him up against the rear door of the car and reached up to kiss him, at the same time grasping one of his hands and placing it between her breasts.

Her lips worked over his, sucking and nibbling. And her hands were all over him, on his buttocks, then between his legs. Long-pent-up sexual desire seized him until he was in a state of helplessness to resist, but then suddenly he was aware of an empty feeling in his left-hand pocket and, with the sure instinct of a criminal who has served time, he knew he had been robbed. His stash of twenties, Ruth Hartwell's twenties, had been taken by this thieving slut.

He peeled her arms away from him and in one easy movement twisted her wrists around her back in the time-honoured manner in which the police and prison officers nick and control wrongdoers. She screamed and kicked out at him with the pointed heel tips of her shoes.

'Give me the money back, you bitch,' he hissed at her. 'Give it back – or you're dead. I've done it once before, I can easy do it again.' He shook her like a German shepherd dog shaking an annoying poodle.

'Jesus!' she yelled. 'Let me go, you bloody maniac.'

He slapped the back of her head hard. 'Where's the money?' he said, holding her fast with one hand whilst the other roamed her body. He felt a square lump on her upper thigh. Wrenching up her skirt he pulled the money from the elasticated top of her stocking and stashed it safely into his pocket.

He kept hold of the woman, fury pulsing through him in hot red waves. He could easily strangle her; she was all flab and no muscle. But the anger wasn't like he had felt when that bastard tried once too often to push himself on to his mum, just to give him, Craig, a load of misery. That anger had been almost sweet in its intense purity of purpose. This bitch simply wasn't worth it.

He knew she'd tell on him, make a fuss, raise the alarm. It couldn't be helped. He thought of pulling her stockings off and tying her legs and arms together with them. It was what she deserved, but there was no point giving the police extra sticks to beat him with, once they caught up with him. Which they would. They always did, didn't they? He'd seen it on the cop shows on TV. They had so much back-up and helicopters and guns and dogs and fuck knows what else. Oh yes, they'd get him. And then what?

The woman was whimpering now, begging him to let her go. He thrust her from him and ran from the car park as though he were sprinting for Britain at the Olympics.

'Jeremy phoned my mobile six times today,' Cat told Swift later on that evening as they ate spaghetti threaded through a sauce of creamed artichokes at the kitchen table. A bottle of cabernet sauvignon stood on the table between them. Outside, the sky was darkening behind the hills in a cradling bowl of glowing orange light.

'And?' he asked.

'And I didn't answer. Then I rang him myself just before we started supper.'

'Taking the initiative,' Swift observed, dryly. 'Often a good move.'

'He wants to meet up. Make things right between us.' She shook her head. 'As if.'

'Does he know where you are?' Swift asked, choosing not to follow up with the more obvious question.

'I guess not. I certainly left no clues for him to follow.'

'But once you meet up?'

'Oh, he'll most probably hire the most expensive private investigator he can find and have me followed. Not being in control is a pastime he avoids.'

So he'll make a nuisance of himself, Swift thought.

'Don't worry, I can handle him,' Cat said.

Swift noted that she had hardly eaten any of her spaghetti. The issue of her and Jeremy's relationship was constantly with her, throbbing in the background. In the past few minutes she had tried valiantly to find other topics of conversation, but Jeremy kept popping up, little fragments of his personality being gradually revealed along the way. And they were not sounding so sweet: Swift was gaining a picture of a controlling, manipulative and possibly ruthless man who liked having his own way.

He laid his fork down. 'Can we talk shop for a moment?'

Her head jerked up. 'Sure.'

'I've been thinking that maybe we need to do a bit more digging regarding Charles Brunswick.'

'Yeah, I'm with you. Go on.'

'Brunswick insists that he hadn't seen Christian Hartwell for a long time. And yet it looks very likely they were at the lap-dancing club together.'

'Maybe Brunswick was anxious for that not to come out. Well, at least the bit about him, Charles, frequenting the club.'

'Agreed. And maybe there was more to it than that. Maybe something relating to the rather amazing story Harriet had to relate about her and Charles's adventures in a North African desert nearly twenty years ago.'

'Ah yes, the desert affair,' she said, swivelling spaghetti strands on to her fork and regarding them with contemplative interest. 'Have you any theories?'

'Not a one. Not yet. Just a hunch we ought to dig a bit.'

She laughed. 'It would be interesting to find out more about what happened according to the authorities in Algiers. Do I need to polish up my French after all?'

'I think it would be helpful for you to make contact with them. And I also think it would be useful for you to speak to Charles Brunswick.'

'Me not you?'

'Uh-huh.'

'Any reason?'

'I think he might be persuaded to be more ... talkative with you.'

She raised her eyebrows. 'The feminine touch, eh?'

'Afraid so. I hope you're not going to get the sex discrimination police on to me.'

'I might find it in my heart to let you off. And yes, I'm up for it. Where and when?'

'At his place, either home or work. I think Ravi Stratton might be persuaded to fork out expenses for the train fare to London and back.'

There was silence for a time.

'Ravi Stratton was wearing a hearing aid, this morning,' Swift remarked, taking a sip of wine.

Cat's mouth fell open. 'So that's the reason for her not seeming quite at the cutting edge of things in review meetings.'

'It's a possible theory,' Swift agreed.

'You know, I've always admired her because she's had a tough time getting to the point she is now. But I could never work out why she just wasn't fully in touch with the snappy style of modern-day police parlance.' Cat grimaced. 'Whatever that is.'

'What sort of tough time?' Swift asked.

'Well, for a start, she's Anglo-Indian and a woman,' Cat explained. 'That's quite a handicap for anyone wanting to break through the glass ceiling which still has a place in the police force. She's married to a High Court judge, which might have its draw-backs. And her first child was stillborn.'

'She's doing pretty well, then.'

As they resumed eating their spaghetti, Swift's phone rang. It was Ruth Hartwell, calling from the hospital. Being Ruth the first words she spoke were an apology for disturbing him at home at such a late hour.

She explained to him what her consultant's current thinking was. 'He's advising me to stay in one more night,' she said. 'My blood pressure's leapt up, which is hardly surprising in the circum-stances. I'm inclined to be compliant about his recommendation but there are so many things worrying me.'

'Just take your time, Mrs Hartwell.'

Ruth began by describing the visit made to her house by the man calling himself Mac the Knife, an account whose details were remarkably consistent with the story Craig had told.

'I should have told you before,' she apologized. 'I buried my head in the sand and pretended that all the nastiness this man had brought with him would simply melt away. But, of course, it was a vain hope. He tracked me down when I was walking in the park and threatened me again regarding these photographs he wanted. He got out some scissors and got hold of my dog. That's when I blacked out.'

Swift fumed silently at the contemplation of the cold cowardice of a man who would stalk a gentle woman like Ruth and make her life a misery.

'Craig came to visit me this morning,' she went on. 'And Harriet arrived shortly afterwards.' She stopped. Swift heard her let out a long sigh. 'You've met them both,' she said, 'you can imagine that it was not a happy situation. Harriet's gone off back to London in a huff and Craig's … simply gone. I'm very concerned about them both. However, Harriet can look after herself rather better than he can. Can you do something to help?'

'We'll put out an alert for him,' Swift said.

'Yes, thank you.' She sounded as though she had little hope of a good outcome for Craig – and Swift was in silent agreement.

'Mrs Hartwell,' he said. 'Regarding the photographs you mentioned, the ones Christian's solicitor gave you? Have you looked at them?'

'Yes, I have.'

'Did they throw any light on Christian's death?'

A pause. 'Not really. No.'

He allowed her time to elaborate, but she remained quiet. He knew that the issue of Charles Brunswick's presence in one of the shots would have concerned her, but decided that if she didn't want to talk about it, then neither would he, not until Cat had done her follow-up on the flame-haired surgeon. What he did tell her was that he was now in possession of photographs found in the kitchen of her house. He gave her a brief description of why and how this had come about. Many of his clients and witnesses would have blown a fuse on hearing how their house had been entered without permission. Threats of recrimination would have ensued. Maybe legal advice sought. He and his colleagues had been through all of this before. But Ruth Hartwell instantly appreciated that the police had been acting in her best interests. But she still made no mention of Brunswick's appearance in the photographs.

Swift could hear the disquiet and fatigue in her voice. He was on the point of offering reassurances of how his team would be doing all they could to further the enquiry and find Craig, and then ending the call when she spoke once more.

'In addition to the photographs, Christian's solicitor also gave me a mobile phone which he had left in her keeping. He had asked her to give it to me in the event of his death.'

Swift felt prickles raise the hairs on the back of his neck.

'I'm afraid I didn't quite know what to do with it. I put it in a drawer in the kitchen. I'm very sorry. I know I should have told you about it. I should have told you everything,' she added, sadly. 'I've been rather stupid.'

'No, you were in a state of great anxiety,' Swift said. 'It's hard to act in a calm, impartial way when you're both grieving and under threat. There's no need to apologize.'

'Did you find it?' she asked. 'The phone?'

'No.'

'I didn't realize you could take photographs with mobile phones,' she said. 'The son of the lady in the bed next to me visited this afternoon, and he was showing her pictures of her grandchild on his phone. And I had this thought that maybe the pictures Mac the Knife wants are on Christian's phone.'

Swift closed his eyes briefly. 'Can you remember exactly where you left it?'

'It's in the kitchen drawer just below the kettle. I keep all my little odds and ends in there. If you want to go back to the house to look for it, there's a back door key underneath the watering can near the outside tap.'

Swift shook his head in quiet despair at Ruth's security arrangements. 'Right, Mrs Hartwell, thank you for that, we'll get on to it right away.'

'You're very kind,' Ruth said. 'I'm rather tired now, so you must excuse me. Good night.'

Swift slid his phone shut, and glanced toward Cat who had been listening and watching carefully.

'So?' she asked.

Swift related the salient features of Ruth's lamentably delayed release of information.

'Our Mrs Hartwell is a glorious mixture of shrewdness, insight and almost childlike innocence,' Cat said.

'Yes. You can't help admiring her,' Swift said. 'And now I'm just wondering who will get to Christian Hartwell's mobile phone first? And whether it will be of any interest.'

'It's either still nestling in Ruth's kitchen drawer near to the kettle, or Mac the Knife has already got it, courtesy of the not so cunningly hidden back door key.'

'Or Craig has it,' Swift pointed out.

'In which case he could be in some danger.'

Swift phoned in to the station and asked for an alert to be put out for Craig Titmus. And a further search to be made of Ruth Hartwell's place.

'Not Craig's good day,' Cat said. 'Destined to be set on by Mac the Knife or the police.' She reached for her glass of wine, took a sip and then fell silent, her features still and reflective.

Swift knew that Jeremy had stepped centre stage once more.

Cat looked across at him. 'I need to see Jeremy before I go to London, face up to things and tell him it's all over.'

'Is there any way I can help?' he said, knowing the question was pointless.

She sighed. 'I don't know, Ed, but thanks for asking.'

She replaced her fork beside the mainly untouched spaghetti on to her plate and took a sip of wine. 'I think I can handle him,' she remarked with a wry grin.

'I'm sure of it,' Swift agreed. 'I've always regarded you as a force to be reckoned with.'

Her grin broke out again. 'Hey, I'm not sure whether to be flattered or not. You make me sound somewhat intimidating.'

'You can intimidate me any time you like, Cat,' he told her, amazed to hear the unmistakable flirtation in his voice.

DAY 10

Craig was exhausted. It was an hour after midnight. He'd put as much distance between himself, the slag who'd tried to get one over on him at the pub, and the market town of Thirsk. He'd considered jumping on a late-night bus bound for Leeds, thinking he might be able to lose himself in a big city. He had money to survive on for quite some time before it would be necessary to get a job. But when the bus opened its doors and people crowded into it, he changed his mind. Someone in that throng might have seen him in the pub, maybe even in the car park with that thieving bitch. Panic had risen up inside him. He'd set off on foot down the road the bus had taken, simply walking, merely taking one step at a time without having any sense of purpose. He kept patting his pocket, ensuring that the wad of money was still there. The mobile was still in a front pocket of his jeans. He realized that if he was caught and searched it would look very bad when they found what he was carrying. But he needed the money, he simply couldn't chuck that away. The phone was another matter. It was no use to him with a dead battery. Maybe he should just ditch it. Confusion and despair held him in their grip – together with an over-whelming desire to sleep.

Cat got the 12.05 train from Leeds. The announcement over the train intercom told her it would get her into King's Cross at 14.20. Which gave her plenty of time to speak with Charles Brunswick, whose secretary had told her that he had a full operating list that day, but that he was usually willing to speak to visitors on urgent matters during the breaks in surgery. Cat had declined the secretary's offer to pencil in an appointment. She didn't want to give Brunswick time to get his thoughts together on what to say to her before they met.

She sat for a while, watching the outside world flash by, the vast, seemingly unending green fields of England. Cows, sheep and horses dotted the landscape like children's toy farm animals. In between her reflections on the Hartwell case, thoughts of her meeting with Jeremy earlier on flashed into her mind.

The interchange between them had not upset her as much as she had feared, although she recognized that she could be blocking the emotion out, putting a stopper on a bottle which could blow its cork later. The main thing was that she had been able to state her feelings calmly and rationally. She had cut short Jeremy's lavish apologies and self-recriminations and told him that woman-bashing was a total no-go area as far as she was concerned. Her work in the police had taught her that violence of an abusive one-way traffic kind was usually addictive. It was there in the perpetrator, it didn't just go away.

He had gone rather quiet after that, perhaps because of the humiliation of being implicitly compared with what he would regard as mindless thugs, members of the lower orders who didn't know how to control their wild emotions. And perhaps, also, because he sensed her utter refusal to continue their relationship. She might be able to forgive him, but she would never let him back into her life.

She had been lucky to bag a table seat on the crowded train and she took out her notebook, laid it on the table and listed the main points the team knew so far about Charles Brunswick. After that, she considered her approach when questioning him, something to keep her mind occupied, even though she knew from experience that an interview always took its own direction once you started, providing you had your background facts and theories firmly lodged in your memory.

She placed her notebook back in her bag and looked out of the window once more. After a time, she became aware that the woman sitting opposite kept taking furtive glances up from her laptop, her gaze irresistibly drawn to Cat's split lip and her blackening eye.

Cat gave her a neutral smile, before putting on her dark glasses and resting her head back against the seat.

The train pulled in two minutes before time. There was a one-day strike in the Underground, so she joined the taxi queue and after a wait of twenty-five minutes was on her way to The Wentbridge.

Her driver apologized for taking a devious route. 'It's a long way round,' he explained, 'but we'll get there quicker in the end. When the tube's not working it's hell on wheels around these parts.'

Cat noticed the *Evening Standard* headlines on the billboards as they drove down the back streets.

'Tipper claims new victim,' she read out loud, aiming to catch the attention of her driver. 'Is this related to the recent drownings in the Regents Canal?' The national news had picked up references to the drownings after a second body had been pulled out of the same stretch of the canal fairly soon after the first. Police are considering foul play, the reporters had written, still in cautious mode.

'That's right. This one's number three. It looks like some nutter has taken a fancy to pushing down-and-out drunks into the drink. The police had the first two down as accidents, but now they're talking serial killing.'

'Have they got any leads?'

'Well, they're not for giving anything away for the moment. Which means they ain't got any, wouldn't you say?'

'Yup,' Cat agreed.

The driver made a series of death-defying right turns and then the front of the hospital miraculously appeared ahead. It always surprised Cat how some of the central London hospitals appeared to simply nestle between the high-street shops, their entrances hardly more distinguishable from their retail neighbours. 'Hey! Good route planning,' she said.

'Yep,' her driver agreed. 'Never mind your sat navs, it's your memory gets you round this city.'

Cat gave him a generous tip and made her way up to the cardio-thoracic department.

Charles Brunswick's secretary was a young brunette: attractive, charming and warm.

Cat introduced herself, showing her warrant and reassuring the secretary that she was making routine enquiries and hoped Mr Brunswick could help her.

'He's due out of theatre in around fifteen minutes,' the secretary said. 'Would you like me to ring through and tell him you're here.'

'No need. I'll just wait.'

The secretary observed Cat's injuries for a few seconds, then jumped up from her desk and took her down the corridor to a small waiting room. 'Do please make yourself comfortable here, Inspector Fallon. Can I get you a coffee?'

Cat smiled. 'No, but thanks for the offer.'

After the secretary had left, Cat positioned herself beside the door, keeping an eye on the secretary's room, alert to any sign of Brunswick's arrival and possibly swift departure when he heard the news of the profession of his visitor.

After fifteen minutes Brunswick duly arrived in his secretary's office, pausing at her desk. There was a short, hushed discussion, after which Brunswick strode forward, heading for the waiting room.

'Inspector Fallon!' he exclaimed, seizing her hand and pumping it warmly.

Bloody hell! He's a bit of a stunner, was Cat's instant female reaction as she ran her eyes over the rangy, muscular frame, noting the bright blue eyes lit with intelligence and charm, the chiselled bone structure, the fantastic crowning of flame curls. He was dressed in blood-stained theatre scrubs which in no way diminished his charisma – quite the opposite. Cat did not envy his wife; this guy must have armies of women drooling over him wherever he went.

'Hope I haven't kept you waiting too long,' he said, gesturing her to sit down. 'Just closing up on a heart transplant.'

As one does, thought Cat.

He smiled. 'Technically, a transplant's not a very difficult procedure,' he elaborated, as though tuning in to her admiration of his prowess. 'You've been in the wars,' he commented, eyeing Cat's facial injuries.

'Yes, I have,' she said.

'Have you been checked out at A&E?'

'Don't seem to have found the time,' she admitted.

He took another glance at the bruising on her face, this time as a professional. 'I think you'll mend quite satisfactorily without the aid of medics,' he told her. He grinned, clearly up for a little pleasurable, flirtatious banter.

'Mr Brunswick,' Cat said, 'when you spoke to DCI Swift a few days ago, you told him that you hadn't seen Christian Hartwell recently.'

The grin faded.

Cat showed him the photograph of himself taken at the lap-dancing club.

'Oh dear,' he said.

'We believe these photographs were taken by Christian Hartwell. And that they were taken very recently.' She waited, wondering if he would try to make a denial which, of course, she could not at this point demolish with the presentation of clear factual evidence. They still didn't know for sure if these images came from a camera Christian had used, or whether he had taken them.

'OK,' he said. 'You're quite right. They were taken a couple of weeks ago.'

'By Christian Hartwell?'

'Yep. He used to carry his camera around with him if he thought there was going to be something of interest to point his lens at.'

'They let him take snaps at a lap-dancing club?' Cat asked.

'Oh, he never bothered about the restrictions of taking snaps, and he never seemed to get caught out.'

'And what were the circumstances that evening you went to this particular lap-dancing club?'

'Chris and I got together with a few pals and went out on the town. We had supper at J. Sheekey, then went on to the club for a few drinks … and entertainment.'

'A boys' night out?'

'Yeah.'

'Nothing wrong in that,' Cat said.

'I'm beginning to think I'm getting rather too old for that kind of thing,' Brunswick admitted, looking boyishly sheepish and totally beguiling.

Except Cat wasn't for being beguiled. She recognized the power of Brunswick's charm, but it cut no ice with her. 'Why did you lie about not having seen Chris recently?'

He considered. 'I didn't want to get involved.'

'You didn't want to get involved with a murder investigation ... is that what you mean?'

'Yes.'

'I'm sorry, Mr Brunswick, but I'm afraid you are involved. But thanks for not lying this time.' She gave him a brief glance of reassurance.

'I've got a big interview coming up for a key post,' he told her. 'I didn't want anything rocking the boat.'

'Director of Surgery,' Cat said. 'We know about that.'

Brunswick registered faint surprise, but said nothing.

Cat was hoping to get him on the back foot, make him wonder if they'd got the information from his wife, or from police investigations. And if the latter, then how much more did they know?

'Were you and Chris on friendly terms?' she asked.

'Sure.'

'When DCI Swift spoke with your wife she told him that the two of you didn't see eye to eye. She said that Christian was very laid back and all for letting things take their course, but you liked to be more proactive.'

'That was a long time ago,' he said. 'We got along OK recently. We haven't met up much but he's always been good as a drinking pal when he come up to town. In fact, I guess I've seen him a lot more than Harriet in recent years.'

'And you saw Chris two weeks ago?'

'Yes.'

'Just the one evening?'

'Yes. And before you ask, he was on good form and seemed his usual relaxed self.'

'Tell me what happened at In Salah.'

The abrupt introduction of the subject brought a startled look to his face. 'It was a very long time ago,' he said. 'What do you want to know?' His tone was now noticeably guarded.

'The circumstances surrounding the murder of one of your friends in a remote part of the desert.'

Brunswick sighed. 'He wasn't really a friend, just a fellow student on a field trip. Harriet has already told DCI Swift about the circumstances.'

'Yes. Now I'd like *you* to tell me.'

Brunswick looked at his watch.

'You can always do it at the local police station, if you'd prefer.'

'OK.' He began to tell the story which began with the appearance of an irate Arab. Cat had read Swift's transcript of the information Harriet had offered several times and she had it almost off by heart.

She was interested to note that Charles Brunswick's account matched that of his wife very closely.

'I had no alibi,' Charles said, as he reached his conclusion. 'I was eventually charged with Hugh's murder but then the police decided to drop the charges.'

'And no one else was ever charged?'

'Not to my knowledge.' He sliced a brilliant blue glance at Cat. 'You can see why I didn't want all this raked up. The press would love it. My interview board would not.'

'I appreciate that.'

The blue eyes were still fixed on her.

'I'm not going to give anything to the press ... not at this stage,' Cat told him. She folded up her notebook and got to her feet.

His lips parted slightly. 'Is that it?' he asked.

She nodded. 'For now.'

She half expected a cheeky grin to break out on his face. Maybe a little quip along the lines of whether he should surrender his passport to the police and on no account leave the country.

Instead, Brunswick looked both solemn and relieved.

Which made Cat pretty certain he had not been entirely generous with the whole truth.

On leaving the hospital, she phoned back to her station in Yorkshire and asked for the address of the nearest police station from where she was now standing. On arriving there five minutes later, she showed the constable on the desk her warrant card and introduced herself as Inspector Cat Fallon.

'What can I do for you, ma'am?' the constable asked, staring at her colourful face with the blend of curiosity and concern Cat was becoming accustomed to.

She told him she was on the investigation team of a murder in the north-west Bradford division.

'Ooh,' the constable said, forming his mouth into a round O. 'The land of windswept moors and curries.'

Cat smiled. 'Indeed. We have excellent facilities up north.' She leaned forward slightly. 'Can you tell me which nick is dealing with the case of the drunks being pushed into the drink … as my cabbie referred to it?'

'Most certainly can, ma'am.' He scribbled a name, address and contact number on his pad, tore off the sheet and gave it to her, his eyes lit up with a curiosity and excitement he did not give voice to.

'Thanks,' said Cat. 'We've got a death-in-open-ground case which is causing us a bit of head scratching,' she explained to him. 'And there's something about this "Tipper" which has set my antennae quivering.'

He gave a broad smile. 'Good for you, ma'am. And good luck.'

'Thanks again.' She started to turn away.

He called her back. 'I hope you won't think I'm speaking out of turn, Inspector Fallon, but I've found in this big city that if you want information straight from the horse's mouth, it sometimes pays not to bother too much with the top brass. Sometimes it's better to go to the man or woman at the bottom.' Whilst speaking, he had transformed his cheery face into a professional and neutral mask.

Cat was inclined to take him seriously. 'Good point,' she said. 'I'll make sure to bear it in mind.'

Whilst Cat had been sitting on the National Express train bound for King's Cross, Swift, not having much confidence in his schoolboy French, was e-mailing the *gendarmerie* in In Salah, requesting any information regarding the unsolved murder of a young man called Hugh Moss in the desert on the date Harriet had given him during their last meeting.

After an hour or so he received an apologetic reply to tell him that the notes on the Hugh Moss case had unfortunately been destroyed – along with a number of other files – by a fire at the local *gendarmerie* some months following the incident.

Swift knew he would simply be banging his head against a brick wall if he followed up on this. When files were said to be lost or destroyed by fire or flood, or some kind of accident, it invariably meant they had been deliberately removed from official records. Which immediately had alarm bells ringing in his head.

He looked again at the notes he had made following his talk with Harriet, then put in a call to the British Embassy in Algiers and was eventually put through to a senior diplomat whom whilst helpful and courteous, was not able to throw any light on the Hugh Moss case. When Swift advised him that his enquiry was prompted by a current murder which could have links to the Moss case, he told Swift he would ask his secretary to access any relevant notes and then phone him back. This he did within twenty minutes.

'We have a record of being involved in advising four students who were on a geography field trip when one of their party was murdered and another member of the party charged with the murder.' He paused for a moment. 'There isn't much detail,' he said, and Swift could tell that he was reading the details as he spoke. 'One of our senior diplomats liaised with a Miss Harriet Hartwell on behalf of the accused man, Mr Charles Brunswick, who was being kept in jail. He then spoke with the police authorities in Algiers.' There was another pause. 'And then it seems that Mr Brunswick was suddenly released. The party were given back their confiscated passports and allowed to go home. That's all there is,' he said, going on to conclude: 'I can't really add anything, I'm afraid. It was twenty years ago. I was still in school then.'

'Thanks for that, anyway.' Swift thought rapidly. 'Do you have the name of the diplomat who helped the student party?'

'Well, yes, I do. I knew him personally. His name is David Colburn. He eventually went on to be ambassador at the British Embassy in Nairobi. Became quite a famous chap within the service, actually. He's retired now.'

'Have you got an address?'

There was a hesitation.

'This is in connection with a current murder enquiry,' Swift reminded him.

'OK, I'll ring through to my secretary.'

Within moments Swift was in possession of Sir David Colburn's home address. Which, most fortuitously, was in the village of Danby Friske, only twenty miles from Swift's station.

Craig tried walking through the fields. He found that making your way through fields of tall, waving wheat and linseed rape was no easy task, and more like wading than walking. He knew that there would be an alert out to find him now. His probation officer would have raised the alarm when he didn't turn up for his weekly meeting, and maybe the friendly police guy called Swift would have done the same. He tried to think things through, his thoughts careering about like a runaway puppy. He was an ex-con, a murderer, a mugger who was carrying a mobile phone and cash which belonged to an old lady who hadn't freely given them to him. He could be in the papers, a mug shot on the front page. They'd use his prison ID photo and make him look like a monster.

He walked on, constantly on watch for irate farmers, or helicopters circling above. He was bitten by a host of insects and overheated by the sun which had decided to make a long-awaited appearance. If he tried to walk nearer the edges of the fields he was too close to the road.

Before long he was hungry, despairing and exhausted. What was the point in walking and walking if you had nothing to aim for?

He sat down with his back against a stone wall and once again reviewed his options. They hadn't improved with time. He lifted his face to the sky and prayed for guidance. No miracles occurred.

He thought of Mrs Hartwell, his one friend. What would she say?

He sat very still, hearing her calm, low voice in his head. And after that he got up, turned around and went back the way he had come.

At a lively, very urban police station close to St Pancras Rail terminal, Cat was ushered into a CID room, where she was advised she would find Inspector Wilton who might be able to give her some information with regard to the Tipper enquiry.

Inspector Wilton was watching out for her, clearly having been issued a warning of her arrival from the front desk. He came forward but did not offer a hand in greeting, until Cat's own outstretched hand and ready smile forced him into it.

Wilton was thick-set, around forty, with a shaved head and a grim, craggy face. Dressed in a crumpled grey suit with a granite grey shirt and tie, he looked like a character from a black-and-white film. His default expression seemed to be an angry grimace and altogether he had the air of a man who was not particularly enjoying his life. 'Inspector Fallon,' he said, 'who's been messing with your face?'

'The hazards of the job,' she said, wondering what he was so angry about.

'I'm pretty busy,' he told her.

'Likewise,' she said, keeping her tone pleasant. 'I've got a train to catch back to West Yorkshire before too long – where my boss and I have a murder case to solve. It's one of those slippery cases where it's hard to get any hard evidence.'

Wilton looked mildly interested. 'And when you do it seems to slip through your fingers like butter?' he suggested.

'You could say that. Our victim is a man in his thirties who got pushed from a high point on a crag. And then set alight at the spot he landed.'

'Not a good way to go,' Wilton suggested. 'And not a case for beginners.' He looked hard at Cat. 'I'm sure you're experienced enough to have a grip on the case.'

She wasn't sure whether he was referring to her war wounds or her bad luck in being on the wrong side of forty. Or maybe he simply liked being unpleasant. 'Your "Tipper" suspect,' she said. 'How did he – or she – get their nickname?'

'Oh, there's no need for sexual equality issues, here. Our killer is definitely a bloke. For a start, women don't go round deserted areas of the Regents Canal after dark looking for random victims.'

Cat mentally filed away the information. 'This latest victim is the third?'

'Been reading the headlines?' Wilton suggested. 'Yep. The latest is number three, and, like the others, an unwashed, homeless alkie in the age range of late fifties to mid sixties.'

'Any witnesses?'

'Nope.'

'Forensics, DNA?'

He gave a hollow laugh. 'What do you think?'

'If it's like our case, then it's a no.'

'We've gone by the book with this investigation. Exhaustive questioning around the area, talking to families. Talking to park patrollers and bedsit landladies. Folks on barges. Oh, and don't forget the profiler.'

'What did the profiler say?'

'What they always say. The bleeding obvious, dressed up in a lot of trick-cyclist jargon.'

'Such as?'

'Loveless background. Rejected by the mother. Taken into care. Never formed any bonds. History of bed-wetting, running away from school. Being bullied then becoming a bully. Becoming independent and living in a bed and breakfast. Can't hold down a job. Psychopathic personality. Or is it sociopathic. I don't know the bloody difference.' He was steaming with self-righteous anger now. He glared at Cat. 'Do you?'

Well, yes, she did but decided to side-step the issue. 'It does all sound rather familiar. Do you have a theory on the killer's MO?'

Wilton raised his eyes to the ceiling. 'He pushes the poor buggers into the water. They're always pissed out of their skulls, so they just slide in and sink like stones. And then some time later they come to the surface and scare the shit out of some innocent dog walker or kid.'

'So, your killer doesn't need to use any strength, he simply puts out a hand and gently tips them in.' She smiled at Wilton, knowing it would annoy him. 'Which is, presumably, why he's called the "Tipper".'

Wilton shook his head in mock wonder at her perceptiveness.

He glanced over his shoulder at a desk piled high with papers.

Cat judged she had got as much from him as she could hope for, and he was prepared to give.

'Thanks for the information,' she said. 'Sorry to have taken up your time. Are you always such a miserable, angry bastard, Inspector Wilton?' she asked, putting a friendly twinkle in her eye and giving him the opportunity to make his peace with her.

He offered a stony look. 'Yep,' he said, turning away and returning to his desk.

Cat headed for the door. As she walked down the corridor, a young CID officer who had been working at a desk near to where she and Wilton had been speaking followed her out and made for the coffee dispensing machine. Cat made her way down the steps, hoping to find the staff exit door without having to go back to the front desk. She heard footsteps following her. 'Ma'am,' a voice called softly.

She turned back. The young officer caught her up. 'I'm DC Quinn. Can we have a word? Maybe in the car park?'

'Sure.'

Quinn led the way to the corner of the car park. 'I was listening in to your conversation with Inspector Wilton. I'd like to ... give you some more information.'

Cat could see this was difficult for the young detective constable, wanting to aid a colleague from another division and at the same time probably worrying about betraying her boss.

'Go ahead.'

'The boss had some bad news this morning. The "Tipper" case has been taken over by a specialist crime investigation team at Scotland Yard. The files were all removed from our nick this morning.'

Cat began to understand why Wilton was in such a foul mood. Is there a question mark over Wilton's competence, Cat wondered. Or something on a wider scale?

'He's pretty cut up about it,' DC Quinn said. 'We all are. We've really worked hard on the last two cases.'

'Did you get anywhere?' Cat asked, bluntly.

'Not really. But we identified that the victims were all local, were all homeless and alcoholics. That the MOs were all the same. That they were all killed by drowning in the Regents Canal in the vicinity of the London Canal Museum. These weren't random killings, they had a pattern.'

Cat thought about it. 'We just have the one victim,' she said. 'So far. I'm taking a long shot in wondering if there is some link here, and it's simply based on the MO.'

'You should never rule anything out,' DC Quinn said, looking doubtful.

Cat smiled. 'Absolutely not. On the other hand, you have to

watch out for getting the wrong end of the stick and keeping on chewing.'

Quinn laughed.

Cat gave Quinn her card. 'If anything interesting turns up on the "Tipper" case would you let me know?'

'Of course, ma'am.' Quinn offered her own personal card in exchange. 'Good luck!' She looked at Cat's bruises. 'And take care.'

Ex-Ambassador Sir David Colburn was standing in the impressive doorway of his small mansion as Swift parked his car on the gravel drive and got out.

Swift had googled Sir David before he set off and discovered that he was seventy-nine years old, had served as a diplomat in a number of embassies and then as an ambassador in a career spanning forty years. He had married a judge's daughter, Lavinia de la Tour, in 1963, and had two sons, one a doctor the other a high-ranking officer in the army.

Colburn welcomed Swift with a firm handshake and a warm smile. 'Come in, come in,' he said, leading the way to an airy drawing room, furnished with Persian rugs and soft sofas sporting worn but spotless chintz covers. There were polished mahogany tables scattered about, bristling with family photographs and views of exotic cities. A huge bowl of casually arranged pink roses stood on the table beneath the long line of windows, nodding to their outdoor relations who were growing in the flower beds which had been dug into the vast front lawn. A huge black dog lay flat out on the rug beside the fireplace, as though it had been recently shot.

Sir David was silver-haired and fit-looking. His manner was both friendly and effortlessly confident and commanding. 'A drink, Chief Inspector?' he enquired. 'Whisky? Gin?'

Swift declined politely. It was only half past two in the afternoon.

'Hope you don't mind if I do.' Sir David moved to one of the mahogany tables, poured himself half a tumbler of whisky and took a cigarette out of a silver case and lit it from a silver table lighter. 'My doctor says I should give up this filthy habit,' he said, taking a long drag on his cigarette. 'And I agree with him. But it's easier said than done. And since my wife died a few weeks ago, I have no one to scold me about it – and not very much else to look forward to either, other than a whisky and a smoke.' He said all this without a trace of self-pity, yet Swift could sense the man's desolation.

'To tell you the truth,' he went on, 'I'm only too happy to help you out regarding any of your investigations. It will make a change from playing bridge and doing the *Times* crossword. Now, when you telephoned me earlier you mentioned the Hugh Ross murder in Algeria twenty years back. And since then, I've been looking through my diaries, and also rifling through my stock of memories, which are still pretty good, I have to say. So! Do you want to start the batting?'

Swift explained that his team was currently investigating the murder of Christian Hartwell, a local journalist, who he believed had been a member of the research trip to Algeria. In an attempt to cover all angles of the case they were interested in any details of Hartwell's past life which might have a bearing on his recent death.

'Ah, yes, Christian Hartwell,' Sir David intervened. 'I've seen one or two reports in the *Yorkshire Echo*. You don't seem to be having much luck.'

Swift nodded. 'Did you meet Christian Hartwell back in 1989?'

'Yes, I did briefly. I went to In Salah and met the remaining members of the field party after the unfortunate Hugh Ross met his end.' He stared down into his glass, and for a moment Swift wondered if he had fallen asleep, or had suffered some minor cerebral incident.

'I had the opportunity a few days ago to talk to Harriet Brunswick, who was one of the party,' Swift told Colburn. 'She gave me some quite detailed information about the circumstances. She told me that one of the party, Charles Brunswick, whom she later married, was charged with Hugh's murder.'

Sir David looked up. 'Yes, that's right. The police were desperate to get someone nailed for the killing. They used to be a bit gung-ho out there about murders committed by foreigners back in the eighties.'

'And then the charges were suddenly dropped.'

'Correct.' Sir David's eyebrows twitched.

'So what happened? Did Brunswick do it and get off after a word from someone in high places? Or did someone else do it and get off for another reason?'

Sir David now had a gleam in his eye. 'No to the first question, and no to the second.' He took a large slug of whisky, and let it roll slowly down his throat. 'Since your phone call, I've been doing a lot of thinking. I've been thinking about my career, and about my small, pathetic and lonely life now, with my lovely wife gone and my sons and grandchildren in far flung parts of the world. And sometimes even when you are as old as I am you can gain a sudden insight into what really matters.'

Swift waited patiently, not very hopeful about quitting this interview in the possession of any helpful information, and probably having to listen to an old man's ruminations and soul-searching, before he could decently leave.

'And as a result I'm going to break the habit of decades,' said Sir David. 'I'm going to divulge some information I would never have dreamed of divulging in past times. Because I think it's the right thing to do: to simply tell the truth for once.' He grinned. 'Just listen to me! A former ambassador committing himself to telling the naked truth!' He stubbed out his cigarette and took another gulp of whisky. 'You came to the right person,' he told Swift. 'No one else would have felt inclined to tell you what I am about to. Indeed there are probably very few people who would have been able to do so because it was all kept secret between myself and one or two other personnel. And you won't find it in any documentation – for the reason that most, if not all of it, has been destroyed and the rest doctored.'

Swift came on the alert. He sensed Sir David was beginning to enjoy himself, and at the same time that he was deadly serious, and knew perfectly well what he was doing.

'You see, there weren't four young people on that trip. There were five. And from what I and my colleagues could gather in liaison with the police and the other students it was that fifth person who was Hugh Moss's killer.'

'Are you going to give me a name?' Swift asked.

'I am. But first, let me tell the whole story. I used to be a rather good raconteur in my younger days, so bear with me. The young person involved was the only son of a multimillionnaire. He was a young man who had been brought up to enjoy huge wealth and privilege. He was also very intellectually able, although he only managed a third at Oxford as he had a disinclination for work and self-application. During his teen years he caused a great deal of anguish for his parents, becoming involved with major criminals, drug dealing and violence. He was always on the sidelines, and never got entangled with the police. Although it's likely he never got caught because of the conspiracy of silence which surrounds people with power and connections and money. Such people should never be underestimated. The current stink about MPs and their wretched expenses is peanuts compared with what goes on with the seriously rich.'

Swift cut in, hopeful to avoid a lecture on the morals of MPs. 'Will you allow me to make a guess at what happens next in your story?'

Sir David grinned. 'Carry on, Chief Inspector.'

'The so-called rich and powerful lobby got wind that this young man was in trouble. Maybe he was the first suspect to be charged … before Brunswick came into the line of fire?'

'Correct. However once the people back home – his parents and their powerful friends – got to hear of it, pressures were exerted, the sharp end of them falling on us chaps at the embassy in Algiers and also the local police. As a result of all that, the young man was released. But the police were still hungry for a conviction so young Brunswick was selected to be put in the frame, on the grounds that he had no alibi for the time of the murder, and that he was a mouthy, headstrong young colt.'

Swift smiled to himself. Brunswick hadn't changed much.

'Fortunately for Brunswick, his own parents were not without influence. They immediately liaised with us, and following some discussion a very sharp lawyer was flown out to Algiers. The Ambassador sent for me, told me that I was one of his shrewdest diplomats, and promptly despatched me to the scene of the action with Mr Smart Lawyer. And the next day Brunswick was free.' He relaxed in his chair, his face lit with a small smile of satisfaction.

'And the name of the young heir to his father's millions?'

'Julian Roseborough, the son of the owner of the Roseborough supermarket chain.' He levelled a glance at Swift. 'And let me tell you this, Julian is dangerous. Plenty of money and influence and very little humanity. When his father inherited the business from his own father, he set about expanding it. He then bought and refurbished Graysham Abbey in Wiltshire, married a minor aristocrat's daughter and did his best to ape the life of a country gentleman. Julian Roseborough was brought up accordingly, mixing with the hunting, shooting, county set and given to believe he had an innate superiority over the rest of us poor peasants.' He stretched his legs out in front of him. 'Was all that of any help?'

'Very much so,' said Swift. 'Thank you for your candour. I have another question.'

'Fire away.'

'Do you have a personal opinion on who killed Hugh Moss?'

'I'm around one hundred per cent sure it was Julian Roseborough. However, I have to say that young British people with their expensive equipment, and their appearance of having endless leisure, do not endear themselves to the poorer Arabs with their vastly different culture and moral stance. They set themselves up to run into hostility and trouble.'

Swift could appreciate the ambassador's point of view.

'Anything else?' Sir David enquired.

Swift considered, making a quick mental review of the interview.

'I did consider contacting you people when I read about Hartwell's death,' Sir David said. 'It took me a while to place the name and match it up with the Hugh Ross murder case, but after that I was able to recall what had happened quite readily. I simply didn't think there could be any connection between what happened then, out there in the desert, and what has happened now. Moreover, I had not yet had my Damascene moment of deciding to reveal a diplomatic secret which has been buried for years. So all in all I'm jolly glad you gave me a call.'

'So am I,' Swift said. 'You've given me some food for thought.'

'Splendid. Pleased to hear it. I don't suppose I can tempt you to join me in a whisky before you go. Just a single, I know you have to work. Not that work ever interfered with a drink back in the good old days.' He got up and made for the drinks table. 'I think I deserve another, at any rate.'

Swift smiled and nodded an acceptance. How could one reject an invitation as gracious and genuinely meant as that?

Craig arrived in Thirsk, tired out, sticky, sweaty and, he feared, smelly, despite his attempts to spruce up a bit in the gents' public toilets in the square. He found the location of the police station and stared it for some time from a safe distance. Various chatting police officers walked in and out, laughing and joking like the end of the world was not about to arrive. He waited, his heart beating a fierce tattoo in his chest. Just do it, he told himself, locked in conflict.

And then his body jerked in shock as he felt a hand on his shoulder. 'Hello, there.'

He swivelled around. The hand belonged to the young woman who had served him in the pub the previous evening. She was carrying some bulky parcels and looked rather careworn, but she was smiling at him, as though pleased to see him again.

'Hi.' He smiled at her uncertainly, trying to think of something else to say to her. 'How are you doing?' he asked.

She shook her head and sighed. 'Not too brilliantly. My dishwasher has flooded the kitchen. I should be opening up in an hour, and my usual helper has rung to say she's sick and can't come in to work.' She put up a hand to smooth her hair, and he saw that her fingers were trembling.

'I'll come and help you clear up,' he said.

She looked at him. 'Are you sure? I'll pay you.'

'You're all right,' he said. 'I'd like to help.'

They fell into step together, making their way around the square. 'I'll carry your bags,' he said.

'You're like a gift from heaven,' she said, handing him the roughly wrapped parcels, which turned out to be a mop and bucket.

'Have you been sleeping rough?' she said, suddenly, noticing the state of him.

'Aye.'

'Have you nowhere to go?'

'Not really.'

They walked on in silence. Craig kept glancing at her. She was small and round like a teddy bear, with plump arms and legs. Her skin was very white and her hair shiny and black like a bird's wing. She was lovely.

Back at the pub he followed her into the kitchen. She gave him the new mop and bucket to use and armed herself with some old towels. Paddling through the lukewarm water spewed out by the dishwasher, they got busy. 'My old bucket's gone missing,' she told him. 'I think my helper might have borrowed it. She does that sometimes.'

'Oh, aye,' said Craig. 'You could do without that.'

She laughed. 'True. She's a nice girl though ... but a bit of a lazy cow!'

They both laughed. 'I'm Josie,' she told him.

'Craig,' he said.

'And where do you come from, Craig?' she asked.

He squeezed the wet mop in the strainer above the bucket. Squeezed really hard. 'Prison,' he said.

She didn't stop, simply went on soaking up the water in the towel she was holding. 'Were you there long?'

'Eight years. I killed someone.'

A short, echoing silence. 'That's some confession,' she said.

'I wanted you to know.'

'Good. That's good,' she told him. She looked at him, her eyes faintly troubled.

'I'll go if you like,' he said.

'No. Don't go.' She said it as though she meant it.

When the floor was dry again, she put on the kettle. 'What would you like to eat?' she said. 'I've got eggs, bacon, sausages. Meat pies to heat up in the microwave. Lasagne, chicken Kiev, garlic mushrooms. And chips, of course.'

He plumped for lasagne and chips. She made thick, strong tea to wash it down with, then sat down at the kitchen table opposite him. 'I took over this pub three years ago,' she told him. 'Me and my partner, Seb. We built it up so we had a good regular clientele, and we were thinking of advertising to do catering for weddings and funerals. And then Seb met someone else and went off to Australia with her.'

Craig looked at her and shook his head in disbelief. How could anyone walk away from a lovely woman like her?

'Well, at least he didn't put his hand in the till. He left me in quite a good position, but all on my own. It hasn't been easy, but I'm still afloat.'

'That's the main thing,' said Craig solemnly, breaking off from wolfing down his food.

She rested her cheek on her hand. 'Yes, it is.' She waited for him to clear up his chips. 'Right! That's a bit of my story. Would you like to tell me a little of yours?'

He dipped his head. 'I dunno.'

'Only if you want to,' she said. 'Finish your grub first.'

They sat without speaking whilst Craig hoovered up his chips. Josie sat quietly watching him and her gaze seemed curiously comforting.

He laid down his cutlery and wiped his mouth on the thick paper napkin Josie had given him. 'I haven't spoken about it for years,' he said.

'Go on,' she urged. 'It'll be all right.'

'It was the day I was twelve when it happened,' he started. 'I was living with my mum in a little terraced house in Bradford. She wasn't very well. She used to stay in bed a lot, and she kept running out of money. I used to stay at home and look after her instead of going to school. We both used to hide when the Education Welfare people called. She had this boyfriend called Barry Jackson. He was right tall and full of himself, driving up to the door in his big Ford Granada and honking the horn to let us know he'd arrived. He'd bought me a great big showy-off birthday card and a model of a Ford Granada. Big deal! My mum was still in bed and she'd forgotten to get me a card, but I didn't mind, because it wasn't really her fault.' He stopped. 'I loved her so much,' he exclaimed. 'I just wanted to stay at home and look after her, and do her shopping and watch telly with her.' He started to chew on his fingers. 'I suppose I was a bit of a wet.'

Josie was very still and quiet. He could tell she was really listening, not just pretending.

'It's special, how you love your mum, isn't it?' Josie said, softly.

'Aye. Anyway Jackson went to get her out of bed, and she came down and sat on the sofa. He showed her the things he'd bought for me, and she said to him, "That's lovely, pet". And for a while things were OK. And then Barry started asking about having some food, like a birthday tea, and mum said she'd got nothing in, and he said she should have made an effort on my birthday, and that the place was a mess and she should be ashamed of herself and pull her socks up.' He took in a shaky breath. 'I could hardly bear it,' he said.

'She got up to go to the kitchen. And then she started crying, and he went to put his arms round her. And then he put his hands inside her dressing gown and started pawing her. He used to do this quite a lot, and he'd look around at me to see how much he was winding me up. My mum started whimpering, pulling away from him and telling him to stop, but he just carried on. And all at once I heard my voice, really loud in the room, like when you turn the telly volume right up. "GET YOUR HANDS OFF MY MUM!" And he turned around and laughed at me, showing all his big yellow teeth. "I'll have my hands on your mum, whenever I like sonny-boy", he said.'

Craig stopped, looking towards Josie, breathing hard, his eyes blazing with the memory. 'I went into the kitchen and took out a knife my mum had bought from her catalogue, thinking she might do some cooking one day. It was called a kitchen devil, really sharp. I went back into the living room and I stuck it in Jackson's back.'

Josie nodded, calm and unperturbed. 'What happened then?'

'He made a sort of gurgling noise and fell on the floor. And then I don't really remember much after that, until the police were there, and someone from the Social. My mum had passed out on the sofa. I told the police I'd stuck a knife in Jackson and that I wasn't sorry. And I hoped he was dead. Which he was.' He stopped. 'That's it, really. And I *was* glad I killed him,' he said fiercely.

Josie spent a few moments considering all this. 'That's what you told yourself,' she said, 'when you were twelve. Because you'd got rid of the man making your mum's life a misery. But later on you'd feel rotten about killing someone. And maybe you still tried to tell yourself you were glad. But deep down you weren't. That's my guess.'

'How do you know that?' he demanded, amazed. 'No one else ever told me that.'

'It's just one of those life things you sort of know, isn't it?'

'Is it?'

'My mum died when I was twelve,' she told him. 'I was the eldest, so I became the little mother … at least that was what my dad used to call me. I started looking after my kid brother and my dad as well. I knew what the suffering of her loss was like for them and I missed her simply desperately myself, so I grew up pretty fast. And, you see, Craig, when you were twelve you did something for your mum which you thought was a good thing to do for her at the time. I can understand that. And you had to grow up all of a sudden too because of what happened after that.'

'But it was wrong,' he insisted.

'Oh yes. But you didn't mean it to be like that. You didn't plan it. It happened, like a wave rolling over you.' She drummed her hands on the table. 'Where's your mum now?'

'Dunno. She doesn't want to see me.'

'You don't know that, Craig. She might have changed. She might be longing to see you. You need to think about that. I lost my mum for ever, and I'd do anything to get her back. But I can't … I can never have her back. And if your mum is still alive, I think you should do anything to get her back. What have you to lose?'

Craig felt suddenly exhausted. He let out a long breath.

'Would you like to stay on and help out here?' Josie asked. 'I really need a good reliable worker. Helping out at the bar, a bit of cleaning work. You could learn to cook if you wanted.'

He stared at her. 'Do you mean that? You don't know anything about me, except I'm a murderer.'

She smiled. 'You can learn quite a lot about a person when you're working as a team mopping up a floor with them. Why don't you give it a go for a few weeks? If you don't like it, you can move on. I pay a pound more an hour than the most of the pubs round here.'

He stared at her, not knowing quite what to say. Longing to stay here and work for her. Not daring to believe he'd been offered the chance.

'I can't start right now,' he said, suddenly remembering. 'I've been on the run. I've got to give myself up to the police.'

Josie's mouth fell open. 'Hey, you're certainly full of surprises.'

'I haven't done nowt wrong again. I promise. Do you believe me?'

She narrowed her eyes. 'Yes, thousands wouldn't!'

'Will you go to the station with me?' he asked. 'Walk in with me? That's all. I'll be all right then, and you can come back here.'

'Well, thanks,' she said, grinning. 'Yes, of course I'll come with you.' She got up. 'Go and have a wash and comb your hair. I'll be waiting for you. And look sharp, I've opening time coming up.'

She was as good as her word. She walked him to the station and up the steps, pushing him gently forwards. And then she turned around and left.

There was a female officer on the front desk. She looked business-like and brisk. She was dealing with an anxious woman who had lost her purse containing all her credit cards. Craig licked around his lips as he waited to be attended to, standing patiently behind the worried woman as though he were in the bus queue. His heart was thumping so hard he was surprised no one had looked around to see where the noise was coming from.

The woman eventually went away, having repeatedly asked for reassurances that her purse would be found. Craig thought this was a pointless exercise. It either would or wouldn't be found whether she kept on nagging the policewoman or not. His heart was galloping like a racehorse now, the tension within building steadily with the waiting and frustration.

He stepped forward. 'Yes,' the police woman said, her tone crisp.

'I'm Craig Titmus. I'm an ex-con and I've come to—'

'Yes?'

'I think there'll be an alert out. I've not seen my probation officer when I should. I think it's today.'

He half expected an army of strong men to burst forth from the innards of the station, push him to the ground and handcuff him.

'Can I have your name again?' she asked, unperturbed, as though he were Mr Ordinary.

He spoke it very slowly and she was tapping it into the computer as he did so. Her eyebrows moved slightly. 'Now then, Craig. You're quite right. There is an alert out for you.' She looked him over, with impartial assessment. 'Well done for coming in. I'm going to ask another officer to come and speak to you. In the meantime, maybe you could turn out your pockets for me. I'll make a note of everything and give it back to you.' She was going on to explain that what she was asking was a safety precaution, but Craig was already doing what she asked. He had been well schooled in obedience to authority. He knew it was invariably the best way to save your skin. He took out his loose change, and then Ruth's wad of twenty-pound notes, followed by the mobile and a half empty packet of crisps he had bought at the pub the previous night. Also the paper napkin Josie had brought him with his plate of food, now grubby and crumpled.

'Any weapons?' she asked.

'No.'

'OK. We'll check further on that later. How come you've got all this money?'

'I borrowed it from my friend, Mrs Hartwell. I got it to keep safe for her. I'm going to give it back.'

'I see. And the mobile, is that yours?'

'No.'

She looked hard at him.

'That's Mrs Hartwell's and all.'

'Really.'

Rebellion stirred within. He leaned slightly towards the woman, looming over her, letting her feel the full force of his big physical presence. 'I'm a murderer,' he told her. 'I'm not a thief.'

She stood her ground bravely. 'OK, just keep calm, Craig.'

'I've done me time,' he said. 'And I 'aven't done nothing else wrong since I came out.'

At that point an impressively burly uniformed officer accompanied by a female uniform were buzzed through the security door and came to stand beside Craig. The woman put her hand gently on his arm. 'We're just going to check you for weapons, Craig. Is that OK?'

'What?' He wasn't used to people asking permission to do things to him.

'We need to be sure you're not carrying anything which could be used as a weapon.'

'Go on, then.' He put his arms out to the side and spread his legs. The male officer stepped forward and ran his hands swiftly and expertly over Craig's body and limbs. 'All clear,' he said. 'Come on lad, let's get you into an interview room and then we'll have a little chat.'

Having sampled a small amount of Sir David's peaty Laphroaig and chatted with him about family and world affairs for half an hour, Swift eventually made his farewells and got behind the wheel of his car once more. Before firing the engine, he selected a CD of Haydn quartets which had come free with one of the big Sundays a while ago. He pushed the disc into the player and the music sprang out, its crispness lifting to the spirit, and in no way interfering with his thoughts on the interview with the amiable Sir David.

He tried to pick out the salient points, the issues to discuss later with Cat.

First of all, why had Harriet omitted any mention of Julian Roseborough in her account of the desert murder. Why omit something so crucial, something which was surely potentially helpful in pulling Brunswick out of the frame.

What role might Roseborough have taken in the murder of Christian? If any? And why?

What might Cat be able to tell him about Roseborough, who was apparently a friend of Jeremy?

He made a small sound of annoyance through his teeth. He could have done without that kind of connection turning up.

A call came through on his bluetooth. It was Ravi Stratton. She told him that Craig Titmus had reported to the station in Thirsk.

Swift disliked driving and talking even with the hands-off equipment. 'Give me a minute, Ravi, I'll park up and ring you back.' He pulled into a conveniently near lay-by and turned off the engine. 'Is he OK?'

'Yes, he's talking to the Thirsk CID now.'

'Did he have anything of interest on him?'

'Two hundred pounds in notes and a mobile phone. He told the front desk both the money and the phone belonged to Ruth Hartwell.'

'Right. Can you get the IT team in Thirsk to access the details from the phone and send them on to us. And if there are any photographs, to e-mail them though to me right away.'

'I've already asked the Thirsk team to get in one of the local probation officers to talk to Craig. Fix up some temporary accommodation in Thirsk if the station don't think it's necessary to keep him.'

'Does it sound as though he's likely to be charged with any offence?'

'They didn't say so. He has broken the terms of his licence, of course. He was supposed to report in to his probation officer earlier today.'

'Right. Well, I suppose we'll just have to see how things pan out. Cross any shaky bridges when we come to them.'

'How did your interview with the ambassador go?' she asked.

'It was interesting. I'd rather not talk on the phone, Ravi. I'll get a report to you as soon as possible.'

Having cut the connection with Ravi Stratton, Swift punched in Cat's mobile number.

She answered almost instantly. 'Ed?'

'How are things going?'

'Not sure. I've seen Brunswick and I had one of those feelings that I was on the scent of something. And then I've been following up a hunch which seemed a bit interesting, but now I'm not so sure about that either.' She laughed. 'But I'm quite enjoying myself, anyway. You know, being on some sort of trail even if it's not the right one. And London is so gloriously big and anonymous.'

He could hear the lift in her voice. Already she was coming round after Jeremy's assault. And maybe enjoying the freedom of being fairly sure he wasn't in the near vicinity.

'Has Brunswick given you anything new?'

'Contrary to what he told us earlier, he and Christian have been buddies in recent years. Drinking partners and so on. Harriet doesn't join in, and probably doesn't know.'

Swift's mind raced. Christian, Brunswick, and Julian Roseborough all on a night out together. What had been going on between them? Both in the distant and the recent past? He decided not to mention David Colburn's account of Roseborough to Cat at this stage. No need to cloud her day, as yet. That would come soon enough.

He told her about Craig and the hopefully significant discovery of the mobile phone. 'Are you coming straight back?' he asked. 'Or taking some time out in Bond Street?'

'What? On a DI's salary? I'm thinking of buying a coffee and a sandwich and relaxing with a stroll along the Regents Canal.'

'Really. Aren't there more exciting sights to see?'

'Time will tell. I'll give you all the details when I see you. I'm aiming to get the 7.05 out of Kings Cross. Be back in Leeds just after nine.'

'I'll pick you up.'

'No need.' She was sounding so much brighter.

'Yes there is,' he said gently. Perhaps more for himself than for Cat.

At the Fox and Hounds Hotel on the north-west section of the Leeds ring road, Lynne, the chambermaid who looked after floor two, was getting a little worried about the state of Room 26. She hadn't been able to get in there to tidy up and put out fresh towels that day. The Don't Disturb notice had still been hung on the door handle at 10 a.m. this morning. And it was now at 6 p.m. in the evening and it had not been moved. At the Fox and Hounds they liked to continue the old-fashioned service of turning down the beds in the evening and ensuring that the fridge, the bar and the tea-making facilities were all topped up. She was keen to get all that done without delay.

She stared at the door for a few moments, then knocked on it with gentle fingers. 'Room service,' she called out, beginning to be concerned. She put her ear to the door. There was no sound. She turned the key in the lock and went in. At least she tried to go in. But there was an obstacle behind the door. She pushed hard, but the resistance was too great. Looking into the room she could see the figure of a man slumped on the carpet. He was fully dressed. neatly pressed grey trousers and a dark-green sweater. He even had his shoes on. He must have fallen forward when he fell, as his face was hidden from view. Around his head was a huge sticky halo of blood. Lynne's hand flew to her mouth but she made no sound. She closed the door and went quickly downstairs to locate the manager.

When Swift arrived back in his office, he went straight to his computer and accessed his e-mails. The file from the IT department in the Thirsk station was the first he opened. He went straight to the section labelled camera storage. Scrolling down the screen he found some stills of the frontage of the London Canal Museum and further stills taken at different points along the towpath of the canal. And then there was a short video. The stills had been taken in the daylight, but the video was shot in fading evening light, making the quality of the picture grey and grainy. It appeared that the photographer had been on the move as he filmed, the images being subject to a degree of jerkiness. But the story told in the film was unmistakably chilling. A stumbling male figure was making his way down the towpath, his footsteps uncoordinated and tremulous. As he weaved his way along there were a number of occasions when he seemed dangerously near the edge of the water and about to topple in. And then, with one clear fluent movement, a man following drew alongside, stretched out his arm hand and simply tipped the drunk into the water with the pressure of his outstretched fingers. As the body slowly disappeared, the killer lingered to watch. He took out a cigarette and lit it, drawing the smoke deep into his lungs as he surveyed his night's work. His profile was in clear view, but in shadow. And then he suddenly turned and faced the camera head on, his body stiffening. At which point, the video came to a sudden end.

Swift's nerves tingled as the grim narrative of Christian Hartwell's death began to fall into place. He was pretty sure who the perpetrator was, but the film had been made at a distance and in half-light, and he needed further clarity. He rang through to Les Patterson, the station's IT wizard, told him what he was looking at and requested a blow-up and a clarity enhancement as soon as possible.

Whilst he waited, he sat at his desk, trying to work out the detailed planning in the lead-up to Hartwell's killing, assessing the killer's motivation, and going on to speculate on the way in which he had chosen to implement his murderous requirements.

*

Cat made her way back towards King Cross on foot. She went into a smart-looking delicatessen and bought a prawn and avocado sandwich and a black filter coffee. By the time she reached the first access point to the Regents Canal she had already eaten the sandwich and was beginning to wish she had bought some fruit or a pastry to fill her up. She hadn't eaten so far today and her stomach was beginning to complain. No worries, she would get something on the train. She crunched up the cardboard wrapping which had held her sandwich and put it in a bin. Sipping her coffee, she strolled along the towpath of the Regents Canal, passing the London Canal Museum and heading in the direction of Islington.

It was coming up to five o'clock and the towpath was quiet, apart from the occasional cyclist and one or two dog walkers. There was a slight aroma of vegetables coming off the water, making her keep away from the edge, to avoid any risk of falling in. The canal made its way through scrubby, dusty bushes, punctuated with occasional illustrated information boards giving details of the area, its history and its flora and fauna. Not far from the museum the terrain became richer and more verdant, almost parklike.

It would be no problem at all for an evil-doer to lurk without being seen, waiting for a suitable victim to appear. What could be easier and less detectable than tipping an unsuspecting, befuddled drunk into the canal? The only problem was to be sure you weren't seen.

She knew she was simply chasing rainbows doing this small piece of informal detective work on the 'Tipper' case. It had nothing to do with her, and probably nothing to do with Christian Hartwell's murder, either. And yet the image of the casual disposal of an unsuspecting victim with the flick of a wrist which had been used on Hartwell and the tipsy tramps was strangely compelling.

She continued her walk. Looking up and ahead she saw a Eurostar train racing away from St Pancras, sending faint vibrations through the ground beneath her feet as its wheels punished the bridge. Her thoughts moved on to returning to Yorkshire, to being met by Ed at the station. And a calm, steady happiness rolled through her.

Swift got a call to go down to Les Patterson's room. When he got there he saw a remarkably well-defined, recognizable image of the canal killer's face up on the screen of Les's wide-screen laptop.

'Good enough for you?' Les asked.

'Brilliant.' Swift never failed to be impressed by the miracles Les performed.

'Good looking chap,' Les said. 'Is he a villain? Looks like a bit of a toff to me.'

'Close on both counts. He's heir to the Roseborough super-market chain.'

'We don't usually attract such exalted company,' Les commented, not inclined to get overexcited by tales of the rich and famous.

'Murder knows no social boundaries.'

'So this guy murdered our Mr Christian Hartwell?'

'Maybe not with his own hands,' Swift said thoughtfully.

'That's toffs for you,' Les said. 'Cute enough to get some lowly minion to do the dirty work.'

'Quite. And powerful enough to cause a lot of grief. Can you keep all this to yourself, Les? Just for the moment?'

'I'll take it to the grave, if you like,' Les said.

'I sincerely hope that won't be necessary.'

Back in his office, Swift sat behind his desk and considered his options for moving forward on the case. But even greater than the need to make the right tactical decisions in gaining a conviction was the awareness that a number of people could be in serious danger and it was imperative to offer them the best protection he could.

It would appear that Julian Roseborough was a cold and calcu-lating murderer, who perhaps regarded killing as some kind of sport. Except his targets were not grouse or foxes or stags, but human beings. David Colburn seemed convinced that Roseborough had been the perpetrator of Hugh Ross's death. Moreover, the retired ambassador had hinted that not only had

Roseborough killed once but that he was capable of more of the same.

He moved on to work with the hypothesis that Hartwell had had his suspicions aroused by Roseborough during his last visit to London. It seemed likely the two had been at the lap-dancing club together, and that Hartwell had been enjoying his hobby of recording interesting events on camera. Had Roseborough spotted this and objected? Or spotted it and been entertained? Was it possible Roseborough had dropped his guard and given Hartwell and Brunswick hints about his liking for flying near the sun. They had both known him in the past, would presumably both have had their suspicions about his role in the Hugh Ross incident. And were the three of them on an arranged boys' night out, or had Hartwell and Brunswick simply bumped into Roseborough at the club?

If Roseborough had a network of henchmen and informers then he would be aware of the progress in finding the incriminating video on Christian Hartwell's phone. Ruth Hartwell, as Christian's named next of kin, had been first in the firing line, the one who had, perhaps, been kept under surveillance and had been seen visiting her solicitor and emerging from the interview carrying a large envelope. After which Mac the Knife had stepped in.

He made a mental note of the names of those currently in the line of fire regarding Roseborough's need to get hold of the video, and also dispose of anyone who might talk in the future.

His list of targets ran as follows:

Ruth Hartwell
Charles Brunswick and Harriet Brunswick. Their son Jake who could be used as a lever.
Craig Titmus, who was potentially at even greater risk, as he had been seen by Mac the Knife who would realize he had access to pretty much everything in Ruth Hartwell's house.

He laid down his pen for a moment. When he took it up again, he wrote:

Me and Cat.

Oh, definitely both of them were at risk. They were probably under the surveillance of one of Roseborough's minions right now. Cat had been talking to Brunswick. And he, Swift, had been talking with Sir David Colburn and even worse was in possession of the vital information Roseborough was desperate to get his hands on. He put a ring round the word 'Me' and pencilled in a question mark and then words 'target number one'.

After talking to David Colburn and before seeing the disturbing video starring Roseborough, it had been in Swift's mind to phone Cat and ask her to go back to see Brunswick and press him on the issue of his and Harriet's silence regarding Roseborough's being a member of the field trip in Algeria.

But now the pressing issue was to get Cat back home and safe.

He rang her mobile.

'Ed?'

'Where are you?'

'On the concourse at Kings Cross. Looking at the departure board along with a few thousand other people. My train's listed as on time.'

It struck Swift that if Cat were one of his next of kin, he would be gripped with the dilemma as to whether or not to tell them of the possible danger they were in. And basically he felt exactly the same dilemma regarding Cat. But Cat was his colleague. She was an experienced officer. She was on the Hartwell case. He needed to brief her. He gave her a quick run-down on his interview with Sir David Colburn and of Craig's appearance at the station in Thirsk. And then he apprised her of the contents of the mobile phone which Craig had been carrying since the previous morning.

There was an intake of breath and a brief silence. The noise coming from the concourse came down the connection as a low, constant roar. 'Did you get all that, Cat?'

'You're saying you have video footage of our rich friend tipping an old drunk into a canal?'

'Correct.'

'Have you a date for it?'

'Five days before Hartwell was killed.'

'Well, he's sent at least one further drunk to his watery grave since then,' she said. 'In the Regents Canal just minutes away from where I am now. Same MO.'

'What?' He was stunned. He rapidly thought through all the implications surrounding Cat's statement. 'Look, Cat. I think we should finish this conversation. I think we're both at risk. Possibly being followed. I just want you back here,' he said. Sweat was dampening the back of his shirt.

'OK.' She matched his briskness. 'You need to contact DI Wilton. He's at the nick in Snowdon Place. I have to go. They've put the platform number up; there's a stampede. If I don't run like hell I'll have to stand all the way to Wakefield. I'll take care – and you make sure you do too.'

She was gone.

He went to Ravi Stratton's office, but she had already left. Which, on balance, he was glad about. It gave him the freedom to authorize whatever he thought necessary. And to keep the explosive revelations of the last few hours between himself and Cat for a little longer.

Hoping to find DI Wilton still at work, he called up Snowdon Place station.

When he got through to Wilton, the inspector's tones were curt and clipped. 'How can I help, Chief Inspector?'

'I think we might be able to help each other,' Swift told him. He outlined the Hartwell case and gave a short but comprehensive account of the recent discoveries.

'Let me just recap, sir,' Wilton said, his tone now enlivened. 'Basically you're thinking that the guy who killed Hartwell is involved in the "Tipper" case.'

'I'm thinking that Hartwell's killer was in the employ of the "Tipper".'

'And you've a video of a drunk on our patch being pushed into the Regents Canal?'

'Yes, we seem to have a picture of the "Tipper" at work – whether he's linked with our victim or not.'

There was a beat of tension. 'That is amazing, sir. Totally unbelievable news.' He paused. 'So do you know who this guy is?'

'We're pretty confident he's Julian Roseborough. Heir to the Roseborough supermarket chain.'

'WHAT? Are you sure?'

'Unless he has a double, yes.'

'Is the footage clear?'

'It's very good. Our IT man worked wonders on it.'

'Admissible in court?'

'I haven't run it by the CPS so far, but I don't see why we shouldn't use it.'

'Have you passed it up the command chain yet?'

'No. There are just me, Cat Fallon our IT guy and you who know about it.' He chose not to expand further, if Wilton had any detective acumen he'd read what he needed into his silence.

'This just gets better,' Wilton said. 'What do you want my help with?'

'I'd like you to go and see Christian's putative half-sister, Harriet, and her husband Charles. I'm going to e-mail some extracts from our files, which will explain the background to my request. I want you to find out why Brunswick lied to Cat Fallon earlier today. And I want to find out what they know about Roseborough. Charles Brunswick was caught on camera in the same club with Roseborough just a couple of weeks back, so there's no point his pleading ignorance.'

'I'm trying to keep up,' said Wilton.

'The material I'm mailing you will tell you what you want to know, plus addresses and contact numbers. Also one of the stills from the video. And I'm on the end of the phone.'

'Right! So, even though I've been taken off the case, I get to do some further investigation on our local killer which is all above board because it's a request from your team regarding your case?'

'Correct.'

Swift expected Wilton to come back at him with some quip about his good luck. Instead, he simply said: 'Thank you, sir, for this. I'll give it my very best shot.' There was a short pause. 'Why aren't you sending Inspector Fallon back to see the Brunswicks?'

'Because she said you were a man of granite, and I know you're very keen to go forward with this case.'

'Right, sir.' Wilton sounded like a changed man from the one who had answered the phone.

'And I want Inspector Fallon back here,' Swift said, cutting the connection and letting Wilton have the pleasure of working out the possible nuances in that statement. Smiling to himself, he rang the local hospital and ascertained that Ruth Hartwell had been discharged some hours before. He arranged for two uniformed PCs to do a home visit, check on her welfare, and reassure her that Craig was safe and well. He also arranged for the two officers to remain in the house for the night.

He phoned Thirsk station to be told that following their investigations Craig Titmus had been cleared of any criminal offences and was about to be discharged to a local bed and breakfast regularly used by the Probation Service. Swift thought fast. 'Titmus is in a potentially dangerous situation,' he said. 'It's connected with a murder case I'm leading which is suddenly hotting up. I'll e-mail you relevant information to put you in the picture. In the meantime, I'd like one of your officers to go and get him and tell him that I've asked for him to stay overnight at the station as a precautionary measure. Let him know he's done nothing wrong, it's simply that we are concerned for his safety regarding a man who calls himself Mac the Knife. I want you to tell him that he can call me personally at any time. Let him have access to a police phone when he wants to make a call and put him in the visitors' suite overnight and give him some breakfast tomorrow morning. Got that?'

'Got it, sir. Shall I ask him which newspaper he takes?' The tone was impeccably polite.

Swift had to smile. 'Watch it!'

Cat took a seat beside the door of her coach. In this way she could see all the way down the coach in which she was sitting and also, by turning around, through into the carriage coupling area and into the coach beyond.

She kept a careful watch, ready for action should anyone approach her. They were nearly at Doncaster and only the ticket collector and the snack trolley service had shown any interest in her. She reminded herself that although they were nearly at their destination it was not yet safe to relax. At Doncaster the doors opened and a trickle of passengers got off and another trickle got on and settled themselves down. After seven minutes, the train was still waiting in the station, and one or two passengers began looking at their watches and frowning. After ten minutes, a steward's announcement apologized to the passengers for the delay in leaving the station. No reason was offered, but there was a caution given regarding any passenger trying to leave the train, and it was pointed out that all the doors were sealed.

At this point some passengers began to look anxious. People started talking in low tones to each other across the aisle. What was going on? Was there a terrorist on the train? These anxieties were voiced readily, but Cat could almost read some of the other passenger's unspoken thoughts. Was there an axe-wielding murderer on board? Or maybe a gunman? Had someone already been killed or injured?

After a second announcement, identical to the first, but even less reassuring given that the train had now been waiting in the station for fifteen minutes, Cat walked down the front of the train to find one of the crew. Tension began to prickle under her arm pits. Having passed the buffet bar which was now closed up, she went into the First Class section. A steward stood barring access to the First Class carriages. Cat took out her warrant card. 'Can I do anything to help?'

'I think it's all under control, ma'am,' the steward said, white-faced.

'What's happened?'

'One of the passengers had a gun. He started threatening the crew. He shot one of them in the arm. Then he said he was going to get off at the next stop and start shooting randomly people at the station. We phoned ahead to Doncaster for back-up. A plain clothes detective and a shrink got on.' The steward began to shake with delayed shock.

'The shrink got the guy talking and the doc managed to jab him in the butt with a needle and he just fell down like he was dead. They've taken him away now on a stretcher. Apparently he's a known psycho from a local mental institution.'

'What about the member of crew who was injured? Cat asked.

'It was just a flesh wound. She's gone to hospital, but she's going to be OK.'

'Are you all right?' Cat asked.

'Yes, thank you. I'm fine. We've got a uniformed PC on board until we get to Leeds.'

193

Cat gave him her card. 'Just let me know if you need anything. Would you like me to reassure the passengers? I think they're getting rather anxious.'

'No, ma'am. Our head steward is just about to make an announcement. We've got it all in hand.'

Cat knew when she was not wanted. But nevertheless, as she walked back to her seat, she gave reassuring nods and words to the passengers whose eyes met hers.

A few moments later the steward's voice came over the intercom, apologizing once again for the delay. There was a creak as the driver released the brakes and the train moved hesitantly forward, as though sharing in the anxiety of its passengers. Gradually it gathered speed as it left the jumble of the urban landscape and entered the countryside.

Cat settled in her seat, watching the calm of the fields and the quietly grazing animals slip by. She punched Swift's number into her mobile and, whilst she waited for his reply, resumed her look out for potential trouble.

Wilton printed out Swift's e-mail. He scanned it through quickly to get a feel for the case and then read it through three more times, before taking up his blue pen and underlining those points he deemed to be most relevant with regard to his forthcoming interview with Harriet and Charles Brunswick.

Wilton was a careful planner and a thorough interrogator. The frustration and disappointment of having the 'Tipper' case wrested from his grasp had been severe and humiliating. And now he was getting a compensatory buzz of anticipation at becoming involved in the case again, coming at it from an entirely unexpected new angle. And with a DCI who seemed quietly determined to get results. Having felt himself rejected and abandoned, and, as he saw it, made to look incompetent in the eyes of his staff, he now felt a new strength of purpose.

He took a bus to Muswell Hill, judging that with the underground still not working, the roads would be totally jammed, and even taxis avoided challenging buses. Which meant that at the moment they got to the destination first.

The Brunswicks lived on the hill itself, their house one of a number of smart residences presided over by Alexandra Palace. It was an end terrace with a candle-snuffer turret. He guessed that even with house prices having taken a tumble it would still be worth upwards of a million. In urban south Yorkshire where he had grown up, you could get a small mansion in good nick for that price. But then, in Wilton's book, there was nothing to beat living in the capital.

A tall, athletic-looking guy with bright red hair and in full evening dress, answered the door. He had spectacularly blue eyes and the kind of nose Wilton wouldn't mind acquiring, but for the money and pain involved. Wilton, however, had a warrant card and the authority of a CID inspector, which he considered gave him an entirely satisfactory wicket to bat on. Holding his card for the inspection of the flame-haired man, he introduced himself and enquired if he was speaking with Charles Brunswick.

'Yes.' For a fleeting second the blue eyes seemed to flicker.

'I'd like to talk to you and your wife about recent developments regarding Christian Hartwell's murder.'

The blue eyes swivelled from side to side, a moving slideshow of anxiety. 'Well, as you can see, Inspector, we're just about to go out. Our taxi will be arriving any time.' Brunswick made a commendable attempt at a confident smile.

'The more you cooperate with my questions, sir, the less time you will have to keep your taxi waiting,' Wilton said.

Brunswick got the drift. 'Right, you'd better come in.' As Wilton followed him down a long hallway, Brunswick was talking at him over his shoulder. 'You do realize that I've already spoken with Inspector Fallon earlier on?'

'Yes.'

On reaching a large, airy sitting room, the two men stared at each other for a few moments. 'Would you ask your wife to join us, sir?' Wilton asked.

Brunswick hesitated, the nuances of an inner debate stimulating his blue eyes once again, together with the muscles of his firm jaw, and for a moment Wilton thought he was going to offer a challenge.

'She is a putative relative of the deceased,' Wilton pointed out. 'And her mother was the dead man's named next of kin.' He lobbed the information at Brunswick with a deadpan face. His eyes were telling Brunswick that he'd done his homework on the case and was not to be underestimated.

'Right,' said Brunswick, trying not to sound as though he were capitulating. 'I'll go and call her.' He glanced out of the window. 'Damn! The taxi's here.'

'Shall I go and ask them to wait?' Wilton asked.

'No, no. I'll go.' He strode from the room.

Wilton went to the foot of the stairs and called out: 'Mrs Brunswick! Harriet! Police!'

There was the sound of footsteps and a rustle of fabric.

A woman's head and upper body leaned over the banister rails. 'What is it? Don't say my car alarm has gone off again.'

Wilton was about to explain, when Brunswick dashed back into the house, sized up the situation and called up the stairs: 'Harriet – darling – just come down; it's important.'

Her face clouded at the urgency of his tone. She came slowly down the stairs, graceful and almost majestic.

Wilton watched her with interest. She was wearing a long blue dress which emphasized the slenderness of her frame. Her dark hair had been dragooned into a complex knot of tresses at the nape of her neck and she wore diamond earrings that flashed like fire. She looked like a woman who liked to be in control. Not his type, Wilton thought. He much preferred his women a little more curvaceous and a lot more relaxed. When she joined her husband, he noted that the two of them made a strikingly attractive picture. They reminded him of A-list couples pictured in the celebrity magazines his girlfriend had a sneaking fondness for. But with brains.

Harriet led the way back into the drawing room. She stood beside the fireplace, strained and tense as she faced Wilton.

'I'm sorry to interfere with your evening, Mrs Brunswick,' he told her. As he repeated the opening lines he had offered to Brunswick, Harriet's eyes widened with alarm.

'Some new evidence has come to light this afternoon as regards Christian Hartwell's death,' Wilton said. He moved his gaze from Harriet to Charles. 'New evidence since Inspector Fallon spoke to you this afternoon, sir.'

Charles looked like a schoolboy caught cheating in an exam.

'Inspector Fallon. Who's he?' Harriet demanded, turning her fierce glances from Wilton to her husband.

'She's on DCI Swift's team,' Wilton said, noting Charles's discomfiture, that he was playing true to form as regards lying and lack of openness – and was probably in for trouble later. 'This new discovery leads us to believe that Mr Hartwell's death and that of the victims of the local so-called "Tipper" here in London could be linked.'

The silence was like a noiseless explosion.

'How so?' Harriet asked.

Wilton saved the answer to that for later. He turned to Charles. 'It also suggests to us that you have both been withholding information from us.' He left a pause for one of them to speak, but they both seemed utterly at a loss how to proceed.

'I'm referring to your trip to Algeria in 1989,' Wilton prompted.

Harriet groaned. 'Not that again.'

'A trip which was made by five people, not four,' Wilton said.

Whilst Charles shifted his weight from one foot to the other, looking as though he would rather be in any situation other than the current one, Harriet dipped her head and took a few long deep breaths. She suddenly swung around to face her husband. 'For God's sake, Charles. We can't keep it to ourselves any longer. It was bound to come out.'

'What was bound to come out?' Wilton enquired.

Charles opened his mouth to speak, but Harriet got in first. 'That Julian Roseborough was one of the party, that he was on the point of going down for killing one of our mates – in the place where we were carrying out our research. And then suddenly he was released and Charles was selected as the killer himself.' She stopped, breathing hard.

A good summary, Wilton thought. 'But Charles was also released,' he said. 'And no one was ever charged for the murder.'

'That's right,' Harriet said. 'We all simply walked away from the situation. We were frightened, and I suppose we were despicable cowards.'

'What were you frightened of?' Wilton asked.

'I, for one, was pretty worried about being banged up in an Algerian jail, or worse,' Charles said with some feeling.

'And we are all pretty scared of Julian,' Harriet said. 'We were pretty certain that he had done the murder. In fact, he boasted about having done it on the way home. He also made it very clear that if any of us ever spoke about it, we'd end up in the same position as our unlucky pal Hugh.'

Wilton looked at Charles. 'What's your version?'

'Very much the same,' Charles said. 'Julian's family has big connections and a great deal of money. They easily got Julian off the hook.'

'As did your parents, I believe.'

Charles pursed his lips. 'Yes. But the police didn't need too much persuading to release me. They knew I wasn't the killer.'

Harriet had been quiet, working things through. She squared up to Wilton, her eyes ferocious. 'Are you saying that Julian killed Christian? And that he's also been pushing drunks into the canal – that he's the "Tipper"?'

Pretty spot on, Wilton thought. 'Let's say we're hoping to speak to him to further our enquiries.'

Harriet snorted. 'OK, we get the message. And don't worry, Inspector Wilton, we won't be mouthing off about this. I won't speak for my husband, but I myself am totally terrified of crossing Julian. He's absolutely mental, utterly ruthless. He wouldn't hesitate to order our demises, or even kill us with his bare hands if he thought we were going to compromise him in any way.'

'Those are strong allegations, Mrs Brunswick,' Wilton observed.

'Yes, and they are absolutely justified.'

'How long is it since you saw him, Mrs Brunswick?' Wilton asked.

'Several years. We've occasionally run into him at social events, but I try to steer clear.'

Wilton turned on Charles. 'But you, sir, saw him quite recently, didn't you? You were both at a lap-dancing club near Piccadilly Circus. We've got photographs to prove it. Photographs which we believe were taken by Christian Hartwell.'

Harriet stared in horror at her husband, then collapsed on to the sofa and covered her face with her hands. Charles rushed to sit beside her, prising her hands from her face and holding them tightly within his. 'Harriet, listen – I met him at Rupert's stag night last month. He got all chummy, wanted me to come to an all-guys night-out he was planning. He made it sound like an order rather than an invitation. He was just playing with me, testing me out to see how much I'd go along with him. Of course I said, yes. What other option did I have?'

Harriet looked at him, her eyes red with unshed tears. 'None.'

'Christian and I had already planned to go out that evening, so I took the risk of inviting him along for a bit of moral support. I guessed Julian wouldn't give a toss. Which he didn't.'

Harriet looked at him, like a stern mother eyeing a child who needs to do a little explaining. 'Is this the truth, Charles?'

'Yes. I wouldn't blame you for not believing me, but that is the truth.'

'OK,' she said, wearily, and Wilton guessed this was a well-practised scenario. On the other hand, he had a gut feeling Brunswick was, in fact, telling the truth on this occasion.

'So you had supper in the West End?' Wilton suggested.

'We went to J Sheekey.'

'Then you went on to a lap-dancing club?'

'The Miranda,' Brunswick said. 'We didn't get around to watching the action too closely because Julian was holding forth. Talking about a bit of interesting "action" he could set up if we were interested.'

'Action?' Wilton broke in.

Charles nodded.

'As in murder?'

Charles grimaced with disgust. 'Julian made it sound like a bit of fun, like climbing up on the school roof at the end of term. But basically what he was suggesting seemed to be some kind of killing club for wealthy guys who'd find it fun to get rid of the capital's down and outs: the drones, the little people. I pretended not to cotton on. He didn't push it, but I think he was more than half-serious. I left as soon as I could but Christian stayed behind for a bit, because he wanted to take photographs in the club. He's an ace photographer, gets great shots and never bothers with any restrictions operating. I guess he'd got interested in what Julian was mouthing off about. And most probably tailed him for a day or two, seeing how many more interesting shots he could get of Julian's law-unto-himself life style. He's a braver man than I am.'

'But foolhardy enough to get himself killed when Roseborough tumbled to what was going on,' Wilton suggested.

Brunswick nodded, his former cheeriness and self-confidence crumbling as the revelations rolled on. 'Have you got hold of some photographs Christian took?' he asked. 'Is that the evidence you were referring to?'

'We have some photographic evidence, in connection with the case, sir,' Wilton told him, 'but not yet confirmation of the person who took the photographs. Did Christian come to see you before he went back to Yorkshire? Did he make any references to shots he might have taken, relevant to the murders?'

'No.'

'Sure?'

'Absolutely. We weren't big buddies. I just saw him occasionally when he came up to London. We'd have a drink together.'

'But you didn't tell your wife about these meetings?' Wilton asked, thinking that Charles must be a man who had a taste for secrets.

Charles shook his head. 'Harriet didn't really want to keep in touch with him.'

'He's right,' Harriet said. 'When I left home and came to London I wanted to leave my peculiar childhood behind me. Christian was fine, an OK person. But he was not my brother, and I suppose I resented what I considered his intrusion into our family, taking up attention from my parents. God knows they had enough lame dogs without him.'

Charles put his arm around her and kissed her on the forehead and then the lips. She kissed him back.

Wilton made a speedy alteration to his first perceptions of this interesting couple. They looked pretty well soldered to each other, for all her high-handedness and his slippery charm.

'What's Julian going to do next?' Harriet demanded, suddenly. 'Who's at risk?' She turned to her husband. 'Oh God, Jake's at a sleepover with Oliver!'

'Where he will be very safe,' Charles told her, soothingly. 'We'll ring to check.'

She rounded on Wilton. 'Well, who's the target?'

'We believe that Julian Roseborough's immediate concerns will be to get possession of the incriminating evidence we have in our possession.'

'So basically DCI Swift is the one who should be looking out for himself?'

'I'm sure DCI Swift is well used to doing that,' Wilton said.

'Julian won't be after our son Jake, or my mother, or us?' Harriet persisted.

'I think that would be very unlikely,' Wilton said. 'Try not to worry, Mrs Brunswick. The police in Yorkshire are aiming to cover all angles, which includes protection for your mother.' How's that for diplomacy, he told himself, guessing that Roseborough had now gone to ground and was lying low.

'Oh, poor Mum, having to cope with Christian's being killed and then getting mixed up in all this.' Harriet exclaimed. 'And I was such a bloody bitch to her yesterday.'

Wilton gave a respectful nod of his head to acknowledge her guilt and grief. He wasn't a psychologist; it wasn't up to him to comment. He now prepared to wind up the interview, judging that things had gone better than he could have hoped for. Anticipating that DCI Swift might give him the pat on the back he had long been short of. That Roseborough might possibly be brought to book. That the big shots who had shat on him from a great height might have some explaining to do to their own superiors. All rather satis-factory, if it could be pulled off. He recalled his surly treatment of Inspector Cat Fallon and felt an uncharacteristic twinge of regret. She'd been the one to pull all this together with her hunch, link the 'Tipper' with the Hartwell case. He had initially scorned her theo-rizing as mere woman's intuition. It seemed like Ms Fallon was one very smart cookie.

As Wilton walked out into the street, Brunswick followed on, the latter paid the waiting taxi driver and told him he wouldn't be needed.

'Time for a night in,' he said to Wilton, his tone of genial superi-ority gradually returning.

Wilton realized that Brunswick, the heart surgeon, regarded him, the police inspector, as just a public servant and a minion. Rather like Julian Roseborough's view, only not as dangerous and psychopathic. It didn't bother Wilton. His view of the world was entirely different. And just at this moment he was in exactly the job and the situation he wanted to be; he couldn't imagine any job more exciting, stimulating and worthwhile. And sometimes, thrillingly powerful.

PC Burns and his colleague PC Jolie were on their way to Ruth Hartwell's house. They had been given a personal briefing by DCI Swift on their job of protecting Mrs Hartwell for the next twelve hours. They had been told that Mrs Hartwell had been discharged from hospital some two hours before and was resting at home.

'The DCI was a bit on the cagey side,' Burns commented. 'I had the impression he was holding out on us, not letting us into the full picture.' Burns was in his twenties, enthusiastic and studying hard for his sergeant's exams. He had attended a number of psychology lectures and been fascinated by what he had learned. Now he was applying his new knowledge to DCI Swift. 'That's not like the DCI. He's usually so straight and up front,' he said. 'This case must have turned into something bigger than he's letting on.'

'He was clearly concerned about Mrs Hartwell's welfare.' PC Jolie commented. Jolie was a family liaison officer and her main focus and expertise lay in comforting the grieving families of victims. She was a dispenser of solace and paper tissues, a sturdy shoulder to cry on and a tower of empathy.

'Yeah, concerned enough to give us a free hand to get full back-up if we had any worries.' Burns was beginning to feel excited. Being a stone's throw away from the cutting edge of catching dangerous villains was setting his adrenaline flowing.

Arriving at Mrs Hartwell's house, they smoothed and straightened their uniforms as they stepped out of the car. On viewing the crumbling villa set in a large rampant garden, they exchanged meaningful glances.

Burns peered at the house's name plate and then pressed the bell.

'Goodness. It's positively gothic,' PC Jolie murmured, tucking a stray hair behind her ear and looking up at the dark bulk of the house from which no sign of light or life emanated.

There was a long pause, the sound of a dog's bark, and then there was the glow of a bulb coming from the hallway. 'I won't be long,' a voice reassured them. The door was thrown open to reveal an elderly woman with a mass of wiry silver hair which was tied back in a girlish pony tail. On seeing the two officers, her face brightened.

'Mrs Ruth Hartwell?' PC Jolie enquired.

'Yes. Come in, come in, I was expecting you.'

She led the officers down a wide, dark hallway into a large, square kitchen. In contrast to the coolness of the hallway, the kitchen was throbbing with warmth pulsing from a wood-burning stove which looked to the two young constables like a piece of engineering which should now reside in a museum. A small dog got up from its bed and greeted the officers with tail wags and kindly looks. Burns, who kept a rather fine German Shepherd, thought this one had the appearance of an animal which had once been squashed by a large object.

'Please sit down,' she continued, gesturing to the assortment of ancient wooden chairs surrounding a large oak table.

The two officers looked around them. More museum fodder.

PC Jolie felt warmth rising up beneath her jacket. The heat from the stove was overpowering, even on a cool July evening.

'You've come to "mind" me,' Mrs Hartwell said. 'Is that the correct term?'

'Yes ma'am,' said Burns.

'Please call me Ruth,' she said. 'Or Mrs Hartwell, if you prefer.'

'We were told a neighbour was staying with you,' Jolie commented, in her gentle, compassionate tones.

'Yes. I sent her home. She needed to prepare supper for her husband. She's very kind but she does like to talk a great deal, and I've got rather a headache.'

'Do you want us to call a doctor?' Jolie asked with concern. 'You've only recently been discharged from hospital, haven't you?'

'I don't need a doctor. I've taken a paracetamol. That should do the trick.' She looked at Jolie. 'There's no need to be worried. I've been fully checked out at the hospital. My CT scan indicated that I don't have any internal head injuries or bleeding into the brain. However, if I sound at all odd, you must bear with me. I had some kind of blackout, and the doctor didn't really give me an explanation of the medical reason for that. I am approaching my seventies, so maybe my brain is giving out, whatever the CT scan says.'

A canny old bird, Burns thought, even though she did look as though she'd got dressed from the contents of a tramp's carrier bag.

'I presume you know that a good deal of trouble has occurred since my informally fostered son Christian was found dead on the crag?' Mrs Hartwell asked them.

'Yes, we are aware of the main facts of the case,' said PC Jolie keeping her voice low and gentle. 'And we're very sorry for your loss.'

'Thank you.'

The two officers smiled, neither of them quite sure how to take her.

'I am extremely worried,' she said, suddenly sounding very serious and very much in charge of her brain. 'If Chief Inspector Swift thinks I need a twenty-four-hour police guard, he must also be very worried.'

'We will make sure you are safe, Ruth,' Jolie said.

'Thank you. It's not me I'm most worried about. It's my daughter and her family. And Craig.'

'DCI Swift is doing all he can to protect your family – and Craig,' Jolie said.

'I know that. But the man who is threatening us is not like other people. He has little regard for the welfare of others. He has the coldest, cruellest eyes I've ever seen.' She put her head in her hands.

The atmosphere grew heavy with tension. PC Jolie did what she often did in difficult and tense circumstances. She filled the kettle and made a pot of tea.

Swift watched Cat walk down the platform and felt almost weak with relief. He pulled her against him for a few moments.

'I could have done without the incident in Doncaster,' she said. 'Me too.'

As they walked down the concourse together, Cat slipped her arm through his. Outside the station, passengers from the delayed train who had missed local connections home were forming a long snaking queue for taxis, their faces drained and exhausted. Swift and Cat headed for his car which was parked in the small private park reserved for station staff.

'How are we doing?' Cat asked, as he steered the car through the traffic, passing supermarkets and car show rooms before climbing the long hill leading north out of the city. 'Any progress?'

'Pin your ears back,' he told her.

Keeping a discreet eye on his rear view mirror to check whether they were being followed, Swift gave her a full and detailed account of his talk with David Colburn, filling in the details which he had not had time to mention when he phoned her at Kings Cross.

She let out a long breath when he had finished. 'That is one chilling story,' she said. 'And you're sounding as though you believe it.'

'Sir David's the sort of guy who you feel you can trust. But, yes, it was just a story; there was no clear evidence to implicate Roseborough.'

'And Harriet, Christian and Charles have kept it secret all this time.'

'They've certainly kept it well hidden from us.'

'Fear of reprisals from Roseborough?'

'That was my theory too. But now we do have some corroborating statements – from the horses' mouths as it were.'

'From Harriet and Charles?'

'Your pal Wilton went to see them after you and I had spoken when you were at Kings Cross. I called him and reeled him in with a mixture of bribes and flattery.'

'I can imagine,' Cat said, grinning. 'And unlucky them! He's a granite man with a heart of iron.'

'Well, he got the job done.' Swift gave her the details which Wilton had e-mailed to him following his fruitful visit to the Brunswick household.

She listened with intense interest, drinking his words in. The revelations about the total silence Harriet and Charles Brunswick had maintained on the subject of Julian Roseborough for so long almost took her breath away. 'And Christian kept quiet too,' she mused. 'Until now.'

'Until he came face to face with Roseborough again and realized that his psychopathic personality had not altered very much. Except possibly for the worse.'

'Sounds like Christian was a true newshound with a nose for wicked deeds.'

'Yes. But unfortunately not enough nose to scent the killer rat, despatched to assassinate him.'

'Poor guy.'

'You realize that all of this represents a possibly significant breakthrough on both Hartwell's and the "Tipper" case. And it's down to you, Cat. You're the one who saw the billboard sign telling the tale of the "Tipper". You're the one who put two and two together, and made just that little bit more than four.'

'No, I wasn't so brilliant as to get that far. I just had one of those hunches we all get from time to time. Mine being: killer tips man into canal, with a touch of his fingers, killer tips man over the edge of the crag in much the same way. Was it the same man? Are the two cases connected?'

'I'm not sure whether Christian's "tipper" was the same man who's been pushing old drunks into the Regents Canal. But your hunch about a link between the two cases is looking spot on.'

There was a short, charged moment as she glanced at his tense face.

'We found the mobile phone which Ruth Hartwell's solicitor gave to her. It contained a short video of the "Tipper" killing one of his victims. We don't know which one yet. But we know the date and the venue of the filmed killing.'

'Sometime during Christian's last stay in London?'

'Yes.'

'Do you think Christian was stalking the "Tipper" – deliberately waiting for a chance to film him committing a crime?'

'That's a difficult question to answer. It's possible he was doing that. However, if he knew the killer was likely to kill again, then in some way he was colluding in the murder of an innocent victim, filming but not intervening, or raising an alarm. Which is, in itself, an offence. But maybe he was taking his time to consider his options, and then was unfortunately stopped in his tracks.'

'I'm assuming that the man on our video is Julian Roseborough?' Cat said.

'It's the same man who you spotted in the photographs we took from Ruth Hartwell's house. Also I've checked it out on our data base and run a check through his background. We are able to confirm Roseborough was the man on the video pushing a drunk into the Regents Canal, and afterwards lingering at the scene for a while before simply walking away. And, interestingly enough, we don't seem to be getting any cooperation from any of the usual channels regarding his current whereabouts.'

Cat muttered under her breath, before saying, 'Was it Craig who had Hartwell's phone?'

'Yes. he turned himself in at the station in Thirsk. Voluntarily gave up the phone and some cash he'd taken from Ruth Hartwell.'

'Do you think he's seen the video?'

'I doubt it. The phone's battery was flat for a start, and it's unlikely he would have been able to get it charged in the time available to him.'

'Right.' She was thinking things through, her teeth biting at her lower lip. 'You're probably wondering if I know anything of interest about Roseborough through his connection with Jeremy. But I don't. I've only met the guy a couple of times. For me, he was just a satellite in Jeremy's entrepreneurial orbit.'

'I appreciate that. This isn't another stick to beat yourself with, Cat. Just an unpleasant coincidence.'

'You've said it! So, who knows about the video?' Cat asked, pulling herself back to the here and now and speaking with a hint of sharpness.

'I do for one and also Les, our IT guy. Harriet and Charles Brunswick know there is new evidence, but not the specifics. Otherwise, I really can't say. We have no knowledge of whether Christian tried to sell it on to the press, or to anyone else. Nor do we know what happened to it in the interval between its being shot and lodged with Christian's solicitor.'

'So the phone's in our secure room?'

'Yes.'

'And who has got copies of the video?'

'Me.'

'Just you? Not Ravi Stratton, or our press officer?'

'So far, just me.'

She was quiet for some time. 'So Roseborough's target has been narrowed down to one?'

'Not necessarily. We don't know what Roseborough knows at this moment. He may not be aware of what has gone on this afternoon.'

'No one has been following me,' Cat said. 'I was very careful after we spoke.'

'No one has been following me, either,' said Swift. 'I'm pretty sure of that.'

'No sign of Mac the Knife?'

'No.' In the past few hours Swift had been thinking that Mac the Knife had been rather quiet for a time, and wondering if his days of paying menacing visits to innocent folks were a thing of the past.

'Let's hope it stays that way.' she said. 'But how long can you keep the vital incriminating evidence secret? If we're going to collar Roseborough, we'll have to share it with Stratton, at the very least. And, of course, she will flag it up with the big boys – and if, God forbid, there's any high-level corruption going on we'll find our case quietly swept under the carpet.'

'That's already happened according to Wilton,' Swift said. 'He's pretty sure the order to hand on the case of the "Tipper" to a specialist team means it's going to be buried. But then Wilton does come across as a somewhat paranoid and defensive character.'

'So,' Cat said. 'If we keep our mouths shut, Roseborough walks free. And if we go public, you get a visit from his band of un-merry men.'

'That's probably the size of it.' Swift said. He reached out and squeezed her hand. 'We'll think of something,' he said. 'Tomorrow's another day.'

He didn't tell Cat that he had already set a hare running. When he had phoned Georgie Tyson at the *Echo* earlier she had been only too pleased to put together a report to go out in the early edition the next day – and alert the news desks at the local London press.

Roseborough wouldn't be able to ignore it. He was bound to come for him.

Some hours earlier, when Craig had been informed that DCI Swift had asked for him to be kept at the station for the rest of the day and the ensuing night, he had not been at all pleased. He couldn't complain about how they had treated him. They hadn't bullied him or beaten him up, but the police were the police, that was all there was too it. You didn't want to spend your spare time with them, especially when they were on their home turf.

'I'm a free man, ain't I?' he demanded. 'You can't keep me.'

'It's for your own safety.' The burly officer who had searched him earlier schooled himself to be firm but kind with the troubled young ex-con.

'You told me Mrs Hartwell had said she trusted me to give the money back. That she didn't want me to get into any bother on her account.'

'Yes,' the burly officer agreed. 'DCI Swift is simply wanting to protect you.'

'I can look after myself,' Craig said. 'There are things I need to do.'

The officer drew himself up, considering the issue.

'I want to see my probation person,' Craig demanded. 'I want to ask him if it's right for me to be kept here if I want to leave.' His eyes were burning with determination.

The officer had hesitated but within the hour the probation liaison officer had turned up to confirm that Craig was free to go, but that he must be sure to fulfil the terms of his licence and report regularly to the probation service. He went on about the details: duh, duh, duh. Craig had nodded agreement until he felt like a toy dog on the parcel shelf of a car.

At the front desk, he was told that the mobile phone had been taken by the Thirsk police to DCI Swift's station for analysis and safekeeping. The money he had 'borrowed' from Mrs Hartwell had been kept in the police safe, pending Mrs Hartwell's wishes regarding its return to her. Mrs Hartwell had told the local police in West Yorkshire that she trusted Craig to return it to her himself.

The desk officer was a middle-aged woman Craig had not seen before. She had cool silvery eyes and a no-nonsense, faintly disapproving manner. She made a meal of unlocking a drawer in a secure cabinet at the back of her reinforced plastic cubicle, then slapped a chubby brown envelope down on the desk. She looked at Craig over the top of her glasses. 'Who's a lucky boy then? To have friends as trusting as that?'

Craig's hackles rose. He pulled himself up short, remembering the anger management courses in the prison. He deepened his breathing. 'Aye,' he said. 'I must have done summat right, at last.'

She raised her eyebrows, and pushed a paper in front of him. 'Sign there, please.'

He did so with something of a flourish. 'I'll be on my way then.'

'Yes,' she said, carefully enunciating that short word. 'Good luck.'

He guessed she would have forgotten about him before he even got through the door. Which was OK. He wouldn't waste time thinking about her, either.

Ten minutes after that he was helping Josie out in the bar of her pub, clearing up the used glasses and plates, taking them to the kitchen and washing them up whilst an engineer was peering into the insides of the dishwasher.

When Josie came through to the kitchen from time to time, she'd smile at him, and ask him how he was getting on. And he would grin and give her the thumbs up. He hadn't felt this happy ever, except for the times he and his mum used to be together on their own. And Josie had said they might be able to find her....

The only thing worrying him was Mrs Hartwell. He needed to see her. To explain, to say thank you.

DAY 11

Swift was up just after 7 a.m., brewing fresh coffee and making toast. Cat appeared ten minutes later, dressed in silky dove-grey trousers and a frilled white shirt. Her hair was still rumpled from sleep, her face free of make-up. Her bruises were beginning to turn a brownish grey, fanning out to a rather fetching shade of lime green around her nose and mouth. 'Hi, there!' she said, stepping up to him and giving him a friendly hug.

'Your face is looking rather colourful,' Swift remarked, thinking that she looked heartbreakingly lovely. He watched her as she walked to the window to look out into the July morning. Today there was a white gossamer mist lying over the fields. And above, a faint silver glow behind the clouds. Once the sun broke through, it would most likely be the sunniest day they had had for some time.

There was the rattle of the letter box as Swift's landlord Richard pushed the morning newspapers through. Having been a sheep farmer for many years, he got up with the lark, whatever the weather, and was at the local newsagents at seven every morning, often before the deliveries had arrived.

Swift went to pick them up. He saw that Georgie's article had made the front page. He scanned it quickly. Under a headline proclaiming, a startling breakthrough in the Hartwell case, he saw that the salient points he had fed to Georgie Tyson were all there.

'DCI Ed Swift has uncovered vital new evidence which is likely to be crucial in identifying the killer of Christian Hartwell who was found dead on Fellbeck Crag ten days ago. Revealing video shots from a mobile phone, believed to have belonged to the dead man, were handed in to the police yesterday. Data available from the phone are under analysis, but DCI Swift said they would be almost certain to provide the vital evidence needed in enabling them to find and arrest Hartwell's killer. Further searches of the house belonging to Mrs Ruth Hartwell, the dead man's mother, will be concluded by this morning, and could well provide further back-up evidence regarding the killer's motives.'

Swift gave a grim smile. Well done, Georgie. He folded the newspaper and laid it on the table by the side of Cat's plate. She glanced at it, instantly noting the headline. Putting her cup down, she picked up the paper and read through the article.

Swift saw that when she replaced the newspaper on the table her hand was shaking.

'He *is* going to come for you, Ed. You've invited him. You've given him the time and venue.'

'Yeah.'

'He's toxic.'

'True.'

'And you're going solo?'

'If he sees any sign of back-up he'll be off.'

'Are you going armed?'

'No.'

'Have you got a plan?'

'Yes.'

'And you're not telling me?'

'No.'

'Because you don't want me involved?'

He smiled at her, his eyes full of affection. 'Of course I don't – and you know why. But I do want you to look after Ruth Hartwell for the day.'

'Consider it done. Do I have carte blanche?'

'Naturally, you're an experienced DI. Just take her and her minders somewhere nice. As soon as you've finished your breakfast.'

'What do we tell Ravi Stratton?'

'Luckily, we don't have to worry about Ravi, just at this moment. I looked in her schedule yesterday and found that she's on a weekend course in Manchester, starting today.'

'And what about Naomi?' Cat asked softly.

'She's grown up now. She'll survive.'

'Dear God! You can be hard when you want to, Ed.'

'Yes,' he admitted. 'So can we all if we survive in the police.'

He looked at her face for a few moments, memorizing its lines and curves. He could think about her when the time came. Not Naomi, because then he might break down and lose it, but if it came to the worst and one of the thugs on Roseborough's pay roll got him, then he could think of Cat and the friendship they had had over the years, the lively banter and the shared anxiety about work. He thought about her wide smile, her strength and optimism. He thought of her personal charm, and the pleasure of being in her presence. And it came to him that they should have been dating long ago, going on holiday as a threesome with Naomi, forming a new family.

When Cat had left he packed his document case with overdue paperwork and then turned on the TV, needing to pass the time, allowing Cat to get ahead and make the appropriate explanations and arrangements with Ruth and her two minders.

The national news was still dominated with Westminster politics. On the Northern news there was a heartbreaking item about two young children having perished in a fire, whilst their mum was sleeping off a binge-drinking session. He sighed, and then came suddenly on the alert when the newsreader started to give details of a man who had been found dead in a Leeds hotel bedroom. He had died from a shot to the head. Forensic teams and the pathology team were still working at the scene and examining the body. The man had been named as Laurence McBride, who lived in North London. His next of kin had been informed. Police had not yet made any statement regarding the possibility of foul play.

Swift aimed the remote and killed the picture. He had the idea Mac the Knife was one enemy he could cross off his list. But liaising with Leeds police would have to wait a while.

In the car, he focused hard on his driving, taking extreme care regarding his vigilance and technique like a teenager taking their first test. Outside the window the sculpted slopes of the gentle Dales rolled softly by, partly veiled in the thinning mist, providing a panorama of majestic beauty. Observing the white glow of the sky, it struck him that the light would have undergone a complete change when he came back. But I may not come back this way, he thought – I may never come back.

He let himself into the *Old School House* with the key which was still lodged underneath the watering can, and went through each room, checking to see if anyone was already there waiting for him. Having ascertained that he was on his own, he settled down at the kitchen table, got out his papers and took up his pen.

Two hours passed. He tried hard to concentrate on the paperwork, looking through the crime detection statistics Ravi Stratton had given him seeking his comments. He tried not to think of Naomi or Cat, just quietly fill in the time whilst he waited for the inevitable.

And then, as though coming seamlessly out of nowhere, there was the sound of wheels on the drive outside the front door, the muffled crunch of the gravel. As the wheels slowed, the engine gave a sudden monster-like roar before being killed.

He closed his statistics file and laid his hands on the table. There was a long, long silence and then a shadow fell over the path leading to the back of the house. A figure walked up to the back door and looked in.

It was Julian Roseborough himself. The organ grinder had ditched the monkeys and come in person.

Swift got up and opened the door. 'I was expecting you,' he said.

'It's good to see you again, Chief Inspector,' Roseborough said, his low drawl amiable, kind even. But his eyes were empty and cold. 'I take it there aren't any other folk here to greet me?'

Swift shook his head. 'Just me.'

'Good. May I sit down?'

'Go ahead.'

Roseborough was dressed in close-fitting jeans, an expensive looking navy jacket with a crisp white shirt beneath. No tie, polished tan brogues. Swift rated him as a handsome guy whom women would fall for, even without the money and position. Tall, good body, blond hair, high cheekbones. Even his daughter Naomi would approve on first sight, give his style a big tick. Cool, knows how to dress, she would say. Yes, thought Swift, and then so much more than that. A fascination with the control of others, for danger, for heartless cruelty and a disregard for the preciousness of life.

Roseborough took out a small gun and placed it on the table top just to the side of his right hand. 'I like to lay my cards on the table, so to speak,' he said. He then took out a silver case, selected a cigarette and lit up. He glanced at Swift. 'Do you mind?'

Swift shrugged.

'So what cards have you got to play?' Roseborough asked.

'No firearms, no knives.'

'That could hardly be said to work to your gain. Have you brought the copies of the video?'

'Yes.' Swift reached into his document case, brought out stills of the video and laid them on the table, arranging them in order for Roseborough to inspect.

'They are a touch damaging,' Roseborough commented. 'But then, no doubt my lawyer could get around the difficulty. Not admissible in court and so forth.'

'No doubt,' Swift said. 'We have to bear in mind that you're untouchable, don't we, Julian?'

'Yes, you do, Chief Inspector.' His features sharpened, wary, wolf-like. 'Have you brought the mobile with you?'

'Of course I haven't.'

'So how much do you want for it? And who else needs a little remuneration?'

'Money's not in the equation,' Swift said.

Roseborough sneered. 'Money's always in the equation.'

'Why are you so worried, Julian?' Swift said softly. 'If your lawyer can get you off, why bother with me?'

Roseborough held his breath, and then exhaled a long plume of smoke. 'Just fucking give me the phone.'

'It was a real blow for you when Mac the Knife didn't find it, wasn't it?' Swift suggested. 'You hired him to kill an innocent man who had been your friend, and then he messed it up. He broke with the clean single shot to the head method, the option your minions are instructed to favour and took a leaf out of your "tipping" method. And after that it all went downhill.'

Roseborough took another drag at his cigarette and stubbed it out in Ruth's pot of pansies which stood at the centre of the table. He bunched the photocopies into a ball, then took out his lighter and held it to the edge of one of the sheets.

The two men watched the sheet of flame climb along the long edge of the sheet, giving birth to more flames which began to crawl and swell across the mass of paper, licking at it, devouring it, until it turned into a grey, charred mass. Roseborough was superbly deft in managing the licking flames, turning and twisting the paper so as not to get his fingers burned. Even the table top suffered little damage, just a pile of dull grey ashes.

'Well, I for one feel better for that,' Roseborough said. He leaned forward, eyes blazing. 'Just give me the phone,' he hissed. 'Shall I come over there and get it? Obviously you won't have sent it on an upward route through the ranks. You'd have worked out they'd most probably destroy it. I have a lot of influence.'

'You won't get anywhere by threatening me,' Swift said steadily. 'You're quite threatening enough already. And you're welcome to search me. It's not here. I told you.'

'Fuck.' Roseborough muttered.

'You never married,' Swift remarked.

Roseborough narrowed his eyes, suspicious but interested in this new tack. 'Have you never heard the one about the simplest way to turn a fox into a cow?' he asked.

'You marry her,' said Swift. 'I've come across that one before. It doesn't convince me.'

Roseborough closed his eyes in a show of boredom which could hardly be endured.

'Are you afraid of commitment? Or maybe simply of not being able to love anyone? Gay perhaps?' Swift went on relentlessly. 'Or impotent?'

Roseborough's features twisted with scorn, but Swift noticed a flicker in his eyes in response to the last question. 'When did not being able to love stop any guy marrying a beautiful girl?' he snapped. 'Cut the psychology crap, Mr Plod. I like to walk alone, always have, always will.'

'I'm wondering why you made the effort and took the risk to come here today,' Swift said. 'You could have sent one of your serfs, but you came yourself. You needed to see things were done properly.

Because this time you're not sure you're going to get away with it. Hartwell's assassination, of course, was not done by your hand. But pushing a harmless drunk into a canal was most definitely you. A hands-on job, caught on camera. You're not scared of a ruined reputation, or of shame and humiliation – they mean little to you. And remorse doesn't come into it. And even though you've access to the smartest barrister on the block and have a few high-ups in the palm of your hand, you're aware that times are changing. Fairness and transparency are the new buzz words in a culture which is uncovering corruption that has dominated the last century. Young people don't revere titles as the previous generation did. They're not hostile, simply not interested. They go for icons like Barrack Obama, David Beckham, Jordan. You could well end up in prison for a long time.'

Roseborough listened carefully, sighed and lit another cigarette.

'You came here because you thought I could be bought off,' Swift continued. 'But I can't. And you would be shooting yourself in the foot if you were to kill me.'

Roseborough's eyelashes flickered.

'I've left documentation at the station,' Swift said. 'I'm a high-profile, long-serving officer. Quite a lot of people who have influence and are not corrupt will be after you. And you could well be tried, convicted and sent down. That's what scares you, isn't it Julian? Being deprived of your freedom. That is not a good prospect at all.'

Roseborough assumed a pained expression. 'And you came along here with the thought you would persuade me to confess. You came to tell me that a free confession, together with my connections, would get me a light sentence.' He shook his head. 'Were you born yesterday?'

Swift could see that self-interest was cutting in with a vengeance. Roseborough was cornered – and at his most dangerous.

As he had been speaking Swift had become aware of a shadow moving towards the door. A figure appeared outside, peering in through the glass. Swift was temporarily thrown, desperately trying not to show the surprise and anxiety he felt.

The figure turned and moved away, only to come back seconds later, holding a huge roof slate. He burst in, panting and raising his arms up above Roseborough's head.

'Craig! NO!' Swift yelled.

As Craig froze, Roseborough swivelled around, levelling the gun at the vistor. 'Steady on,' he said to Craig. 'Drop the weapon.'

Craig's eyes blazed with anger. 'Fuck off,' he said, having been used to being shouted at for years and become heartily sick of it.

Roseborough fired a shot at the ceiling. It made a muffled, almost watery sound. Both Swift and Craig gave an involuntary grimace. 'OK, no more messing me about,' Roseborough snarled. He pointed the gun at Craig. 'Sit down next to the chief inspector,' he said. 'You can hang on to the kiddy's toy if you must. I'm tracking every movement you make.'

Craig was looking thunderous, but he did as he was told, still clutching the slate.

Roseborough levelled the gun at Swift. 'I want to tell you something,' he told the detective. 'Something about killing. Killing is the highest, purest, sweetest form of pleasure. It's something so few people ever get to understand, the sheer beauty of having life and death under your control. Of toying with someone else's life. The ultimate sin, the most irreverent act one can contemplate. I've had all the psychiatric and psychological assessments you can think of. I know all the jargon. Psychopathic tendencies. Sociopathic tendencies. A detached personality, with a contrasting ability to come across as sociable. Gratified by violence. Cold, arrogant, detached.' He gave a wry smile. 'My parents paid for those assessments and reports. Perhaps they thought that if I ever got into a tight spot, my brief could plead madness rather than badness. What do you think, Chief Inspector?'

'I think you've dug yourself into a deep hole, Julian.'

'You're a guy who can put on a brave face, I'll give you that.' Once again he made use of the bowl of pansies to grind out his latest cigarette.

'You know, some of the reports put my "disorders", as they termed them, down to a failure to make significant bonds in childhood because my parents left my upbringing to a succession of nannies, and subsequently pals and tutors at Eton. And others put it down to genetics, opining that I am constitutionally programmed to behave the way I do.' He made a show of considering this choice. 'I can see some validity in both views. My parents were neglectful and cold and my father is a pompous twat and my mother is a selfish, vain and self-regarding monster. So you see, what chance did I have?'

Swift kept silent, willing Craig to do the same. It struck him that Craig's arrival had changed the dynamic of the duet being played out between him and Roseborough, and brought about a flicker of hope. He and Craig just needed to live through the next few moments until Roseborough saw the futility of his own situation. That is what he told himself, but another part of his brain was saying good-bye to Naomi, trying to picture Cat....

'So now, which one of you do I kill?' Roseborough mused. 'Neither of you mean a jot to me; you're of no more consequence than the arse shit under my shoe.' He swivelled the muzzle of the gun between his two potential victims. He did it several times. He did it very slowly. 'Who shall it be? Or should I simply shoot you both?'

Swift heard Craig's breathing rasping in his chest. He tried to force his brain to come up with a way forward.

Roseborough continued his little piece of choreography with the gun. Without any noticeable pause in the flow of the dance, in one smooth movement he opened his mouth and took the gun into it. There was another muffled, watery noise and then the crash of his chair falling on the floor.

White bits of gristle flew up into the air. A pool of blood began to seep from Roseborough's head.

'Jesus!' Craig said.

The two of them sat together for a time, staring at the body on the floor, temporarily numb with shock.

Swift snapped back into professional mode, planning to call Cat, get back-up. His hand shook as he grasped his phone, whilst his fingers of their own accord pressed Cat's name. As he waited for her to answer, he looked at Craig. 'Are you OK?'

Craig stared at him and then his face lit up in a way Swift had not seen before. 'Bloody glad to be alive!'

Cat arrived before the back-up team. She stepped carefully around Roseborough's corpse and blood, put her arms around Swift and drew him against her. And then opened one arm and brought Craig into the embrace.

Swift tried to think of an appropriate comment. Recalling Craig's last remark, he decided he couldn't better it. So he didn't try.

Some hours later, Swift faced a stern and shocked-looking Ravi Stratton, who had hot-footed it from her conference in Manchester in order to hear his account of the events at the *Old School House* earlier on.

Swift offered a clear and detailed account of what had been said and done.

'You went against all police procedure,' she pointed out. 'You broke so many rules.'

Swift knew this episode could bring disciplinary proceedings, maybe lose him his job. Taking events into your own hands, metaphorically shooting from the hip like a sheriff in a John Wayne movie, was not highly regarded in the higher echelons of any organization, let alone the nation's vehicle of law enforcement.

He declined to make a protest, crediting Ravi Stratton with the intelligence to work it out why he had chosen to go it alone. He did, however, point out that through his actions a serial killer had been identified, a killer who would no longer be continuing in his evil career.

'I shall have to make a full report to the chief constable,' Stratton said, giving him no quarter, her face a mask of solemnity and fore-boding.

'Of course.'

Stratton walked to the window and stood there for a few seconds. She turned around. 'Well done, Ed,' she said softly.

He nodded, made no comment.

'Do we know how many people Roseborough has killed?'

'Inspector Wilton has a list of unsolved cases in the Kings Cross area which he's examining in the light of what we now know. Of course, he's likely to come up against resistance, high-ups manip-ulating and exerting pressure to keep the damage limitation on Roseborough as contained as possible.'

Stratton sighed.

'You've no need to discuss this with me, Ravi,' Swift said. 'You have a job to do. A career to pursue. We're not going to agree on the rights and wrongs of concealment of information about the rich and powerful. And maybe this is the time for me to bring my police career to an end and move on to something else.'

At this, she looked seriously perturbed and about to protest.

He held up a hand and stopped her from speaking, warning her not to pursue that issue.

'Go home, Ed,' she said kindly. 'Get some rest.'

He got up. 'Thanks for that.' He headed for the door.

She called him back.

He turned.

Stratton was again sitting at her desk. 'It'll be no surprise to hear that I made it my business to familiarize myself with my colleagues' methods of working when I first stood in for Superintendent Finch. And it appears that you have a record for a certain liking for going off on trails of your own.'

'That's true.' Swift smiled, recalling Superintendent Damian Finch's taking him to task more than once on that particular point.

'And maybe it's a quality which has some merit,' she said.

'I'll bear that in mind,' he said. 'If I were an eager young constable, this is the point where I'd assure you I wouldn't let you down, which would basically be asking you to trust me not to do anything daft. But as I'm no longer young, and hopefully a touch cynical, I won't insult you with such reassurances.'

She looked steadily into his face. 'No.'

'I'll try not to get out of hand,' he said. 'Whatever comes next.'

In the car, he called Cat to discover her current whereabouts. She told them she'd booked Ruth into a small country hotel in Burley-in-Wharfedale and the two of them were there now. 'She'd like to see you, Ed,' she said. 'Are you up to it?'

He felt himself vibrating with the need to sleep. 'Sure.'

Ruth and Cat were sitting together in a cosily furnished bedroom on the first floor of the hotel, Ruth's dog at her feet. Ruth jumped up when she saw him and greeted him with a vigorous handshake.

'How are you?' he asked.

'Much better for knowing my family are safe. Cat has given me all the details of what has emerged from your investigations and prompt action. Thank you so much.'

Swift rather liked her description of his method of nailing Roseborough. 'How will you feel about going back to the house?' he asked her. 'We will clean it and get it back to how it was.'

'I'm not going back,' she said. 'All these deaths, all this sadness, and the menace and the evil. It's been a lot to come to terms with. And the poor parents of the man who killed so many people and then himself. How will they ever come to terms with that?'

Swift and Cat maintained a respectful silence.

'Harriet has asked me to go and stay with her and Charles and Jake for a time – she's even invited Tamsin,' Ruth continued. 'And I've decided it's time for a new start. I'm going to sell the *Old School House* and get myself a little place near my family. I've been doing a great deal of reflecting over these past days since Christian was killed, and I feel that many of the complaints my daughter has made to me have some justification. My daughter is not an easy person, but I love her and I'm very proud of her. And I can see how she would have felt pushed to one side by all the people my husband and I helped along the way over the years, and it must have been hard to accept Christian as an adoptive brother so late in her life. I want to learn to be closer to her, and I'll be able to spend time with Jake. And I'll try not to be too much of an ogre with Charles. It'll probably be a touch hellish from time to time, but that's life.'

'Yes, indeed,' said Cat.

'Ah, and regarding Craig. I shall of course keep in touch with him, but he needs to make his own way now. I've contacted a friend who works in Social Services and asked her to give him support. I've also asked her to reintroduce him to his grandparents who were apparently estranged from his mother and prevented from making contact.'

'When did you do all this?' Swift asked.

'Today. Whilst your colleague was looking after me. And when she wasn't explaining all I wanted to know about what has been going on the past few days.'

'Nothing like keeping busy.' Cat said.

'I rather think Craig is already making a move towards building a new life,' Swift told Ruth. 'He's got a job and bed and board in a pub in Thirsk. And I rather suspect he and the landlady have taken a shine to each other. We'll arrange for you to see him when he's finished making his witness statement.'

'A lady friend. Well, good for him!' Ruth said. 'Maybe she's what is now termed a "yummy mummy". He could do with one of those. I shall keep my fingers crossed for him.'

'Here, here,' said Cat.

'I'll be a rich old bird when Christian's money comes through,' Ruth said. 'And I've promised myself to be a little frivolous for a change.'

'May I enquire in what way?' Cat said, genuinely curious.

'Oh, I'll pop into the West End and get my hair done at a top stylist's. By the top man. Harriet will be astounded.'

'I like your hair now,' said Swift.

'Don't worry, I shall still be eccentric, just expensively so.' She suddenly looked hard at the two detectives. 'You both look totally exhausted.' she said. 'Go home. Right now.'

They duly departed. When Mrs Hartwell used her mother-warning voice, you had no choice.

THREE MONTHS LATER

Swift woke with the autumn morning on his face. Outside, a layer of white mist as high as a field wall had risen up from the ground. Above, the sky formed a delicate canvas of palest blue on which were painted a thin rind of silver moon and one tiny star.

He gently touched Cat's shoulder. 'It's a new day.'